The Colour of Pride

Hi Ursula

Tks. for your support as fellow writer, but, most importantly, as friend.

Best.

David

The Colour of Pride

David Floody

Implosion Press

First Edition.

Cover Illustration: Joanna Streetly.
Layout: First Choice Books.
Author photo by Dolores Baswick.

Library and Archives Canada Cataloguing in Publication

Floody, David, 1946-, author
The colour of pride / David Floody.

Issued in print and electronic formats.
ISBN 978-0-9919004-3-5 (paperback)
ISBN 978-0-9919004-2-8 (pdf)

1. Riots--Michigan--Detroit--History--20th century--Fiction.
2. World Series (Baseball) (1968)--Fiction. I. Title.

PS8611.L65C64 2016 C813'.6 C2015-908082-7
C2015-908083-5

Published by Implosion Press,
P. O. Box 653, Tofino, British Columbia,
Canada V0R 2Z0
defloody@telus.net

Printed in Victoria, BC, Canada
on 100% post-consumer waste recycled paper.

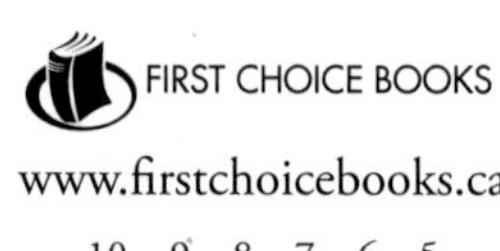

www.firstchoicebooks.ca

10 9 8 7 6 5

For Eileen, always. And for those who stand against racism everywhere.

We've got a lot of pride at stake, and we're representing the American League, and we just want to do a better job than we've been doing.

—Al Kaline, 1968 World Series

I look to a day when people will not be judged by the colour of their skin, but by the content of their character.

—Martin Luther King, Jr.

part one

FRANK

one

Windsor, Ontario – 1968

"Wow! She's goin' for it, Larry! She's gonna steal third!"

On the grass behind home plate, fourteen-year-old Frank Phelan jumped to his feet and hauled Larry up beside him. Together they watched the drama unfold between second and third base through the wire mesh of the tall backstop. Frank was a ballplayer too. He knew it would be close.

The determined black girl, in pinstripes and Detroit Junior Tigers ball cap, did everything right: she watched the blonde third baseman's eyes follow the throw from his catcher to his second baseman behind her; saw the final position of Blondie's outstretched glove; used her body to block his view of the throw from second; extended both arms and dove flat out for the base.

The hard throw flew between Blondie's hands like a cowhide cannonball and slammed into his chest. "Oomph!"

"Wow!" Frank punched Larry's arm.

"Safe!" the umpire yelled from behind home plate.

Loud groans went up from the clutch of Canadian fans

rooting for the Windsor Hellcats beside the third baseline of the Atkinson Park ball diamond. Along the first baseline on their right, the few dozen American fans from Detroit cheered for all they were worth. The girl's teammates whistled and clapped from their bench. They were all guys, all black.

"You know, Frank, that steal was pretty good." Larry allowed.

". . . for a girl." Frank heard his best friend's unspoken words.

"No, Lar. That steal was perfect. We should do so good next season." *Attaway, babe!* Frank silently cheered.

Then Blondie brought his steel-cleated baseball shoe around and spiked her in the face.

"Ah-h-o-w-w-w!" she cried out in a clear voice that soared above the crowd, a mixture of pain and surprised disbelief. Blood jumped from the wound and ran down her cheek in a bright crimson curtain. The cheers from the American side turned to loud gasps and then heated shouts of "Foul! Foul!"

Frank saw a black couple stand up in the front row of the American crowd and grasp hands. The woman's eyes widened and she called a name Frank couldn't make out. Her solemn companion put a large hand on her arm to restrain her. He wore a round white collar and spotless black shirt, like a minister or something.

The girl's parents?

"Whoa! Ok. A spike is never good," Larry said. "Could be an accident, though?"

The wound on the teenaged girl's cheek bled heavily. But she stood up, took a wad of Kleenex tissues from her pocket and held it against the side of her face. Blondie waited behind her, his hands on his hips and his face expressionless. The girl waved off her coach and the umpire, who was about to stop play. With one shake of her head, she persuaded her parents to sit down again.

Frank had watched it all. It was no accident. "Now that takes real guts, Lar."

After the final out, when the girl was left stranded on third base, Blondie must have said something to her. Frank saw the girl turn to stare at Blondie, her shoulders stiff, and her eyes tracked him back to his teammates on the bench, a smirk on his face. The Windsor Hellcats sniggered behind their gloves.

The girl caught the eyes of her teammates taking to the field. The tension in their faces was a living wave that washed over the black crowd so they shifted in their seats. Her parents leaned forward with a question on their faces, but again, the girl shook her head.

The second inning was over, but Frank had the disquieting feeling this wasn't the end of the incident, not by a long shot.

He pounded his fist into his Al Kaline glove and wished it were Blondie's face.

The early fall afternoon was perfect for baseball. The weather cooled off and a slight breeze blew in moist and sharp from the Detroit River a block away through the autumn maples behind the neighbourhood playing field. The arching black shadow of the Ambassador Bridge framed the scene. Frank took a deliberate breath through his nose and smelled the heavy sweetness of cut grass, smelled the sizzling onions and patties of fried beef from families who had set up grills in the surrounding park.

It had taken a lot of persuasion to talk Larry into biking over here to Atkinson Park to see this near-end-of-season exhibition game between the Hellcats from Windsor and an unknown team from the Detroit Junior Baseball League. This Saturday was only two weeks before the Labour Day long weekend, the last weekend before school began again. Every day was a precious nugget of time not to be wasted. Playing Junior League baseball was Frank's first love. Watching Junior League baseball was a close second. And he was curious about the American team.

"You still cool, dude?" Frank asked Larry after returning from the refreshment stand with two bottles of the Double Cola they both liked, his treat.

"Hell, man! I will be after you give me the pop and get off my friggin' back about not wantin' to come."

Frank laughed at his friend's discomfort. "Just checkin'."

"So, who you rootin' for, Frank?"

Larry's question was a good one and his best buddy might not like the answer. Frank took a swallow of cola and shrugged a shoulder. He might have been neutral before, but after the girl's spiking in the second inning, Frank wanted the Junior Tigers all the way. It might not matter. Now with only two innings left the Detroit Junior Tigers were down 7-3 against the Hellcats. New York Yankees catcher, Yogi Berra, liked to say, "It ain't over, 'til it's over." Frank thought this game was pretty much over.

Larry pointed his chin at the American crowd. "And that—did you expect it?"

Larry was talking about the Detroit Junior Tigers and their fans all being black. Yet when Frank thought about it, why should it be surprising? He drove the Ambassador Bridge across the Detroit River a dozen times a year with his father and grandfather to see the games at Tiger Stadium. Thousands of black and white fans filled that ballpark to cheer on Al Kaline and the Detroit Tigers. "Expect it? Not really. But so what?"

"You tell me, dude."

"Well, the guy at the refreshment stand thought it might be some kind of goodwill gesture, you know, after . . . after the damn race riot last year!"

"DETROIT BURNS!" Larry raised his voice to quote the oversized *Detroit Free Press* headline from the previous July. "So that's what's goin' on out there."

"Ell-ie! Ell-ie! Ell-ie!"

Sudden chanting and whistles from the American side broke out before Frank could say more.

"Geez, I don't believe it, Frank! Are they bringin' in that girl—to pitch? No way, José!" Larry collapsed on the grass for a few moments before hoisting himself up again to sit with his legs crossed.

The black girl took up her position on the pitcher's mound. "Looks like it," Frank said. It was unexpected. She had been playing at first base. And his best friend was skeptical of a girl pitcher.

"At least we know her name's Ellie."

Frank nodded and watched the girl named Ellie take the ball from her coach and begin her warm-up pitches. For just a moment there, when she trotted out to the mound, Frank thought she looked familiar. He flashed back on the Detroit riot. *Nah.* The coincidence would be too much.

"Play ball!" the umpire shouted.

"Crazy," Larry said. "Down four runs with two innings left to play? Just crazy."

"Yeah, I hear you, Lar. Now put a sock in it, will ya?" Larry flipped him the bird, took a pull on his cola and drew out a long burp like a drunken frog.

Frank ignored him. All his attention was on the pitcher's mound.

Before her first pitch, Ellie fingered the ball a few seconds too long. Frank thought she looked nervous. Who could blame her? It wasn't just the pressure of coming in to pitch relief with her team losing badly, or playing in a different park, in a different city, in a whole different country. No, it was the thing from the second inning. Which was really two things Frank decided: the spike to her face and whatever Blondie said after. Sure enough, the girl brought her hand up to her face, realized she held the ball in it, and dropped it down to her side once more. The nasty cut high on her right cheekbone was still ugly, the blood dried and crusted-over in a dark scarlet smear.

"That's gotta be hurtin'," Larry said.

"Yeah," Frank agreed, "gotta be."

Then, like she couldn't resist, the girl shot a quick glance at third base. Third base, where the Hellcats base runner, that same Blondie, took a long lead from the bag, crouched low and worked in his spikes, ready to dig for home. The smirk was back on his face.

Frank's fist pounded his glove like a piston, waiting for the thing he was sure would happen. The crowd on both sides was tense now, silent. When he looked over at the girl's parents, he saw that her father was holding her mother's hands in both of his, each of their faces stiff as an African mask.

Frank no longer cared about Canadians against Americans, blacks against whites, girls playing with guys.

Get 'em, babe. Get 'em good.

After Ellie struck out the first Hellcats batter on five pitches, Blondie increased his taunts from third base and shouted encouragement to his team's next hitter at the plate. "Attaway, Buck! No pitcher out there! Yeah, nothin' but a girl!"

Frank had watched those first five pitches and was impressed. The girl didn't throw as hard as most guys, but Frank judged she threw smart and read hitters well. After that first strikeout, Ellie's movements became fluid and precise on the mound.

Frank looked sideways at his best friend. "So what d'ya think, Lar? Mixes a wicked curve and slider with that floating change-up? Makes her fastball look even faster."

"Ok, so she can pitch, already." Larry was the talented catcher for the Windsor Werewolves, their team. He knew pitching and didn't often give compliments.

"Yeah. She can pitch." Frank watched the girl throw over to third base twice to keep Blondie close.

"Gotta be the sacrifice, man," Larry said.

"Yeah," Frank nodded and pounded his fist into his glove. Anyone who knew anything about baseball knew that the sacrifice bunt down the first baseline to score Blondie from third was coming. "Gotta be."

"You got her, Buck!" Blondie shouted and lengthened his lead from the base. "Bring me home, now! Girl shoulda worn a dress!"

Ellie didn't look rattled. Just intense. *And maybe something else*, Frank thought, every time she looked over at Blondie.

Ellie worked fast, not giving Buck time to think and little chance to check his manager for signals. She took him to one ball and one strike with a slow-breaking curve, and a fastball kept high and off the plate. The third pitch was a beautiful change-up that had him swinging way out in front and looking stupid.

"One ball, two strikes!" the ump confirmed, and the American fans cheered.

The Hellcats manager was slapping his cap against his thigh, muttering under his breath.

"Well?" Frank cocked an eyebrow at Larry.

"Yeah, so maybe not the sacrifice bunt."

"Come on, Bucky," Blondie yelled. "Good eye! Good eye! They're all girls out there!"

Ellie waited until Buck set himself at the plate, rocking back and forth on his toes—then surprised everyone, Frank included.

"Time, ump?" She held up her glove and pointed to some problem with the rawhide ties in the webbing.

"Delay of game! That's delay of game!" The Hellcats manager jumped to his feet, slapped his cap and gestured at the mound.

"Time out!" the ump said, and Frank thought the manager's hairless head would explode like a fat red hand-grenade.

Ellie went to one knee on the mound to work on the glove. Her tall catcher and the other infielders surrounded her. After a few seconds, she stood up, held the glove in front of her mouth and said something to all of them. A moment later, her teammates turned as one and stared at Blondie on third base. He tried to ignore it. But when five black guys are looking at you like you're ripe dog dirt, it was too hard to ignore. Blondie decided to bend down to tighten the laces on his spikes.

"Time's up!" the ump said.

The Junior Tigers infielders threw more daggers Blondie's way and went back to their positions. Ellie made a fist and held her arm straight up for her catcher. He made a fist back, nodded once and trotted to his place behind the plate.

Yeah, it's comin', Frank thought.

Larry looked at Frank. "Weird, man. What was all that about?"

"Not about her glove," Frank said.

Frank didn't tell Larry what he remembered. He'd seen that arm and raised-fist gesture on television once before—from a wild-eyed black guy standing in front of a burned-out cop car in the middle of the Detroit race riot. Maybe the girl's father had seen it too. He was halfway to his feet, with a haunted look on his face.

Like he saw ghosts.

This time, his wife restrained him.

Ellie received the sign from her catcher, nodded her head, wound up and delivered a fastball, high and inside, right at Buck's eyes. He flinched back and away. The catcher wheeled, threw a low bullet down to third and almost caught Blondie, his eye on the girl and his concentration on the orders of his third base coach.

"Boo! Boo!" The Hellcats fans were on Ellie for the too-close pitch. She ignored them and threw another fastball. Buck squared around to bunt. The infield shifted toward home, and Buck went for it. Almost. He pulled back in time and watched the ball miss the outside corner.

"That's three balls, two strikes! Full count!" the umpire said. The crowd responded with groans or cheers.

"Attaway, Bucky! Good eye! Just a girl!" The rest of the

Hellcats bench added their taunts to Blondie's. Now the skin was electric along Frank's arms and he flexed his fingers to stop the muscles jumping.

The umpire must have felt it too. There was more than just baseball going on here. He called time, to brush the plate and give the crowd a few seconds to calm. "Ok, let's play ball!"

On the mound, Ellie made the quick fist again. Frank thought he saw the catcher dip his head in response.

Frank knew something was coming.

But what?

With the count full, Buck resumed his stance and pointed the bat at the girl as if it were a weapon. Frank left his glove and cola on the grass, and stood up to get a better look. He worked his fingers through the rusted wire of the backstop and brought his nose close, as though looking through a cage at exotic animals.

Ellie went into her wind-up. Paused. Checked Blondie on third. Delivered the pitch.

And then it got weird.

Frank watched the ball come off her fingers in an odd way, in a low arc toward the batter. The ball wobbled in the air and Frank could see every seam in its slow rotation. It wasn't fast, but it wasn't the change-up either. Frank had waited for a thousand pitches, in a hundred games, on a dozen fields. This throw wasn't any of them.

Buck squared around again and the infielders leaned forward on their toes. Ellie sprinted in from the mound to follow her pitch, ducked low and spread her arms to field the sacrifice bunt. Larry jumped to his feet beside Frank.

At the last moment, Frank saw the ball twist crazy at the plate.

"Damn knuckleball!" Larry said in wonder.

Buck pushed out his bat and connected. He popped the ball up behind the catcher, dropped the bat and dug for first base, head down and arms pumping. The Junior Tigers catcher slipped off his mask, turned and looked up for the ball. Frank's eyes followed his toward the backstop, along with every other eye in the crowd.

Four feet in front of Frank, the catcher grunted and lunged with his wide glove extended as far as his body and arm could push it, lips pulled back, teeth and eyes very white. The catcher watched the ball fall into the pocket and squeezed it hard for the second out. The American crowd clapped and whistled their admiration.

Behind her catcher, Ellie was going to her knees in the dirt, blocking the plate and yelling desperately for the ball. "Home! Home! H-O-O-O-M-M-E!"

Frank's eyes were on Blondie.

The Hellcats third base coach judged the distance, saw the opposing catcher on his stomach in the dirt and faced away from the plate, scrabbling at the ball in his glove. The coach threw his right arm down like the starter at a hundred yard dash and sent Blondie off from a big lead, shouting at him to "Get home! Haul it!"

With a move Frank had never seen another player make, the Junior Tigers catcher twisted his long body around and used the cat-like motion to make a flat, sidearm throw back to Ellie at home.

Twelve feet from the plate, Blondie went down into a left

hook slide. Aimed to slip in behind home plate and just brush the corner with that left foot or following hand. Blondie's mouth was open, angry and wide. It shouted words Frank couldn't make out against the freight train roar of the crowd.

"H-O-O-O-M-M-E!" In a roil of sweat and grey dust, Ellie caught the ball and covered the plate on her knees.

A second after Frank, Larry saw it too and grabbed Frank's shoulder. They watched in slow-motion horror as Blondie raised his right foot and aimed the spikes at the black girl's face once again. Frank could already picture the torn flesh, the rush of blood, hear the screams. He pressed his forehead against the rough wire of the backstop and tore at the mesh with both hands. "No-o-o-o!"

The spikes were two feet from her face when Ellie ducked her left shoulder under Blondie's leg and lifted it high, spreading his legs like a wishbone. Now Ellie was swearing too. In a blur of dust and emotion Ellie jammed the ball right up between Blondie's legs. It wasn't his jaw she was aiming for. Combined with Blondie's sliding momentum, the brutal jab was a short, savage punch to his privates.

"A-A-A-H-H-H-G-G-H-H!" Blondie's swearing changed from threatening to intense, screaming agony two seconds later. The dust cleared to reveal Blondie writhing in the dirt like an animal in its death throes. Half the crowd, the white half, was on its feet in angry, vociferous protest.

Frank and Larry watched in silence, their mouths gaping open, as Ellie stood up, held her right hand high in the air and showed the umpire and the whole crowd she still had the ball.

"Yo-o-u-r-r-r out!" the ump declared.

Her face set, blood crusted on her cheek, Ellie tucked the

ball into her glove, raised her right arm in a fist and turned to face her black teammates. The crowd went still, as one by one, they raised their fists in return.

The inning was over.

Frank stood in the still eye of a storm of sound. Wild cheers, whistles and foot stomping from the Americans. Rabid shouts of "Foul! Foul! Not fair!" from the Canadian fans. Both teams poured onto the field to argue their sides, followed by the whole crowd.

"Well if the dumb bastard's gonna slide into home plate like that, he should wear a damn jock strap!" Frank could just make out Ellie defending herself to the ump and the growing mob. Half the mob, the white half, didn't buy it.

Just when Frank thought undeclared war had broken out, the solemn black man in the white collar and black shirt fought through the close-packed bodies, stood between the two contentious sides, raised both arms in the air and turned slowly in a complete circle. The first fingers of both hands formed the symbol that was the sign of the sixties, the response to the war in Vietnam, to the shooting of Martin Luther King just four months before.

"Peace," Frank mouthed the word.

That's when the umpire raised his own arms and voice, and declared he was ending the game.

"He can't do that!" Larry exclaimed.

"He just did, Lar."

Frank saw Ellie shrug away her father's arm and head off the field: past her teammates, past her mother and through the park toward the Detroit River, like she would swim home. The only things she carried were her glove and the fateful ball.

BR-R-O-O-M-M!

The deep horn of the Great Lakes freighter sliding under the Ambassador Bridge rolled over the park and almost swept Frank away with the sound. He stood rooted against the blast and watched Ellie disappear through the trees.

He had never felt so white.

two

"Man, Lar! Is that what I think it is?"

Twenty minutes after the excitement at Atkinson Park, Frank stared through the window of Marentette's Sport and Hobby Shop. He said the words as much to himself as to Larry.

"C'mon, Frank. It's just a fielder's mitt." Larry looked at his watch. "We told the east end guys we'd be at Holy Name School for the Strike Out game at three-thirty. It's already five minutes after."

"Then it was good the ump stopped the game early, wasn't it?"

"Dude! What's with you today? Quit raggin' on me."

"Ok, Lar. It's supreemo difficult, but I'll try." Frank still didn't look at his best friend.

"Great. Let's haul butt. We got five bucks each ridin' on this game. It's one of our last chances for some fast cash. School starts again in, like, a couple weeks, man!"

Pop Marentette must have heard Frank's question about the

glove. He materialized like an aging elf in the shop's doorway, watching Frank over the rims of his heavy black glasses. "Yep, that's the latest model Al Kaline fielder's mitt. Just got her in yesterday."

Frank spared him a quick glance. "Is that the real thing, Pop?"

"Course it's real, 'at sucker's personally autographed by Kaline himself. Yep. Man only signed ten for the whole Canadian market. Lucky to get even one 'fore those big outfits in Toronto and Montreal snapped 'em all up."

Frank couldn't take his eyes off the golden glove. He was afraid to ask.

Pop guessed it. "Yep, 'at sucker didn't come cheap, neither. Can't let it go less 'an $39.95. Nosiree. Kaline and the Tigers make the World Series in a few weeks, glove like 'at be worth a small fortune. Yep. Tigers win the World Series, be a large fortune. Mebbe good for Detroit city too, after them bad race riots last year. Yep."

Larry banged the front wheel of his CCM bicycle against the brick wall. "Ok, now you know, Frank. We're gonna miss that easy money, man. Let's make like bananas an' split."

Yet the rare treasure held Frank in its golden grip. The glove, the autograph, the price, all left him a little dazed. Frank told himself he shouldn't stay. The message didn't reach his feet. "You go on, Lar. Start warming up. Tell the other guys I'll be there in fifteen minutes, latest."

"Geez, Frank! Sometimes I just don't . . . " Larry didn't finish. He banged the wheel against the wall once more, muttered to himself, hopped on the bike and rode off.

Again, Frank knew he shouldn't. This time his mouth

betrayed him. "Think I could try it on?" Pop made him wait long enough to ask twice. "C'mon, Pop."

"Yep. Guess that'd be ok." Frank followed him inside and waited until he took the fielder's mitt out of the window. Then waited once more while Pop fussed with it. At last Pop put the mitt into Frank's eager hands.

That first touch was all it took.

The golden glove was a bit large, sure, but as soon as Frank slid his hand into the buttery leather fingers and inhaled the sharp smell of the newly tanned hide, he got testosterone fever no guy could withstand.

This newest Kaline glove had it all: the patented "Lock-Tite" web; the "Grip-Tite" pocket; the "Snap-Action" close and the "Hold-Tite" strap, to keep the glove snug in any position. But the best, the absolute best, was the all-star right fielder's handwritten autograph in black Sharpie pen above the stamped, mass-produced signature in the palm of the glove: *"Al Kaline 1968."*

"Yep. She's somethin', ain't she?" Pop said.

Frank could only nod like a bobble-head idiot.

From that moment on, Frank couldn't stop thinking about the beautiful mitt, calling out its siren song from the window of Marentette's, where any guy could hear it and see it. He imagined some other guy's hand slipping it on, being captured by its promise and walking it out of his life forever. It made him physically sick with worry and longing. When Pop reached out and pulled the glove off his hand, Frank felt like his guts pulled out with it.

"Yep, 'at sucker won't last long," Pop said.

Frank knew it was true. With a supreme effort of will, he

made himself get back on his Raleigh racer and head down Wyandotte Street toward Holy Name School. He didn't hear the noisy Saturday traffic all around him. When he stopped at the next lights to look back, Frank could still see the Kaline glove glowing in the window like a yellow jewel.

"Maybe I'll be lucky. Maybe."

But Frank knew it would take a whole lot more than luck. It would take, like, what? He couldn't shape the thought. Frank's mind groped for a solution.

The light changed to green and the idea hit him like a fastball to the head: the east end guys, the Strike Out game, five bucks waiting to be won. It was a start. "Do it, man! Work for that money. You want that glove? Just do it!"

Frank clicked the gearshift into high and sped off on wheels of fire.

It became his routine.

Each Saturday morning, Frank rode his Raleigh racer the same eleven blocks down busy Wyandotte Street from his house on McKay Avenue. He dreaded the day the glove would be gone.

"Lucky! Lucky! Lucky!" He matched the incantation to his pumping of the pedals.

Frank raced past his J.E. Benson Junior High School, the Kehoe Apartments, Katz Brothers Wholesale Grocers. Tore past Bookwin's Shoe Store, with the black X-ray box that turned your feet green and revealed the gray shadows of your bones fitted inside a pair of new shoes. He dodged around Mr. Katchen, the butcher, or tried to. Katchen spent more time in the street chewing the fat with Miss Gottlieb, while she shined the windows of Gottlieb's Fine Ladies Wear, than cutting it off of his meat.

Both storeowners knew Frank and his family well, and he offered only a quick wave the first time he flew by. "Goin' to a fire, Frank?" Katchen shouted, standing under the shade of the store's faded canvas awning and wiping big hands on his bloodstained apron.

Frank didn't have time to answer.

He willed the stoplights to be green, his legs to work faster, his luck to hold. One day his mother got wind of his bad manners and lectured him about his rudeness to Mr. Katchen and Miss Gottlieb. "I want you to explain and apologize, Frankie." He hated it when she called him Frankie. He was fourteen already.

Frank forced himself to stop and apologize that next week, but kept the reason vague. "Uh, you know, Miss Gottlieb, just meeting with the Bridge Avenue guys at Atkinson Park for some late season ball practice."

"If you say so, Frank." She raised one thin eyebrow and shook her head in amusement. "And please tell your mother I have in the first of that new line of Cantrece pantyhose I've been waiting for. Very chic. Your own wife might like them, Mr. Katchen." The butcher blushed as red as the blood on his apron and retreated quickly into his shop. Miss Gottlieb actually winked at Frank.

"Uh, I'll tell her, Miss Gottlieb." What the hell did he care about pantyhose? Thereafter, Frank spared them quick waves and shouted greetings.

"Lucky! Lucky! Lucky!"

Frank worked around the neighbourhood, took any job he could find. Cut grass, pulled weeds, painted steps, cleaned junk out of garages. Every Saturday Frank continued to pump his legs and chant. Miraculously, the golden glove was always there. Yet the $39.95 it cost was a fortune for a Sandwich West guy like him. Still, he had won that five bucks from the Strike Out game with the east end guys.

And that's when Frank had come up with "The Plan."

Frank yakked about the fielder's mitt incessantly to his dad. Took every opportunity to bring it up. Saved his best efforts for the dinner table where his father and mother were captive. "My old Kaline glove's ok, Dad, but it's almost three years old now. I've grown a lot since I was eleven. See how big my hand is." Frank spread his fingers as wide as he could. "And now I'm playing right field in the Windsor Junior League. It's a lot tougher than Little League. Some of the guys are two years older than me and got better equipment too. Got more expensive stuff."

"They *have* better equipment, Frank. They *have* more expensive stuff," his mother corrected, when she arrived with the bowl of whipped potatoes.

"That's right, Mom. They do," Frank agreed. His mother shook her head at him. She did that a lot lately.

His father finally looked up from carving the roast chicken. "More expensive doesn't always mean better, Frank. Now pass me your mother's plate, please."

Frank did, and made his best argument.

"And the glove's a good investment, Dad. Pop Marentette says if the Tigers make it to the World Series in October, the glove'll be priceless."

This last was clever, Frank calculated, his dad being Chief of Accounting for *The Windsor Star* newspaper. But maybe not. Because that was when his dad, the caring parent, the careful accountant and a double die-hard Tigers fan, had made him "The Deal."

"Fifty-fifty, Frank. Cash on the dinner table," his father announced. "You get your three dollars allowance every Friday evening, as usual. But we'll match any additional money you earn doing jobs around the house and the neighbourhood too."

"This way, Frank, you'll earn the glove," his mother added, "and come to value it more."

Frank groaned.

School and homework were on the horizon. His time after class with Larry and the guys was short enough, and his weekends were more precious than gold.

But gold was what Frank needed.

"You'll never do it in a hundred years, Frank!" his younger sister, Fancy, crowed. She wanted to say a lot more, but a look from his mother warned her. "Well, he won't."

The special Kaline glove was within reach. Maybe. But with this deal, his dad had hit the ball right back into Frank's field.

"What have you got in your pocket?" his father asked.

"Two bucks. For cutting and raking the de Sousas' grass."

"Since when?" His mother's eye was heavy on Frank now. He'd known it would be a problem when she found out and wished he'd picked a better time. Their next-door neighbors were elderly, and Mr. de Sousa had a bad heart. His father had cut their grass at first, but his mother assigned Frank the job the summer before. They were neighbours in need. Frank's mom had been very clear no payment from the de Sousas was expected. So Frank took a chance.

"I didn't ask or anything, Mom. Just told Mr. de Sousa about the glove. I guess he wanted to help."

"Isn't that taking advantage of his condition, Frank?" she said.

"Yeah, Frank. That was just mean." Fancy got in her two cents worth.

"Do I have to give the two bucks back?"

"I'll talk to Paulo and see," his mother decided.

But his father had taken his wallet out of his pocket, opened it and laid out a crisp new two-dollar bill. "Here's my half until then, Frank." Frank saw his parents exchange a look and decide something without using words. He got a bad feeling. "And we'll let your mother hold the money, like a savings bank."

Man, how did parents do that look?

"What if someone buys the glove first?" Frank said.

His dad had looked at his mom again and something else was decided. "There are no guarantees, Frank, in this or in life," he said. "The sooner you get to work, the better the chance you'll get the glove before it's sold."

Fancy smirked at him across the table but said nothing. Shirley Temple's evil twin.

Frank held out his plate for a helping of chicken. "I guess." There was no sound, but Frank knew Fancy was still laughing at him. He ignored her and bit down hard on his piece of chicken—right through a sharp bone. "Ah-h-h!"

When Frank pulled it out of his mouth, it was the wishbone. *Weird.*

The Deal had been just the beginning. Besides all the extra work for the glove, it took almost four weeks of bitter deprivation, a lifetime. Fewer hits of Milky Ways, jujubes, sponge taffy, licorice whips, roasted sunflower seeds, Peerless Dairy milkshakes and the other things that made school and sisters bearable. Frank even gave up the two packs of Topps baseball cards he'd bought religiously every week for years. In short, The Deal meant Frank made major league sacrifices.

Even Larry Teeples, Frank's best friend from across the street, didn't really think he could do it. And near the end, Larry even questioned whether the glove was worth it. "Man, it's just a glove. And me an' the rest of the guys are gettin' tired of sharing out our candy and smokes and stuff after our scrub games."

His best friend and he didn't understand! The doubt only made Frank work harder to prove Larry wrong.

"Lucky! Lucky! Lucky!"

On the morning of Saturday, the fourteenth of September, Frank had the full $39.95 amount in his jeans pockets. Refusing the company of Larry and his other friends, he rode his Raleigh racer to Marentette's Sport and Hobby Shop all by himself to claim the golden glove. It just had to be there.

"Had to! Had to! Had to!"

Frank hopped off his bike, dropped it against a lamppost and didn't stop to lock it. He turned and sprinted to the shop window. Along with the dollar bills, the quarters, dimes and nickels in both jeans pockets bounced against his thighs. The bouncing stopped and Frank's heart stopped with it.

The display stand was empty.

"No-o-o!" It came out as a low moan of denial.

Frank closed his eyes and squeezed his hands against the sides of his head to keep it from exploding. The hope. The Plan. The Deal. The sacrifices. The weeks of guy-sweat. It was all for nothing. Frank felt like he'd crashed his bike and his life head-on into the brown brick wall of Marentette's. He sagged forward and let his aching head bang against the bricks. Then punched the wall so hard he thought he'd broken his hand.

"Damn it!"

"Thought 'at was you out here, Frank. Tryin' to break down my wall? Find out what's harder, them bricks or your head?" Pop Marentette let out a self-satisfied little chuckle. He stood at the doorway in his narrow-brimmed felt hat and baggy grey sweatshirt. On the front of the shirt was an image of teenaged Farina, his black face split by a wide grin that Frank recognized from the old *Our Gang* TV series. In that episode, the teacher asked Farina to use the word "isthmus" in a sentence. The words underneath said: "Isthmus be my lucky day!"

Perfect.

"You sold the autographed Kaline glove." Each word was a brown brick on Frank's tongue but he managed to say it. He rubbed the bruised knuckles of his hand.

Pop's heavy black glasses slipped farther forward on his nose. He looked over them at Frank. "Mebbe." Then he turned and went back inside. Frank followed him in. But what was the point?

Pop perched like a leprechaun in his usual position on the wooden stool behind the glass-topped counter. It displayed a selection of intricate Cox model airplane engines in silver and black.

It was torture, yet Frank had to ask. "Can you tell me who bought the glove?"

Pop took out one of the engines and began fitting a piece of clear plastic tubing onto the fuel intake stud. He didn't look up. "Oh, a young Tigers fan from the neighborhood. 'Bout your age, I 'spect. His mother called."

"What? When?"

"Oh, mebbe ten minutes ago, give or take. Yep." Pop picked up a small silver fuel tank and fitted the other end of the tube over the outlet stud.

Frank didn't want to believe it. "So I must've just missed the guy?" It was even more devastating to come that close and lose the golden prize.

"Oh, I don't think so . . . "

"What do you mean?"

And that's when Pop began to cackle. And cackle. And cackle. "Mother name of Mrs. Laura Something. Phelan might've been. Yep." Pop dropped the parts onto the glass counter and added knee slapping to the cackling.

Frank could hardly make his mouth work. "You mean . . . ?"

Pop was now cackling, slapping and nodding. "Yep. Really had you goin' there. Look on your face? Shoulda took a picture. Yep."

Frank wanted to murder the old geezer. But he was too happy.

Thirty seconds later, he was wearing the golden glove. It was his. His!

Frank shoved his face deep into the yellow pocket and inhaled the intoxicating scent for a long minute. The scent of power. Of possibility. Of the Major League baseball he loved. And last, doubting the truth of his own eyes, Frank traced the indelible, black Sharpie miracle of the handwritten signature with a slow index finger:

"Al Kaline 1968"

"Lucky. Lucky. Lucky," he whispered the magic words to himself.

And Pop must have heard. "More lucky than you know, bub. Yep." He looked at Frank over the black glasses again.

"What do you mean?"

Pop only winked and laid a sly finger against the side of his nose.

three

"They clinched, Mom! The Tigers clinched the pennant race! Pop Marentette was right. The Tigers, Kaline, they're going to the World Series. 'Gainst the St. Louis Cardinals. Man! Bet my autographed Kaline glove's worth, like, a hundred bucks now, easy." Frank forced out the words between panting breaths.

It was Tuesday, September seventeenth, but not just any Tuesday. Earlier that morning, Frank took a chance and smuggled his small black and white, Sony portable transistor radio to school in his jacket pocket, to listen for news of the Tigers in the pennant race. It was easy to conceal, the size of a Rothman's cigarette pack.

At the sink, his mother stared at him. "Did you just run all the way home from school, Frank? Sit down at the kitchen table and catch your breath."

Frank struggled to keep his expression neutral, so his mom wouldn't guess he'd broken the rule about taking the Sony to school. It didn't matter.

"Your father called me from work with the news. I'm very happy for you and your father and grandfather. I know how much you were all hoping." She turned ominously away from the dishes and gave Frank the full effect of the heavy eyeball. He knew he'd blown it.

"Frank? Don't tell me you took your transistor radio to school, after we agreed last year that it was not appropriate under any circumstances?"

Damn! He should have waited until he got home and pretended he heard it on the clock radio or something, or just let her tell him. He was too hyped.

"C'mon, Mom. Just this one time, honest. It was the pennant race, the World Series. I didn't listen in class."

His mother wiped her hands on the dishcloth, put one hand on her hip and held out the other with a snap of her fingers. "Give me."

Frank let out an exaggerated sigh and handed it over. He and Larry had used the radio to listen to the reports of the Detroit race riot, far away from home and the prying eyes of their parents and younger sisters. Frank never regretted the decision to spend some of his hard-earned savings on it. And a year later, it still came in handy for situations like this.

When I'm not stupid enough to let my mother figure it out.

"One week," his mother decided. "You get it back next Tuesday."

"Aw, Mom."

"THE YEAR OF THE PITCHER"

That's what all the sports headlines were calling the 1968

baseball season. Frank knew it was the year of two pitchers: McLain and Gibson.

Detroit boasted Denny McLain, the right-handed hurler who awed Frank, his father and grandfather, and proud Tigers fans on both sides of the river, by becoming the first thirty-game winner since 1934! And in this same year, farther south in St. Louis, the Cardinals Bob Gibson had produced an earned run average of only 1.12 in over three hundred innings pitched, starving opposing batters of hits. It was a major league record. Gibson gave up earned runs like a miser gave up pennies. Batters waited all game for a single decent hit and were still disappointed.

How perfect then, that when the regular season was finally over, the Fall Classic, the 1968 World Series, would match St. Louis against Detroit. And when the starting pitchers for the opening game were named, well, Frank thought God must love baseball, because McLain was on the mound for Detroit, and Gibson was toeing the pitching rubber for the Cardinals.

Frank crossed the fingers on both hands and prayed with all his might that God loved teenaged ballplayers too, and that his mother would let him watch at least one game on TV. When it came to issues like this, his mom was tougher on the mound in her home stadium than McLain and Gibson combined. Frank's grandparents had come down from Peterborough for the series, and Frank brought in his grandfather David to pinch-hit for him and manage the major league argument he knew was inevitable. Frank, his father, his grandmother Norah, the old black Lab, Cobb, and even the year-old, constantly curious Lab pup, Kaline, observed their difficult conversation from a distance. Fancy, holding her half-Persian cat, Mr. Nibs, got as close as she could while his grandfather came to the plate to bat for Frank with his mother.

"A Detroit World Series opening game, Laura. It may never happen again in Frank's lifetime. In his whole lifetime. I know he'll miss an afternoon of school, but his dad and I will see that he makes it up with extra math work at home. So, please, Laura, just this once, let Frank be home to watch the game on television with us. Let us be true Tigers fans, a family, Phelans together."

Instead of answering his grandfather, his mother exchanged a second's look with his grandmother Norah, like a pitcher looking for the pitch sign from the catcher. Something flashed between them, invisible but palpable nonetheless. Was it women's secret code or something? Frank actually bit his tongue to keep from speaking out and hurting his cause. His mother looked over at his sister holding her stupid cat and screwing up her face like Elmer Fudd on the verge of a tantrum at this favouritism. His mom considered the decision for a lifetime. Couldn't she see the desperate need in his eyes? His grandmother gave the smallest of nods, and it was like his mother didn't have to see it to pick up the sign. "So, this one time, Frank. And you're only missing your afternoon classes. Understood?"

Fancy's response was immediate. "No, Mom, no-o-o-o!"

When his mother held up a hand like an umpire to silence Fancy, Frank felt a ton of dread slip from his shoulders. "Understood, Mom, thanks," he said, "and I will do that math work, promise."

She nodded and turned to his grandfather. "Very well, the first game, David. But I want you and Frank and his father to understand, this will not, not, become a habit."

"Understood." His grandfather practically saluted.

Frank's mother turned to his sister and Mr. Nibs. "I know it's not fair, Fancy, but it's very, very important to your brother, dear. Can you understand that?"

It was Fancy's cue for the drama to begin. She went right into her Shirley Temple's evil twin act, just as Frank knew she would. "No, Mom! It's not fair I have to go to school and Frank doesn't. It's not fair!" She actually stamped her right foot and jostled Mr. Nibs. Frank rolled his eyes at his mother. He could act when needed, too.

"I said it isn't, sweetie. But it's what I decided."

Fancy pushed out her lower lip and said nothing more. She hugged Mr. Nibs and did the tragic-victim-on-the-verge-of-tears thing until they all felt guilty. Frank knew it was intentional. He never doubted his sister was clever. Yes, the decision was made. Yet Frank could tell Fancy filed away the injustice for future considerations. She whirled around and exited the stage to go to her room in a petulant, full-lipped pout.

For Frank, his father and grandfather, not to mention the dogs, Cobb and Kaline, lying at their feet by the living room couch, the opening game of the 1968 World Series on the afternoon of Wednesday, October second, represented a legendary "Clash of the Titans." Frank wore his number 6 Kaline jersey, his Tigers ball cap and, of course, his lucky, personally autographed Al Kaline fielder's mitt. His grandmother surprised them with a six-pack of Double Cola and shot a shrewd glance at the players from each team lined up on the baselines for introductions. She winked at Frank like they shared a secret. Frank remembered that slight nod to his mom a few days before. He began to suspect there was more to Grandma Norah than met the eye. But what?

The first pitch was thrown at Busch Memorial Stadium in St. Louis, and three generations of Phelan males clinked bottles and toasted a Detroit Tigers victory. Twice Frank caught his grandmother cocking an ear to the action, beside his mom in the kitchen, when he went to the refrigerator for quick snacks. *Huh?*

Clash of the Titans? It was anything but.

Frank was sure that the agony of witnessing that first game on television with his father and grandfather would be a gaping wound at the heart of his memory for the rest of his life.

McLain gave up three runs to the Cardinals in the fourth inning. The first was on a costly misplay by the normally reliable Tigers left fielder, Willie Horton. Horton's misplay made Frank wince, and his grandfather shake his head in disgust. "Ok, but everybody makes mistakes, Frank. The game's not even half-over."

It got worse from there.

By the eighth inning, the Tigers were down 4-0. The Cardinals Gibson had struck out thirteen Tigers hitters and was closing in on Sandy Koufax's World Series pitching record of fifteen strikeouts. The Phelan men groaned collectively as Gibson retired the first Detroit Tigers pinch-hitter, Eddie Matthews, in the eighth. They cheered when he gave up a single to Tiger Mickey Stanley in the ninth. And Frank cheered again and drove his fist into the deep leather pocket of his new glove. His idol, big number 6, Al Kaline, nicknamed "Mr. Tiger," came to the plate with his dangerous bat and dug in his spikes.

Frank thought Al Kaline looked supremely confident. But so did Gibson, standing tall on the pitcher's mound like some invincible African god in his Cardinals white and red.

McLain was long forgotten. For Frank, this was the ultimate Clash of the Titans! "Kaline will do it. We can come back. You'll see," he assured his father and grandfather with a confident look to match the expressions of the two Titans on the screen. Frank leaned forward in expectant awe and watched the duel play out.

It took barely two minutes.

When it was over, Frank marched up the stairs, retired to his room and locked the door without saying a word. Downstairs, he left his prized Al Kaline fielder's mitt and his teenaged faith lying abandoned on the floor in front of the television set.

"It's just the first game, son. Tigers pride, remember?" But Frank didn't hear his father. Gibson had, indeed, equaled Koufax's record of fifteen strikeouts.

Al Kaline, his invincible hero, had fanned.

Gibson would go on to retire Norm Cash for strikeout victim sixteen and Willie Horton for an amazing seventeen. The Titans had clashed, and the Tigers humiliation was recorded for evermore in annals of World Series history. The St. Louis Cardinals had soundly defeated Denny McLain, Al Kaline and the Detroit Tigers in the first game of the 1968 World Series, completely shutting them out 4-0.

And that wasn't the end of it.

"Frank?"

More than an hour after the crushing Tigers defeat, there was a knock on his bedroom door. Frank expected it would be his father or even his grandfather, coming to commiserate. But it was his mother's voice on the other side.

"Frank? May I come in please?"

He'd been swearing under his breath every time he recalled Kaline's humiliation and didn't care that his mother may have overheard him. Frank hesitated but unlocked the door. Fancy overhearing him would be bad. He didn't want to give her the satisfaction of seeing this vulnerability. Yet his sister was nowhere in sight. Later, Frank figured it wasn't an accident. His mother was smart about that stuff. Seeing her standing in the open doorway holding his autographed Kaline glove was disconcerting.

Frank was suddenly ashamed.

His mother joined him, sitting on the side of his bed, and together they stared in silence at the brown wooden headboard. It was completely covered with baseball and Detroit Tigers memorabilia. The carefully framed and almost priceless pair of mint condition, #240 Topps Al Kaline rookie cards were front and centre. Frank spoke at last, if only to confirm the disaster.

"How far did Gibson go?"

"He struck out Cash and Horton and bettered Koufax by two, at seventeen," his mother said.

"How could Kaline do it? How could he let it happen? I counted on him." Frank waited, not expecting any kind of real answer.

"I think what's important here, Frank, is that Kaline tried his best, his very best. But on this one afternoon, with this one pitcher and this one at-bat, Gibson was the better player. Today Gibson was unbeatable. It happens, Frank. But Al Kaline is still a great player and a great sportsman. He didn't go down easily.

He went like a champion. And like a man. But we're all human. We all fail at times."

"This was the World Series!"

"I know. A very important game. But still only the first game, as your father said. That's why they call it a series. There'll be at least three others. And Kaline will be in right field or on first base and stepping up to the plate in all of them."

Frank let himself fall back on the bed. His mother had to turn and look down at him.

"Gibson struck Kaline out, but he didn't defeat him. And you have to respect Gibson's performance this afternoon. It was his moment, Frank. For a while, Gibson took pitching and the World Series to another level. I think Kaline is the kind of player who would respect that, congratulate Gibson and then be proud to say he was part of it, even in a losing cause." She waited, but Frank could think of nothing to say.

"Isn't that why you admired Kaline in the first place? Wore his number? Worked so hard to earn his glove?" Frank had to admit it was true. Still, it was tough. But his mother hadn't finished, and that's when guilt really started to weigh Frank down hard.

"And speaking of this Kaline glove, Frank, I'm going to tell you something I intended to keep to myself." His mother laid the golden glove on Frank's chest. "Not even your father knows this." Frank was suddenly very attentive. "That night, more than a month ago now, when your father finally made the fifty-fifty deal with you about the glove, well, I got worried. As you said, the glove might be sold to someone else before you had enough time to earn your share and buy it. I phoned your grandmother."

Now Frank held the glove and sat up again, to see his mother's face.

"So the next morning, after you and Fancy left for school, I walked down to the sporting goods store and made a deal with Mr. Marentette. I put a deposit of twenty dollars on the glove to hold it for a month. I told him that if you didn't buy the glove yourself by then, he could keep the money and the glove. So he couldn't lose."

"You did that?"

"Yes, I did. Mr. Marentette shook his head like I was some kind of crazy mother, but he agreed. I walked back to collect my twenty dollars the following Monday, after you bought the glove. It was one of the proudest walks of my life. The look on Mr. Marentette's face when he handed the money back? It was respect, Frank, for both of us."

Frank was silent again, struggling mightily to process this. No wonder the glove was always there each time he rode over and checked. *"More lucky than you know, bub."* Pop Marentette had said.

"But Mom, you knew I was worried about the same thing. And I was always riding over to make sure it was there." This was really a question.

"I know I did, Frank. But you had to earn that glove on your own. Work hard for it. So when you finally got it, you'd truly appreciate it. Then it would be your glove in a way it could never be if we just bought it for you." His mother placed her hand on the Kaline mitt in Frank's lap. "It's a beautiful glove. And Kaline's autograph? When I saw it, I understood right away why you had to have it."

"You could've just told me."

"No. I couldn't. I don't know if you can understand this, but my role was to give you the time you needed to earn it. And you did, Frank! I am so very, very proud of you. You showed guts and commitment. I'll always have faith in you." Frank felt the slow resurgence of his own pride. "Do you know why I'm telling you this now, Frank?"

He could only nod and say a single word. "Kaline."

"Exactly. You're too smart for this, Frank. Kaline deserves another chance. He just needs time. Sometimes, especially when it's hardest, that's when you most have to believe." His mother gave Frank's shoulder a quick squeeze. "I love you, son." Then got up and walked to the door. "Dinner is in fifteen minutes. I expect to see you down there washed and at the table."

And that was it. Guilty—and feeling stupid too.

Fifteen minutes later, Frank was seated in his usual place. He was wearing his number 6 Kaline jersey, and the autographed Kaline glove was beside him on the floor. Frank directed a private smile at his mother and received one in return.

From the other end of the table, his grandmother winked at him.

four

"Ok! Listen sharp all you fans and fanettes out there. 'Cause it's noon on the clock and Daddy's ready to rock. I mean it's time for the 'Scheib Series Special,' baby!"

Frank reached over and adjusted the tuning-dial on his transistor radio beside him on the bed. Every time he listened to a Detroit radio station, it brought back the disturbing memories and images from last year's riot, burned scary-bright into his mind forever. Literally. Back then, every chance they'd had, for most of five days, Frank and Larry sat under the Ambassador Bridge with the small black and white radio, and with thousands of other Windsor spectators. The crowd went for miles along the riverbank. Across the familiar river, hardly a stone's throw away, Frank and Larry listened and watched as Detroit burned.

Now, more than a year after the riot, the little transistor filled Frank's bedroom with the voice of Motown's most popular black deejay.

"All right, Dee-troit! This is your lover-man, Smooth Daddy

Groove, comin' at ya from WSMU—that's Smu-u-u-th Radio! The mainline station for particular picky people who like their Motown lowdown."

"Yes, Gwendolyn, you're gettin' it straight-no-chaser, from the Dad with the Bad on the Rad! We *are* the heart in the heart of Motown. The beat for the street, up top the Penobscot Tower, so high in the sky even birds don't fly! But I got my eye on you from WSMU-U-U, baby!"

When Frank and Larry left school to go for lunch, only Frank's grandparents were at home, Norah in the kitchen, David reading the papers at the dining room table. His mom was out walking his grandfather's two black Labs, with only the pup, Kaline, needing a leash. Fancy was eating across the street with Larry and his sister, Carol. On days like this first Friday in October, his dad always worked late at *The Windsor Star* newspaper and wouldn't be home much before six o'clock.

"I hear ya, Smooth Daddy!" Frank said to the radio.

Around him, Frank's huge collection of baseball memorabilia decorated the room like a shrine. His dozen Detroit Tigers pennants, his rare 1955 Al Kaline rookie cards, his Tigers ball caps, his souvenir Tiger Stadium bats, a bobble-head doll for each American League team and two shoeboxes full of stacks of Topps major league baseball cards going back nine years. Frank had the best collection among all the guys he knew. He dared to think it might be the best in the city, maybe the whole of Canada!

Two years before, his grandfather had given Frank a cool pair of old black and white photos: one of Ty Cobb, nicknamed "The Georgia Peach," at Navin Field; the other of great-grandfather Wally, smiling under his fat walrus moustache. They were to remind Frank of the long history of Phelans and Tigers baseball in Detroit. Great-grandfather Wally was a carpenter from Windsor and helped build Tiger Stadium back in 1912, when it was called Navin Field. His Phelan sweat was soaked right into its wood.

Wally actually saw Ty Cobb play!

Pop Marentette was so right more than a month ago just before school started. The Detroit Tigers had made it to the World Series. Now Frank's beloved Kaline glove was beside him on the bed with Al Kaline's autograph staring back at him like baseball magic. Frank damped down the uncomfortable memory of that first-game Tigers loss.

He fluffed the pillows behind him and settled back against the headboard. "Ok, Smooth Daddy, who's gonna crash and burn today?" Frank knew this daily chance to win a pair of the impossible Tigers World Series tickets came from Detroit's Earl Scheib, the well-known owner of Scheib's Auto Body and Paint Shops.

Right on cue, Smooth Daddy let Earl make his pitch. "And before we get to today's question, babies, ya'll give a close listen to our favourite sponsor, Brother Scheib."

"Yes, sports fans," the transistorized voice announced, "my name is Earl Scheib and I will paint any car any colour for just $29.95 using my exclusive 'Diamond Dust Paint.' That's no lie, so stop on by! Go Tigers go!"

"Geez! Get on with it already!" Frank shoved half of his tuna sandwich into his mouth, followed by a swallow of Fancy's chocolate milk. He stole small glasses of it almost every week and she never noticed. *Sweet.*

Frank nudged up the volume on the transistor by a hair and prepared himself.

"Ok, babies! The Tough Tigers Trivia for today is . . . get ready for it! Daddy G is wishin', an' hopin', an' waitin' for thee."

"In 1905, what uniform number did the Tigers give their new rookie, Tyrus Raymond Cobb? Here be your choices: number 6, number 36, number 12, or number 24? That's Ty Cobb, 6, 36, 12, or 24? Daddy G is pullin' for thee!"

"1905?" Frank whispered. This one was sure enough tough. He looked at the facing view photo of Cobb on the wall, but the number would be on the back of his jersey and could change. Something tickled at the back of Frank's memory. "Cobb's number? Sixty years ago?" After a few moments, Frank just took another sip of Fancy's milk and waited.

"Takin' caller number three! Number three!"

Some die-hard Tigers fans out there might know, he thought. Yet Frank was pretty sure most of them were actually dead. They wouldn't be picking up a phone any time soon unless the universe was a lot stranger than he figured.

"Ok, brothers and sisters! Now get off the lines and don't give me no whines. Smooth Daddy has caller number three, lucky number three on the phone right now! Where are you brother and what is your handle, p-u-l-e-e-a-se?"

Frank picked up the radio and put it on his lap. There was a short hesitation while the caller cleared his throat. Two seconds later, Frank pitched forward and sprayed tuna fish and chocolate milk all over himself.

"No friggin' way!"

Riveted by the voice and drama playing out with Smooth Daddy Groove, Frank made no attempt to clean himself up. *Can't be!*

"This is David, uh, Edwards," the caller began, "phoning from a cottage near, uh, Peterborough. In Canada."

But it is!

"Hot damn!" Frank grabbed the Kaline glove and the fish and milk-spattered radio and shot out the bedroom door so fast, it slammed back against the wall. In an adrenaline rush, he took the stairs two at a time, burst into the living room and—stopped. No way could Frank accept what his eyes saw and his ears heard.

"Grandpa?"

His grandfather David stood hunched over next to the clock radio on the buffet sideboard in the dining room with the phone to his ear. The expression on his face was super-tense, and he made frantic "quiet down" motions with his free right hand. Frank's grandmother Norah stood in the kitchen doorway wiping her hands on a dishtowel and shaking her head at her husband. The slight smile on her face suggested the shaking was not displeasure. Sure enough, she winked at Frank.

What a surprise!

Frank slid, lungs panting and heart hammering, into the nearest chair at the dining room table and shook his own head from side to side in complete denial. Didn't his grandfather David know that what he was doing was, like, very, very illegal? Of course he did! Frank's father worked at *The Windsor Star.* Didn't he sign a contract? No one in the family was allowed to enter this kind of contest. And calling from Peterborough? Wouldn't everyone know that was, like, impossible?

Smooth Daddy's voice came in stereo from the clock radio and Frank's transistor he forgot for a moment he was still holding. "Oh yeah . . . yeah, baby," continued Smooth Daddy, "the great Canadian metropolis of Peterborough—never heard of it! Hey, just messin' wit' ya. You there, Brother Edwards?"

"Right here, Smooth Daddy."

"Ok, Country Canada! You heard the question. You know the rules. Cobb's number, 1905? Wanna take you a try, or roll over an' die?"

"I believe I'll try," David said.

"Then lay it on us, Canada!"

"It'll be nothing, Smooth Daddy."

"What say, brother? Don't even wanna guess?"

"No, Daddy. It's not a guess. I know for a fact that Ty Cobb never wore one of those numbers because he never wore any number at all on his Tigers uniform, ever."

"O-O-O-E-E! That yo' shot Canada?" Smooth Daddy's voice went up in pitch like a rising fastball.

"Yes, sir."

Frank hung his head and felt stupid. He knew that! Were all these questions tricks?

"Well, Smooth Daddy is very, very sorry, Brother Edwards. Cause it hurts like hemorrhoids to have to tell the box office to hold on to these two fine Tigers World Series tickets—so they can give 'em to you and a lucky amigo from some boonie-burg in Canada I ain't never heard of! Congratulations, Canada! You are abso-positively correct! You won, baby. You're goin' to game five of the 1968 World Series on Monday. Daddy G is proud of thee!"

"Wow, Grandpa!" All Frank's worries about the illegality of the thing vaporized in an instant at the mind-blowing possibility of actually being there. At the World Series! With his beloved Tigers! With his hero, Al Kaline! It was too much.

WE WON THE TOUGH TIGERS TRIVIA!

The words exploded like cherry bombs in Frank's imagination. Two tickets to the World Series! Frank couldn't help it. He jumped up from his chair, whooped and began throwing punches at the air . . . until his grandfather's one hand shot out to grab him by the shoulder and force him down into the chair again.

"Uh, Smooth Daddy?" his grandfather continued.

"Right here, Canada. How does it feel? You be a winner, baby!"

"It feels great, Smooth Daddy. But I believe now I'll go for the 'Double Or Nothing Big Bonus Question.'"

What? Frank's incandescent joy vanished in a heartbeat. His mind went dark with dread. *What?* Before he could open his mouth to protest, his grandfather dug fingers into his shoulder so hard, Frank squeezed his eyes shut against the pain and went limp.

"What say, Brother Edwards?" Smooth Daddy asked, as if he too didn't quite believe it. "Hey-y, you some crazy cat dude up in Canada there, Dave! No cool cat, no cool kitten, I mean no one baby, in two whole weeks, has dared to try Smooth Daddy's Double or Nothin', be lyin', die cryin' Big Bonus Question. Last guy to try went down in flames. I mean he was crispy, brother. Only guy who didn't fry was this sports historian dude from

Michigan State University the week before. You sure 'bout this, Brother Edwards?"

"I believe I am, Daddy. I can't use just two tickets."

Frank took his grandfather's hand and gave out soundless protests with his mouth. His grandmother stepped forward and pulled Frank's hand back. Now she made quiet down motions.

"Ok, Dave. I get the groove. It's go big or go home, baby! You got some *cojones* Canada! Just like old Tyrus Raymond. So here she comes, brother!"

Frank groaned and closed his eyes, unable to watch the disaster unfold. "No. No. No," he said under his breath. This was insane! His grandfather had the tickets—illegally, but he had them for a moment. Nobody wins in the Double or Nothing Bonus. Nobody but that Diamond Dust huckster, Earl Scheib!

"The question be: What for and where was 'Cobb's Lake'? That's Cobb's Lake. What and where?" Smooth Daddy intoned.

The silence lasted an eon. Frank's mouth was a black hole sucking all available oxygen from the room.

"Try or die, baby!" Smooth Daddy warned.

Frank cracked an eye. Sure enough, his grandfather looked panicked. All was lost! For a few miraculous moments, they had had a pair of rare Tigers World Series tickets. Two Phelans were headed for the big game. Now they were headed for disaster.

That's when his Grandma Norah stepped forward and whispered into his grandfather's ear for a few seconds.

Huh?

Grandpa David's eyes went wide. Then his grandfather was actually smiling? He kissed his wife's cheek and mouthed a silent thank you. Frank knew what was coming next. His grandmother knew he knew, and winked at him anyway.

Who was this woman?

"You standin' by, Brother Edward?"

"No, Smooth Daddy, I'm keeping faith."

"What faith is that?"

"The faith of my father."

Frank opened the other eye.

"You one crazy Canuck loon," Smooth Daddy declared. "But *tempus fugit*, brother."

"Just messin' with ya, Daddy."

Frank felt the hair prickle above his shirt collar. Was his grandfather talking about his own missing and presumed dead father from years before, great-grandfather Wally?

"Cobb's Lake, what and where?" his grandfather echoed the question. "Well, the 'where' was right in front of home plate in Tiger Stadium, when it was still called Navin field in the 1920s. The 'what' was that Ty Cobb made the grounds-keepers wet down this area and keep it a bit muddy. Slowed down his bunts and increased his on-base percentage and successful sacrifices to advance his runners. Drove the opposing teams crazy."

Now like his grandfather, Frank leaned forward and widened both eyes in wonder at the obscure baseball lore his grandmother must have, like, at her fingertips.

"That yo' shot, Canada?" Smooth Daddy asked.

"That's it, Smooth Daddy."

Frank balanced on a double edge: one of disbelief, one of desperate hope. There was no breathable atmosphere in the room.

"O-O-EE, O-O-EE, DIS CANUCK IS KILLIN' ME! You hit it, Dave-baby! YOU! HIT! IT!"

Frank collapsed against the chair in dazed disbelief.

five

"You were awesome, Grandpa! I mean, four World Series tickets! How sweet is that? Too sweet, that's what!" Frank's energy had come flooding back electrifying every cell in his body. He jumped up and continued to shadowbox with the air in a flurry of quick jabs and uppercuts.

"Frank!" His grandmother surprised him, grabbed him by an upper arm a second time and held his shoulders with unexpected strength until Frank focused on her face. "Enough, Frank! Just cool it."

"You were awesome too, Grandma! How did you know about that Cobb's Lake thing?"

"You think I lived with three generations of Phelan males, rabid Tigers fans, and didn't pick up everything I needed to know to keep up?"

His grandfather laughed and gave his wife a joyous embrace. "Your grandmother knows more about the history of the players and the game than most male fans, Frank. She just doesn't show off about it like us Phelan males, or get all worked up and grouchy when things don't go the Tigers way. Still, the Cobb's Lake detail surprised me too. Like the most important things in my life, I couldn't do it without your grandmother."

Frank's grandmother blushed and pushed her husband away. "Ok, don't embarrass him, David."

This time it was his grandfather who winked.

In the brief interval, the unpleasant reality struck back, and the impact knocked Frank into the same chair. "But it's illegal! Illegal!" he almost shouted. "Dad works at the newspaper." Torn by an agony of emotion, Frank shot to his feet again and began to stomp back and forth, shaking his head.

David's expression was dead serious. "Frank! Frank! Stop this right now! I mean RIGHT NOW!"

Whoa!

His grandfather never raised his voice. Not to his grandmother, not to his parents, not to his two black Labs, not to Frank, not to Fancy—and that was saying something. Frank's whole body slumped, sagged like a beat up base leaking sawdust. "Er . . . ok Grandpa, sure!"

"Then I want you to get whatever stuff you need and get back to school." His grandmother crossed her arms and nodded her agreement.

"What? No! No, Grandpa! It's Friday. End of the week. I can miss an afternoon. It's the World Series." His grandfather backed Frank into the chair and brought his face close. His intense Phelan-blue eyes stared deep into Frank's own Phelan-blue eyes. It was no contest. Frank hung his head and his grandfather gripped Frank's chin and forced it back up. Frank's eyes stared straight into his.

"No, Frank. Missing school is exactly what you cannot do. What I just did on the phone was . . . questionable. No one must know. No one. Not Larry. Not any of your friends. We keep this strictly in the family.

"Listen to your grandfather, Frank," his grandmother said.

"But Fancy? You know she'll . . . "

David continued. "I know we'll have to discuss this, as a family, and Fancy is part of the family. But we'll do it tonight, after supper. Until then, you button your lip. You go to school. You do nothing different. You do nothing to raise suspicion. I'll tell everyone when we're all home together, not before.

"But . . . "

"The only but I want to see is your butt heading out the door five minutes ago. Get Larry. And get back to school. Now."

Frank did, and the joy warred with the dread as he contemplated the now unacceptable possibility that things could all go to hell. That he could come this close to being there, in person, at the 1968 World Series with Al Kaline and the Detroit Tigers, and blow it!

By the time he finished school; by the time Fancy got home; by the time his mother and grandmother made dinner, and his father arrived from *The Windsor Star* at six o'clock; Frank's brain felt the size of an over-inflated Zeppelin. It was about to burst into hydrogen flames with the pressure of uncertainty. David gathered them all together around the dining room table, asked them to seat themselves, took an audible breath and made the momentous announcement.

In the middle of the stunned silence and the dozen questions that followed, Frank couldn't help it. He broke loose from his family, paced around the table and pounded his fist into the Kaline glove for emphasis. "We won! We did it! Grandma and Grandpa got the Double or Nothing Big Bonus Question! Screw you too Earl Scheib!" That drew a warning look from his mother.

It didn't stop him. Cobb barked again and again, and Kaline was at Frank's heels, jumping up with him and filling the rooms with her wild puppy yips. At last, his mother corralled Frank and forced him into his chair. Fancy picked up Mr. Nibs, marched out to the living room couch and disdained it all.

"Hey! Geez! I just have to tell Larry! He'll like . . . like . . . " Frank couldn't think of anything monumental enough to describe Larry's surprise and envy, and jumped up and was off again.

He made it to the front door before his father's strong arm persuaded him back to the dining room "Just cool it, Frank. It's not that simple."

"Aw crap, Dad!" Frank said, when his father reminded him of the ticket dilemma in a voice loud enough for the whole family to hear.

"You know I work for *The Windsor Star*, Frank, a big newspaper tied in to all the media networks in the area, including Detroit. Other newspapers and magazines, radio and TV networks, as well. I'm an insider, son. We'll hash it out after supper. Now is not the time."

Frank wanted to swear with teenaged frustration. Punch out the universe. Instead, he slouched back to the living room and flopped down on an over-stuffed chair across from his gloating sister. Kaline licked his hand in sympathy. He couldn't stop himself. "Crap!"

"Frank David Phelan!" his mother warned from the dining

room. "If I hear that word or another like it one more time, you will spend the weekend in your room with your math book improving your mark. I will not have another C when your father is an accountant who works with numbers for a living and is ready to tutor you." Frank knew his mother would do it too.

Fancy smiled her annoying smile and thoroughly enjoyed his upset and reprimand. Frank could practically see the golden halo as his sister walked back to the table with her fat fur-ball of a cat and reminded his grandmother Norah: "I got an A in math, Grandma. I always get As. Want to see my last report card?"

"I know, Fancy, dear. I'm very proud," Grandma Norah said. "You can show it to me, again, after dinner."

It was true, and Frank hated it.

Just shut it, Fancy!

"Why don't we eat then?" his grandfather suggested. David was usually the final authority in matters concerning baseball plans, but Frank caught his grandfather's quick look to his mother, who nodded in agreement, but slowly.

Grandma Norah clapped her hands to get them all moving. "I'll mix the salad and season the potatoes, Laura. Frank, Fancy, you two get out of your school clothes and clean up. David, you can turn on the coffee percolator and carve the ham. The extra sour-apple dressing is warming in the oven." Frank's grandfather nodded and began sharpening the carving knife with loud sandy scrapes.

At least it wasn't chicken again. Frank remembered the wishbone. He didn't feel lucky, and he didn't feel all that hungry. His stomach was empty of food but stuffed with anxiety.

"Fine, Norah," said his mother. The two women were

suddenly busy, happy to do what they took pride in. Yet his grandmother had surprised Frank that afternoon, really surprised him. Now Frank looked at his mother, as well, and wondered what surprises she, too, might have in store. He still couldn't get over the glove thing with Pop Marentette.

Who were these women? Frank would never take them for granted again.

Frank's dad relaxed for a moment, then sneaked a quick look at the latest World Series news from the sports section of the *Detroit Free Press* he'd brought home from the clipping room at *The Windsor Star.*

Frank returned from the upstairs bathroom eager for news from Detroit. But his mother wouldn't let the three men of the house bring the paper to the table, not even his grandfather. Fancy put down Mr. Nibs and gave Frank a dirty look as she headed for the main bathroom. She returned a minute later and sat at the table with her hands folded in front of her, the innocent angel from heaven above, about to say grace.

"Aren't you eating tonight, Frank?" Fancy asked with a coy smile. Frank hung back and was the last one to the dinner table. He took his place across from his sister, but said nothing.

"Cat got your tongue, Frank?" Fancy giggled and crossed her eyes at him.

Take poison, Shirley!

six

Frank's mother insisted that the whole family would finish the first course like "civilized people" before discussing the ticket situation over dessert and coffee. For the next twenty minutes, everybody mostly watched their plates and concentrated on eating. The couple of times Frank did look up, his sister smirked and crossed her eyes again.

Was there still hope?

Frank was bursting with his opinions and ideas, but one hard look from his mother and he knew to wait and not risk it. His mom did allow him to change into his number 6, Al Kaline jersey, but refused to let him bring his cap and his new Kaline glove to the table. Frank still believed the glove might be a little lucky, even though he now knew the real story behind it.

Lucky! Lucky! Lucky!

He didn't really feel it now, and trying to force it made it worse. When the platter of sliced ham came to him, his stomach rebelled, and Frank was careful to take only half the number of slices he usually did. Still, the wonderful taste of his mother's baked ham and his grandmother's sour-apple dressing helped put down the rebellion, and the tightness in his stomach lessened a bit. Over the cup of coffee and cream that his mother had allowed him since he turned fourteen, and his grandmother's deep-dish apple pie with wedges of old cheddar that he'd loved as long as he could remember, Frank could almost hope.

What conversation there was seemed meaningless to Frank: training the pup Kaline to retrieve ducks, the condition of Mr. de Sousa's heart, starting the new school year and so on. Frank took no part and gritted his teeth while Fancy chattered away about her new teachers and the compliments they had already given her about her work. Finally, his grandfather carefully positioned his knife and fork on either side of his now-empty dessert plate, and his face became dead serious again. He looked at each of them before he spoke into the lull. "To go or not to go? That is the question."

The words dropped like doom.

The drawn-out silence that followed his grandfather's pronouncement was too much even for Fancy to challenge. She buttoned her busy lips at last. It was Frank who couldn't believe his family's hesitation. Even after his father's words before the meal, he couldn't accept the unacceptable possibility that he and his father and grandfather would not go to a World Series game, and such a crucial game at that. He had to speak up.

"We gotta go! We gotta!"

His family eyed Frank as if he were an alien from the planet Pluto that had landed at the dinner table. Even Cobb and Kaline, stretched out on the floor beside his grandfather's chair, looked at Frank as if he were a stranger. Looked, but couldn't see: there were four incredible Tigers World Series tickets waiting for "David Edwards" at the stadium box office under a secret identification number Smooth Daddy had given to his grandfather, privately, off the air.

Yet Frank knew his father felt it necessary, his duty as the family breadwinner and the nominal head of the household, to remind everyone of the unpleasant truth once more. The weight of it caused his father to hang his head a moment before he looked up and could begin. "Our family is not eligible, Frank. You're not eligible. I work at the newspaper and can neither take part in any media contests, nor benefit from them. It's part of my employment contract. I signed it to give my word. I'm considered an insider, with unfair advantage. I must remain objective and apart. So must anyone related to me."

His father looked at each of them in turn and added the final truth, the heaviest of them all. "A scandal like this could mean my job, our family's income and my complete disgrace."

Damn! Frank had never considered that.

The women nodded, especially Fancy. Like she was a woman-in-waiting. Still, his sister said nothing, and that worried Frank. This was not the super-calculating Fancy he knew and . . . well, "despised" was too strong a word; "suspected," maybe.

Frank's dad went on to say that it would be "unethical" to go. An important principle was involved. Their "integrity as a family" was involved. Frank knew what that meant. All it implied. But when he tried to interject, his grandmother held up a hand to silence him.

"Your father has a point, Frank."

Were they thinking the unthinkable?

Frank appealed to his grandfather. "But you called the radio station, Grandpa. And you knew all that." The tension deepened. Frank had never seen his grandfather avoid his look. Never. He saw it then, and it shocked him to silence—and his grandfather to an ominous pause.

Now he did meet Frank's eyes. "Yes, Frank. I admit it. I may have been wrong. It wasn't just the tickets; it was my pride, a most deadly sin. Wanting to beat the question, to flaunt my knowledge of baseball and Tigers history before an audience of thousands of fans and listeners. When I got through, no one was more surprised than I was. What were the odds? And then I lied about who I was, and deepened my sins." His grandfather took a drink of black coffee, grimaced as if the taste was bitter on his tongue. He glanced at the black telephone a few feet away and met Frank's eyes again. "But I won't lie now, Frank. And I'm not just talking about who I am and where."

"Then what, Grandpa?" Fancy asked, before Frank could get the words out.

"About the strange thing that happened when I heard Smooth Daddy say Ty Cobb's name. Impossible as it sounds, I suddenly felt . . . my father's presence. Your great-grandfather Wally's presence. Right there, right beside me. Like time ran backwards and it was 1920 and I was eight years old and we were sitting on the old benches at Navin Field again. I swear I smelled his cigarettes, smelled wood-shavings and sweat and beer. We were looking at home plate and at the greatest Tiger to ever play the game, Tyrus Raymond Cobb, squaring around for the bunt. My father Wally was trying to tell me something. And he used that special word, the word he never dared to use in front of my mother, your great-grandmother, Lulu Pearl.

The word that was a secret only between us. And then Smooth Daddy used that same word, like baseball magic, to describe the risks Cobb often took at Navin Field. '*Cojones*.'"

Frank's mother and grandmother gave David a very severe look.

"That's crazy, Grandpa," Fancy said. "And what's *cojones*?"

Frank was about to enjoy telling his sister, when his mother shot him an equally severe look. "Nothing you need to worry about, Fancy."

"Yes, maybe it was crazy," his grandfather admitted.

Frank didn't think it was crazy at all. The exact opposite. Like it was meant. "Cobb's Lake," Frank exclaimed, "that's how you knew!"

His grandfather forced down another long swallow of coffee, like atoning for his sins, and looked all around the table. "Not exactly." He reached across and took his wife's hand and kissed it. Frank was embarrassed by the intensity of the look in their eyes. Your grandmother reminded me." Norah smiled but said nothing. "So I don't know what I knew, Frank, then or now. It doesn't change the situation we're in."

But Frank knew it changed everything! Crazy or a ghost, magic or a miracle, he and his dad and grandfather were destined to go to game five of the World Series.

His mother spoke first, looking over the heads of Frank and Fancy. This was bad. "David, we have to consider the example we would be setting." The other adults turned solemn, looked down and nodded.

Of course Fancy took the opportunity to nod her own agreement. "That's exactly right, Mom." Fancy declared, eyeballing Frank like Mr. Nibs did a cornered rat.

"Ah, no, Mom, no-o-o!" Frank pleaded. "This is different. One time. Just this one time. Please. We'll be all right. But we have to be there on Monday. We just have to."

"It's wrong, Frank. W-R-O-N-G, wrong!" Fancy leaned across the table to spell it out. "And you know it."

BUTT OUT, FANCY!

Frank wanted to shout it out. Shouting it would feel so good, but make his chances so bad. Frank bit down hard on a piece of sharp-tasting cheddar instead. Fancy wanted to say more, but his father put a hand on her arm and squeezed her to silence.

Grandma Norah spoke into the silence. "It is a once-in-a-lifetime opportunity, Laura. Frank's right about that."

Hope? Frank was already exhausted, felt the second helpings of ham and pie crawling out of his stomach, and took a quick slug of coffee. Even with the cream, the taste was harsh on his tongue. This was just the opening round of the argument. The debate went on. Even his sister, who couldn't care less about baseball, had her full say. Under the table, Frank kept pounding his fist into his hand, as if he were getting ready to snag a high fly ball, one that was drifting out of reach overhead, and him without the Kaline glove.

Lucky! Lucky! Lucky! Had Frank's luck run out at the worst possible time in his life?

Frank was almost ill from the argument. In the end, after almost an hour of give and take and several re-orders of pie and coffee from the adults, his grandfather David hauled himself up at the side of the table and reviewed the important points, ticking them off with his fingers.

"We are Phelans. People of integrity. Honest, hard-working people, with the respect of our friends, neighbours and colleagues to consider. We are responsible parents and grandparents with children to consider. Norm is chief accountant at *The Windsor Star* with his position, his career, and his family's income to consider. The prohibition policy is crystal clear. I blame my pride for the fall from principle. We could be risking it all: our well-earned reputation, the respect of our kids, our economic security, if the fraud became public and Norm's employers were forced to respond to the scandal."

Each point was a railway spike of despair pounded into Frank's brain. The answer was inevitable. The issue decided. Frank could no longer bear to watch, to hear. He pushed back and let his head fall against the table edge with an audible thump.

David dropped his hands to his belt and looked at the other adults. The silence hung like God's judgment, or the Devil's. Until David's hands crashed down on the table and rattled the cutlery and jolted Frank's aching head.

"But damn it! I say we go. WE GO!"

Cobb jumped up and barked. Kaline added her energetic puppy yips, sensing the excitement.

"Wha-a-t?" Frank managed.

His mother looked hard at his grandfather. Laura Phelan would have the Last Word at this table, not God or the Devil. The thing was, she didn't look surprised.

Under the table, Frank couldn't stop driving his fist into his hand.

His dad and grandmother, Cobb and Kaline, Frank and Fancy, now looked at his mother too. She looked down at her empty dessert plate, crossed her arms, looked up at all of them. "Oh, very well, David," she said at last, like the words hurt, and sank back in her chair, the weight of her decision too much for her. "I realize how important this is to the family, to you and Norm both, and especially to Frank. But I'm afraid. We must be careful. His mother loomed forward to direct her warning to each of them in turn. "Very, very careful."

Frank closed his eyes, misjudged the distance and let his forehead hit his sticky dessert plate in supreme relief. Bonk! He wiped apple pie off his face with his napkin to the general amusement of the table.

Frank David Phelan didn't care.

Frank could find no words and stumbled out of his chair to drop onto the front couch like a pathetic Pinocchio with his strings cut.

His grandfather stretched over from the side of the table and took his mother's hands in both of his. "Thank you, Laura. Thank you sincerely for this."

Frank closed his eyes and let his mind drift free of the tension.

Family history continued to repeat itself, and Frank was never more grateful. They were Phelans, all of them together. Phelan men were Tigers fans. Always had been, always would be. Some Phelan women, right back to his strict, Irish Methodist great-grandmother, Lulu Pearl Phelan, might disagree, but in this one area at least, the current Phelan women supported their husbands and sons. The Tigers were in World Series competition, up against the St. Louis Cardinals, last year's winners, last year's Titans. This was the chance of a lifetime, Frank's lifetime. Phelans should be there to support their team, in body and spirit, even if the cause was already lost.

And it might be.

Frank hunched forward. The Tigers were already down

three games to the St. Louis Cardinals. Only two teams in the whole history of baseball had come back to win the World Series after losing three games. If his Tigers lost on Monday, they would lose the series. And Frank would be there with his idol, Al Kaline, and have to experience it with every nerve in his body vibrating with the agony of ultimate defeat. The very thought made him grimace and grind his teeth.

Frank roused himself. "Yeah, thanks, Mom. Thanks, Grandma." He got up and moved around the table and embraced them both. His father nodded at Fancy. Frank knew better than to try and embrace her.

"Thanks, Fancy. I really appreciate this. I mean it." Frank looked his sister in the eye and stuck out his hand.

Fancy waited an age before she took it and gave it a single shake. "I guess," she said.

Would this change the endless rivalry between them? Lessen the divide? Probably not. At least Frank would have the whole weekend to anticipate and savour the luck or the miracle or the destiny or whatever it was. Fancy would see it as a personal defeat, and maybe it was. Then Frank fully realized the implications and understood his sister's suppressed anger. Fancy would be in school! Knowing Frank was at the game and unable to say a word about it to anyone. *Sweet!* Frank couldn't resist the pleasure of the thought.

"And no one must know," his grandmother echoed to him and Fancy. "Not Larry Teeples. Not Carol Teeples. No one! You two must keep this as a family secret, always. Promise?"

Frank nodded solemnly.

Now it was Fancy's turn. "I wanna go if Frank's going," Fancy insisted. "It's not fair. There are four tickets."

Geez no! That was, like, crazy!

Frank was ready to shout it out and do some serious pleading himself, when his mother's firm touch on his arm cautioned him to let her handle this.

"You have a point, Fancy. It isn't fair. You've been collecting Barbie dolls for years and are as proud of your collection as Frank is of his baseball cards. So, 'Ash Blonde T 'N' T Barbie.' Pink bow, two-piece swimsuit, earrings, blue eyes, toe and fingernail polish, maybe some accessories."

Fancy's own blue eyes went as wide as the doll's she coveted.

Yeah, Frank remembered, the newest "twist and turn" model Barbie. Fancy wanted this doll as much as Frank wanted his Kaline glove. Fancy didn't play with her Barbie dolls and only collected the rarest, most expensive, limited edition ones. Her Barbies were displayed on her bed's headboard like the baseball trophies Frank collected. But his sister was still negotiating the allowance conditions and the other expectations with their parents, holding out for something better than the fifty-fifty deal Frank accepted.

His sister considered the offer, playing it for all it was worth. Which for Fancy was plenty. "If this is such a big secret, Mom," his sister argued, "a once-in-a-lifetime secret like Grandpa says, then Barbie should have her new boyfriend, too." Fancy folded her arms and sat back.

His mother must know what Fancy was getting at. Frank was the only one who didn't laugh. He couldn't believe it. His mother and grandmother actually looked proud of his sister.

"All right, 'Bend Leg Ken,' as well," his mother agreed,

"the red trunks, monogrammed jacket, red cork sandals and standard accessories."

Frank was impressed, in spite of himself.

Geez! That huckster, Earl Scheib? He should adopt Fancy and put her on the payroll.

"And the gold stand instead of the black one?" his sister continued.

"Don't push it, Fancy." Fancy looked at her mother's face, then over at Frank with a superior smile. She waited just long enough to annoy him again.

"I guess so. May I be excused?" When their father nodded, Fancy left the table and went out to the kitchen. Kaline followed. Frank glimpsed Fancy sneaking a slice of ham, putting it into the pup's slobbery mouth, and looking right back at Frank as she did so, challenging him. Feeding Kaline human food from the table was absolutely forbidden. But after this delicate negotiation, Frank decided to say nothing. He pursed his lips and Fancy crossed her eyes over her little victory.

She really is evil.

Mr. Nibs watched it all from his pillow on the couch and got up to follow Fancy into the kitchen. The spoiled fur-ball was probably worried the new pup would get in ahead of it with Fancy. When the cat passed in front of him under the table, Frank gave him a little kick in the butt to help him on his way. The cat let out a yowl, but Frank only smiled innocently at the adults, who watched Mr. Nibs hastily disappearing into the kitchen.

Two can play at that game.

Frank settled on the cat's still-warm pillow and picked up the *Detroit Free Press* for the latest news on the Tigers. In spite of his fears for Kaline and his team, exhilaration began to build in Frank and his face flushed with heat.

He felt like . . . like rounding first base after hitting a game-winning grand-slam in the bottom of the ninth, with two out, the crowd on its feet roaring, and Larry and his Werewolves teammates waiting at home plate to slap him on the back and congratulate him.

The sweetest of all!

seven

"Geez! What now?"

Frank slouched down in the back seat of the family's '66 Ford Galaxie and shot anxious glances toward the front door. He was impatient for his dad and grandfather to get in the car so they could go. Larry and his friends would soon leave for school, but Frank would not be walking with them. His reason was a good one, unique in fact, but an absolute secret.

Yet Frank was taken completely unawares by the guilt, the disconcerting nervousness he felt at being healthy but not in school on a Monday morning, even after the huge discussion and argument the Friday before. "Hang loose, man. You got your parents' permission, for chrissakes," he whispered.

It didn't help. The big bowl of Cheerios and brown sugar, along with the tall glass of orange juice he'd wolfed down for breakfast, now curdled in his stomach. On the other hand, he reminded himself, Fancy did have to go to school and keep her big mouth shut about it, had sworn to say Frank had a stomach ache. It helped.

"Sweet!" Frank said it again.

But hey, could Fancy keep quiet? Wasn't like she practiced it. Telegraph, telegram, tell Fancy. She was only eleven, and loved to be seen and heard.

Frank leaned back, kicked his brain into neutral and tried to let his mind idle.

He couldn't remember a time when he didn't love baseball, worship Kaline, and live and die with the Detroit Tigers seasons of play. They were like malaria in his blood and no cure. All the Phelan men were bitten early. Frank's infection was just as fatal as his father's and grandfather's, going all the way back to great-grandfather Wallace George Phelan revering Ty Cobb in the 1920s. But for Frank, in 1968, there was only Al Kaline, Detroit's Mr. Tiger.

With that thought, his mind slipped into gear again. "C'mon, Dad!" Frank yelled from the Galaxie. His father had phoned his boss early to request one of the personal business days his contract allowed, no explanation required. Frank pounded his fist into the golden glove. He was doing a lot of pounding lately.

Frank watched Cobb and Kaline come spilling out the door onto the front porch, their paws dancing with excitement. The dogs always seemed to sense when something big was up. The whole family followed.

Frank's father went down on one knee to say something to Fancy, while his grandfather, grandmother and mother looked on. Fancy was holding Mr. Nibs like a fat fur basketball. Even with the Barbie doll bribes, Fancy and her dumb cat wore the same wounded expression. It figured. Frank almost felt sorry for her. Almost.

"Let's go, Dad! We'll miss batting practice." Frank's second shout drew a warning look from his mother. His father ignored his impatience. Frank knew his dad cared about things like that, fairness and taking time to explain. Both his parents did. His parents caring and making him The Deal were the reason Frank had got the chance to earn the Kaline glove.

Frank saw his father hug the tearful Fancy while his mother and grandmother each kept a hand on her shoulders. A minute later, his father was behind the wheel and his grandfather was in the passenger seat. *At last!*

The women waved goodbye when the car pulled slowly away from the curb. Old Cobb sat and whined after Frank's grandfather. Kaline shook with her usual nervous energy and gave out anxious puppy yips.

Frank looked back to see his grandmother leave Fancy, bend down and put her arms around Kaline's neck to reassure her. The young Lab gave her face wet puppy licks in return. Frank thought Fancy whispered something into Mr. Nibs' furry ear. Then his sister turned her back on everybody and went into the house.

"Have fun at school, Fancy," Frank whispered. "Sweet!"

Frank stretched out in the seat, acknowledged the guilt, stowed it away deep, and seconds later, welcomed the pleasure of delicious anticipation that rippled up from his toes to his head, under the Tigers ball cap. In the short weeks since Frank first slid his fingers into the smooth leather of the Kaline mitt, it had all come together, and the Phelan faithful would be there: Tiger Stadium, in Detroit, for game five of the 1968 World

Series of baseball. Frank loved history, especially Phelan family history. *Super-sweet!*

Frank realized he had wanted the Tigers in the series even more than he wanted the Kaline glove. That was a lot of wanting. Yet right up to his team's American League pennant win, he was careful never to make a big deal about it publicly. In case his saying-so jinxed Kaline and the Tigers. And it worked! That was the incredible thing.

Incredible until the great play of Al Kaline and the Detroit Tigers had fallen apart and disappeared down the rabbit hole, back when he'd first got his glove. The Tigers collapse had taken little more than a week after that first disastrous loss. Frank recalled his mother's uncomfortable talk and surprise revelation in his bedroom, and silently vowed to offer his idol and the Tigers this other chance of game five. And yet, as his dad drove south down McKay Avenue, toward busy Wyandotte Street, Frank felt the elation drain out of his body as quickly as it had come. It lay in a black pool at his feet.

Yes, the Tigers had made it to the World Series to play the St. Louis Cardinals. They were the World Series champions from last year, and this year's odds-on favourite to repeat the win. Now the big question was: Would the worst of the worst follow?

Right there in the back seat, Frank's own triumph with the wonderful glove turned into the slow agony of terrible doubt. The odds-makers were right. Al Kaline and the Tigers had gone down three games to one against the Cardinals from Busch Stadium in St. Louis. The 1967 World Series Champions were indeed formidable.

Vow or not, Frank couldn't get the thought out of his mind. If the Tigers lost game five today, it would all be over. Worst of the worst? Frank would be right there, forced to watch his beloved team and his baseball idol go down to defeat in the most important game of all their lives. Could Frank endure such agony? The hammer blow to his pride? The everlasting distress the memory would cause him?

Lucky! Lucky! Lucky!

Which way would the luck go?

eight

Frank's father turned right on Wyandotte Street toward the black spans of the Ambassador Bridge standing thirteen blocks west beside the University of Windsor. All of Windsor's rush hour traffic headed downtown in the opposite direction. Frank still felt strange as they drove right past the block-long, fortress-like mass of his J.E. Benson Junior High School. When he caught sight of the early-arriving students sitting on the front steps, Frank slipped down in the seat.

"That new pup, Kaline, looks to be smart as nine whips," his father said. "Will she be ready to take over the pointing and retrieving from old Cobb, now that you've retired him as your duck-hunting dog?"

Frank guessed his father needed to pick a safe topic. He too, didn't want to speak out loud about the possibility of a Tigers defeat.

His grandfather went along with it. "Kaline's smart, all right. Had her six months and she's taken to retrieving like a duckling takes to water. It wasn't but one week before that pup wormed her way inside her great-granddad Cobb's affections and Norah's too. Then old Cobb wouldn't settle down at night till Kaline was there beside him. I finally made a new sleeping box big enough for both of them. If I don't remind Norah, she talks to Kaline like a baby. Kaline just laps it up."

It sounded like his grandfather was complaining, but Frank could sense the deep affection, for the pup and for Norah both.

"Just last night," his grandfather continued, "Mr. Nibs was caterwauling and carrying on at the back door, wanting out. There was Fancy in the backyard about to give Kaline chicken dressing right off the serving spoon. They both knew it was wrong, and they both acted as innocent as God's little angels. I felt about the same as Mr. Nibs, betrayed."

Frank knew his sister was never innocent. "Maybe it's because Fancy and Kaline are both girls. You know, devious," Frank said.

Both men stiffened in the front seat. His father shook his head and spoke without turning around. "Now watch that type of talk, Frank." Both Frank's parents were strict about stuff like that. He still wasn't sure what the big deal was. Guys and girls were different, that's all.

His grandfather did turn around in the front seat and looked serious. "Well, Frank, I believe it may be the opposite."

"How granddad?"

"It may be because Cobb and the rest of us are all men. Selfish and too full of ourselves. Sometimes we deserve the criticism that comes our way when our heads swell up and get too big for our baseball caps."

That drew a laugh, even from his father.

When the Galaxie turned onto the Ambassador Bridge and began to take them high over the Detroit River, Frank could forget about his sister. He cranked the passenger-side window handle and leaned out with the cool breeze on his face. He tried to catch a glimpse of the old Irish, Corktown neighbourhood in Detroit that contained the ballpark. Frank wanted to be the first to catch sight of the big banks of lights above Tiger Stadium, and then, the huge spread of the American stars and stripes on top of its lofty flagpole in centre field.

"Tiger Stadium," Frank announced, with deliberate premeditation, "house of the gods." Now he leaned forward, between his dad and grandfather, and said it again, as if he'd just introduced the Taj Mahal. That's how his grandfather had announced it to him, when he and his father had taken Frank to his first game there, when he was four years old. Frank knew his grandfather couldn't resist such an opening.

He wasn't disappointed. The familiar ritual and incantation began, and Frank's doubt about the Tigers receded, at least for the moment.

"Your great-grandfather Wally was a master carpenter before the First World War," his grandfather said. "He took the Detroit ferry over to Corktown every day in 1912 to help build the new ballpark."

"When it was called Navin Field?" Frank prompted.

"That's right, Frank."

Frank's father joined in. "And your grandfather here was born that same year. He and Wally watched Ty Cobb, Babe Ruth, Honus Wagner, Walter Johnson, Nap Lajoie, all the other greats of their day, play at Navin." His father shook his head in admiration of the experience. "Yet all of those players, great as they were, Frank, they still stood in the six foot-one-inch-long shadow of Tyrus Raymond Cobb. He was the Georgia Peach or just Peach. The one. The only."

His father drifted off, probably remembering those few years in the middle of the 1930's depression when Wally, David and the young Norm Phelan, three generations, sat together in the park to enjoy the game and the team they loved.

Frank hesitated, then prompted again. "Until 1937."

"Yes, until then," his father confirmed.

The mood shifted. Frank waited, but his father still didn't want to talk about it. Neither would his grandfather. Frank knew only that two bad things had happened during that long ago fall season in 1937. First, that the heavily favoured Detroit Tigers had lost the 1937 World Series to "Dizzy Dean" and the "Gashouse Gang" of these same St. Louis Cardinals. Second, and more disturbing, that his great-grandfather Wally, in his duck-hunting boat, had disappeared on Lake Erie. The grave in the Windsor Memorial Cemetery had a headstone but held no body.

Frank needed to break the solemn mood. "What kind of things did you and Wally and David talk about, Dad?"

"The same things," his father said, finally.

"The Georgia Peach or the 'Bambino'?" Frank suggested. "The greatest hitter? Cobb's 5,325 base hits, 1937 RBIs and .366 lifetime batting average? Or Ruth's 4,229 hits, 2,213 RBIs and .342 average?"

"Wow, you've been listening, Frank," his grandfather said. "But remember Ruth's 714 homers and the great pitching in his early years on the mound."

"But Ruth never managed the New York Yankees the way Cobb managed the Detroit Tigers." Frank said.

Frank's grandfather turned in his seat. "But in 1935, at the end of his career, Ruth crushed that last home run so hard, he hit the ball right out of Forbes Field in Pittsburgh. The first hitter to do it. The Pirates pitcher, Guy Bush, tipped his hat to him as he hobbled around third, and the Babe saluted him back. That's pride and respect and history, Frank. It's the discussions more than the answers. I miss them. And Wally."

Frank didn't know what to say.

Frank had been seven in 1961, when Ty Cobb died, the same year they renamed the park Tiger Stadium, after being Briggs Stadium since 1938. Each name marked an important era in the site's baseball lore and history: its own heroes, own records, own triumphs, own scandals. Frank had only been one when twenty-year-old Al Kaline became the youngest player to win the batting title in 1955. Tiger Stadium was the name the park would probably carry until its close. And Al Kaline, the player Frank would come to revere, started his Tigers career and took up the burden Cobb laid down when he left the Tigers in 1926. Frank, a fan and ballplayer too, thought these events marked his era. He was proud of Al Kaline. Proud every time he attended a game at Tiger Stadium and wore Kaline's number 6 jersey.

Frank wore his Kaline jersey now.

He was surprised at how much Ty Cobb's death, so far away in Atlanta Georgia, had affected his dad and grandfather. They'd talked about it on the phone for almost an hour, his grandfather calling from Peterborough and running up a big long-distance bill.

Frank's mother had continued reading her latest Agatha Christie mystery and hadn't interrupted.

nine

Frank wondered where Al Kaline was in these hours before the opening pitch. He imagined his idol gathered with his teammates, in their dressing room at Tiger Stadium, listening to manager Mayo Smith laying out his strategy for this do-or-die game. If so, just what was Kaline thinking and feeling before he took to the field?

Frank couldn't imagine that.

"Whoa!" His father hit a rough gap in the black asphalt and ironwork of the Ambassador Bridge, high over the Detroit River, and immediately slammed on the brakes. All three rocked forward and back. "Sorry about that. My thoughts were elsewhere for a moment there."

More than a moment. Frank was afraid to ask where. Probably still with Ty Cobb and Wally, their lives and deaths. He shivered just thinking about it.

Frank slid over to the driver's side of the back seat, cranked down the window and stuck out his head. The wind swirling at this height tore away his breath. "Geez, Dad! There's already a monster line up!" Frank worried it might be other baseball fans in a snail-stream of vehicles that lead over the bridge and all the way to Tiger Stadium, still miles distant.

"Relax, Frank," his grandfather said, turning. "It's just the commuters and the early morning transport truck traffic heading to the Detroit auto plants. No point in complaining."

"FORD MOTOR COMPANY." The familiar blue-and-white logo spread across the tall rear doors of the transport truck ahead of them. The truck lurched forward with a belch of noise and black diesel smoke. Frank hastily cranked the window closed again, but not before the acrid smell got all the way up his nose. His dad hung back and let the high winds on the bridge whisk away the smell and smoke.

Unlike the slow-moving bridge traffic, still more questions zoomed around in Frank's head and made his stomach ache. Would Larry bug Fancy until she told him the real reason for Frank's absence? Would the World Series tickets really be waiting for them? Were the seats as good as they sounded? Would his idol have a good game? Would the Tigers squeak out a win? And one more, the inevitable question that Frank had asked himself for years, ever since he and his father and grandfather began making their trips across the bridge to enjoy a Tigers ballgame.

Will I finally, just one time, successfully fight my way through a hundred Detroit baseball fans with the same idea and get Al Kaline's autograph? Finally?

Sure, Frank now had the autographed Kaline glove. And it was, like, incredible. But Kaline wasn't there in person. Frank didn't witness him signing it. Didn't hear Kaline ask for his name or utter just a few words directed only at Frank. In the end, somehow, the autograph on the glove, cool as it was, wasn't the same. Still wasn't enough. *Geez!*

Would this game be the one? The game when Frank, at last, got Al Kaline's autograph on the brim of his Tigers ball cap?

In each of those previous ten years, ever since his grandfather suggested that he attend the Tigers pre-game batting practice, when Kaline and the other players were most available to their fans for autographs, the answer had always been a big fat NO! No personal autograph. Again and again.

"Aw, crap!" Frank mumbled and pounded his fist into the Kaline glove. At this rate, he'd wear out the glove or scrape all the skin off his knuckles before he succeeded. Frank squeezed his eyes shut tight and kept them shut against the vision of his past failures and loss when Kaline had overlooked him at the fence and given his coveted autograph to other lucky fans.

It wasn't fair. Didn't great-grandfather Wally help build the damn stadium? Wasn't his Phelan sweat soaked right into the very wood? Didn't Frank's grandfather and his amazing grandmother just beat Earl Scheib at his own game and snag those priceless tickets? Didn't Frank's father sit with his own father and grandfather and witness the incredible feats of some of the greatest ballplayers in the history of the game? Wasn't Frank about to do the same thing with his own father and grandfather? It was his turn.

I gotta try. Gotta make the luck happen.

Frank sat up straight and opened his eyes.

The trip across the Ambassador Bridge was always memorable. Frank gave in to the slow pace of the stop-and-go traffic on this Monday morning and allowed the crossing a chance to work its sublime magic. Maybe it was the effect of the god-like height.

Frank moved to the passenger-side window, rolled it down again to brave the swirling wind and let his gaze travel slowly east, along the brown and grey thrusts and angles of the Detroit skyline. In spite of the buffeting of the strong gusts, his eyes rested long moments on the skyline's most distinctive feature, at least in Frank's mind: the tall, artillery-shell-shape of the Penobscot Building, with its triangular steel skeleton supporting the big flashing red light on top. A warning to Detroit Metropolitan Airport traffic, his father had said. And, Frank judged, a fitting advertisement for Smooth Daddy Groove, who made his WSMU radio broadcasts from his studio there.

Thanks for those cool tickets, Smooth Daddy!

Two white, Bob-Lo Island passenger ferries were tied up at the docks nearby, rocking on the whitecaps that looked like stiff whipped cream. Frank had taken the ferries to the special holiday island downriver a dozen times for weekend picnics with his family. He'd ridden the high wooden rollercoaster, The Wild Mouse, till he was literally sick to his stomach, a bit like now. Still, it was a good memory.

Behind Frank, farther west to the left, thick streamers of grey smoke from the foundries on Zug Island blew sideways in the winds. Blew above the ferries and up against the fat cement cylinders of tall grain elevators and into the downtown Detroit office towers behind. Traffic moving along highway three looked the size of Dinky Toys. A bit farther over on his right, Frank could almost make out the distant shape of the huge Stars and Stripes on its tall pole in centre field at Tiger Stadium. At least he thought he could.

BR-R-O-O-M-M!

"Geez!" Frank flinched, as the whole bridge vibrated to the deep tones of the horn of a Great Lakes freighter. "Geez!" The last time that surprise happened was at Atkinson Park, the day the black girl got spiked and crushed Blondie's privates.

The dingy black and white freighter, with a ribbed steel deck crane lying along its spine, slid out from under the bridge below him. It gave out a sudden series of shorter blasts to warn away the score of smaller white pleasure craft zipping at high speed around it, and up and down the length of the steel-coloured Detroit River.

In the watery sunlight, even this late in the year, many of the sleek boats revealed flashes of sunglasses, streaming hair and bright foul-weather gear. The smaller wakes of the speedboats also cut those of the drab black Canadian National Railway ferries. More Dinky Toy creations like floating serving trays bearing their loads of freight cars ponderously cross-river to serve the demands of the sprawling Ford, GM and Chrysler auto plants that made Detroit the "Motor City." The car plants had been there almost as long as the Tigers and the stadium.

Frank's grandfather risked rolling down his own window halfway. The winds and the complex river and heavy industry smells they bore filled more of the car. "The river seems too busy for this late in the season, especially the speedboats and cabin cruisers so early in the morning."

"Want to get their last fill of it before the real cold sets in, I guess," said Frank's dad, as his grandfather cranked the window closed again.

Now Frank wished he was already at the ballpark. He wished the game was over, and that he knew the outcome.

Lucky! Lucky! Lucky!

The world curved away around him, filled with the sights and sounds of the busiest international waterway in the world. None of it mattered. Frank just wanted to leave it all behind and get to Tiger Stadium.

If only I was moving like one of those speedboats. . . .

"Get the birth certificates handy. And remember, be polite."

Frank's father reached into his back pocket to check for his wallet, and Frank and his grandfather did the same. It seemed a little early to Frank. They were barely at the midpoint of the crossing, still caught in the snailing lineup of truck and commuter traffic. He couldn't even see the Detroit Customs booths yet. But crossing the border would never be the same.

How could it be?

ten

Frank knew the "be polite" was directed at him.

And how could he ever forget the terrifying Detroit race riot that had, like, blown his mind to smoke and smithereens that last week in July the year before? How often had Frank jumped awake in the early hours of those mornings to discover he'd kicked off the bedclothes in the grip of a fire-filled nightmare, the sound of machine guns and helicopter gunships rattling his brain?

Too often.

Now, five hundred yards from Detroit Customs, Frank flashed back to the most disturbing dinner conversation of those times.

When the family had gathered for dinner that first Sunday, after the riot had erupted on Saturday night and into the early morning hours of Sunday, July twenty-third, Frank had had no appetite. His mother had made one of the family's favourite dishes, Betty Crocker's cheese-flavoured Noodles Romanoff.

But even his mom had hardly touched her plate. Frank's safe, predictable world of school, friends, family and baseball had shifted underneath him and opened his eyes to a new reality of riots and racism.

His parents' own uncertainty had made it worse.

Frank's dad had put down his fork and said, "It's like we've learned nothing from the Watts riot, in Los Angeles, in 1965. Six days and thirty-four dead, all because a white California Highway Patrol officer got into a confrontation with a black driver over a traffic violation."

The lyrics from Gordon Lightfoot's song, *Black Day In July,* had seared the memories of the Detroit riot into Frank's brain forever. To make the whole experience even worse, the race riot had meant the sudden end of the 1967 baseball season for fans like Frank. Thankfully, this 1968 season, they were going to the games again! Yet, now, even a year later, headed for Tiger Stadium, Frank had to admit he felt very white and more than a little nervous.

Frank leaned out the window to look ahead as his dad continued in the long line leading to the customs booths. Frank could just make out the booths. All the Detroit Customs officials he could see were black. No surprise.

Not just the world had changed. Frank had changed.

After the fires, the gunshots, the violence, the naked hate, the deaths, Frank had come to count on his beloved Tigers and the sight of his favourite player, Al Kaline, to reassure him. Now at least, Frank didn't fear losing his life. Not really. But people had died in the riot, forty-three people: thirty-five blacks and ten whites. Maybe more. Frank had seen all of the images on television and in the newspapers, and it really panicked him knowing it was stark reality and so close by.

Their impending arrival at Detroit Customs must have affected Frank's dad, as well.

"I was barely into my twenties when the 1947 race riot broke out across the Detroit River," his father spoke into the strained silence of the car.

Frank actually welcomed the chance to talk, even about such a painful subject.

"There was another Detroit riot before this one?"

"Well, it was World War II, Frank," his father continued. "There were so many good manufacturing jobs created that I'd almost been tempted to quit the Canadian Bank of Commerce and work here, in a Windsor auto plant. In the United States, something like fifty thousand blacks had migrated north from the southern states and moved into white neighbourhoods—or became homeless. I still remember how outraged the white community had become." His father shook his head. "For me, the extent of the racial tension had been unheard of. A downtown brawl between blacks and whites had turned into a twenty-four hour riot. I looked it up in the newspaper's archives: twenty-five blacks were killed, seventeen by police; and nine whites, none killed by police.

"Wow!" Frank said.

Now Frank's grandfather turned around to look at him. The depth of concern in his voice was clear.

"And many of the same problems exist today, Frank. What can we expect? A history of segregated housing and schools. High black unemployment. Police mostly white and often brutal. That's why it's important to be civil when we get to customs."

"Sure, Grandpa."

But Frank was still nervous as hell, every time he crossed the river.

Over the course of the week of the riot, Frank had discovered things about his parents and the world that he wanted to forget.

Now, headed for game five of the 1968 World Series, Frank had figured that fear was the major effect of the latest riot. It made him appreciate how easily he could lose the things he took for granted: the simple pleasure of a trip across the swaying span of the Ambassador Bridge; the fascination of visiting a foreign country; the thrill of attending a Tigers game, of experiencing the incredible play of Al Kaline, live and in person. It just wasn't the same on television or his transistor radio.

Yet maybe the other, the even more disturbing effect of the riot was harder to admit, harder to talk about, even to his parents or grandparents. Even to his best friend, Larry.

The race riot, only a short river crossing away, had brought home to Frank, with devastating clarity, just how white he was.

When he let himself think about it, really let himself think about it, like now on the bridge, Frank thought of the word in capital letters: WHITE. The other fans in Tiger Stadium or the people on the streets of Detroit were no longer Negroes, no longer black. They were BLACK. But what did that mean?

And the Detroit River still flowed between them. . . .

eleven

"Frank? You stay away from that river now," his mother had warned at the start of the 1967 riot. "Betty Teeples is telling Larry the same. It's not healthy. Watching the news on television is as close as I want you and Fancy to get. You hear me?"

"But it's across the river, Mom. A whole mile away. I bet everyone else will be right there watching. Hundreds of people. It's, like, you know, a riot!"

"It's heartbreaking, Frank, and you will not be gawking with the rest of them. Stay above University Avenue or go south to Wilson Park to play ball with Larry and your other friends. You promise me, now."

Frank had hung his head to wait his mother out. His mother was having none of it. She took his head firmly in both hands and held him more urgently than he could ever remember her doing before. Until Frank looked right into her eyes and about pissed himself from the shock. His mother's eyes were stone.

"Promise me, Frank." It wasn't a request.

"Ok. Ok. I promise." What else could he say?

Yet Frank had already planned to break his word. A riot was, like, major. Like . . . once in a lifetime, too important to miss. Larry would do the same, Frank was sure. Didn't mean it was easy. The conflict unnerved him.

"I'll watch him, Mom, don't worry," Fancy piped up. Yeah, Fancy and Carol, the sisters, would be the biggest problem—after the guilt.

"So we ride, man," Larry had advised Frank, later. "Get on our bikes, head to Wilson Park, then turn west and haul butt for Atkinson Park and the Ambassador Bridge. The crowds will be so big around there we can disappear, easy."

"Right you are, pal," Frank agreed with more enthusiasm than he felt. *So just do it, man!* In the end, they had exchanged a big thumbs-up and cackled like idiots at their cleverness in deceiving their parents and interfering sisters.

Frank and his friends had settled in for hours under the shadow of the Ambassador Bridge. They pooled their money and continually argued about who should go back to Martineau's candy store, up on University, to bring down more orders of Hostess shoe-string potato chips, Crispy Crunch and Hershey's chocolate bars, sponge taffy and jelly babies and sunflower seeds, Double Colas and Hires root beers.

At least Larry had been right about blending in. Frank figured hundreds, maybe thousands of Windsorites kept the same vigil for miles along the Windsor waterfront. Brought their blankets, picnic baskets and portable radios, for news and updates. Along with Frank, the crowd had marveled that a once-familiar Detroit skyline could so suddenly become an alien, smoke-shrouded urban landscape, the tips of familiar skyscrapers only just visible. The blinking red ball on top of the Penobscot Building repeated like a lonely distress signal ignored by the raging blacks and whites below.

Frank was luckier than most. His dad had just begun working for *The Windsor Star,* where the latest news came over from reporters at the *Detroit Free Press* and *The Detroit News,* who called in directly from the scene. After dessert that first Sunday evening, still at the dinner table, his father had told them all he'd learned going in to the paper on an unbelievable weekend shift. It was, like, real inside information Frank had before most other people. His mother was too silent. Frank could tell she disapproved of his teenaged thirst for details.

Man! How could she still not realize? It was a RIOT!

"Three-fifty this Sunday morning," Frank's father had recounted, "that's when it really exploded. The Detroit police raided a 'blind pig' in the mostly Negro neighbourhood around Twelfth Street and Clairmont Avenue. It spread from there."

Frank's dad explained that a blind pig was slang for a late night drinking hangout selling booze illegally. Supposedly, the drinkers were celebrating the safe return of two black soldiers from the Vietnam War when the police struck. A raucous crowd gathered as officers arrested and took away almost a hundred partying drinkers.

"The cops were white," Frank's dad said. "And I guess some unidentified bystander threw a bottle into the rear window of a police car. That turned the watching crowd, all Negroes, into an angry mob. I told you earlier about the Watts Rebellion in Los Angeles two years ago. Well, it took two days for the fires there to be set." His father had pointed his dessert fork north, toward Detroit. "But this time, across the river, whole Detroit neighborhoods were torched within hours."

Frank hung on every detail.

Two thick black words had filled the entire television screen after dinner that Sunday evening:

"DETROIT BURNS!"

On the Monday, Frank and Larry and the rest of the guys saw and smelled exactly that: a city of more than one-and-a-half million people in flames.

"Man, check out the smoke!" Larry had pointed north and a bit west across the river. A grey and black thunder-smear of smoke grew steadily larger and would hang above the Detroit skyline like a giant door into hell for days. Then the looting and rooftop sniping began. People on the riverbank said Detroit Mayor Cavanaugh had had to call in the State Police to help protect his own, endangered city police, firemen and ambulance crews trying to bring the flames under control. They failed.

"That's a not a firework, Frank!" Larry had leaned forward with his bottle of Double Cola halfway to his open mouth. Frank and the others stopped their snacking and leaned forward too.

"Jesus, Lar! Frank declared, "I think that's gunfire. They really are shooting each other!"

Frank remembered collapsing against one of the big cement blocks of the riverfront parking lot in amazement, like he himself, had taken a bullet to the brain. He'd looked straight up at the slow-moving white clouds in the Canadian sky that was still a clear blue above him and tried to imagine it. What a difference! "Wait 'til I tell my dad. I wonder if he knows at the newspaper?" Yeah, of course he would. More pops and crackles from across the river had followed.

What was it like to be shot? Really shot? This wasn't TV stuff. It was happening!

"Yeah, but wait," Frank said. "My mom will kill me if she finds out I broke my word and sneaked down here to watch. Yours too, right, Lar? I mean she made me promise." Larry and his friends had nodded. And on their way home, Frank had stopped at Marentette's Sport and Hobby Shop and laid out fifteen bucks of his hard-earned cash for that cool little Sony radio. "It's worth it, Lar."

Only later, did Frank realize he'd picked out a black and white model.

twelve

So that Monday evening, the second day of the riot, Frank had been careful to let his dad tell it all as if hearing it for the first time. And more annoying, he'd had to beg his mom to let him watch the television news. Fancy was scared, but curious too. Yet Frank's mom wanted to see and hear the latest reports herself, as much as he did, even if she worried it was "unhealthy" for him and his sister.

"Laura," his father had said, "I don't think we should try and hide what's happening."

"Oh, very well. But it's so disturbing."

"Agreed," his father had said. "I'll be like Sergeant Joe Friday, Badge 714, 'just the facts, ma'am.'" That was a joke about the popular cop show, *Dragnet.* Frank's mom hadn't laughed, but she did let his dad tell the family what he knew.

His dad sighed and began the update of that Monday's events. "Ok. The rioting's spread to the greater Detroit area, to the cities of Highland Park and Hamtramck. Sheriff Buback has ordered a nightly curfew, nine o'clock in the evening to five o'clock in the morning, across the whole of Wayne County. He's also set up roadblocks to try and contain the crisis." All the Detroit and Windsor television and radio stations carried versions of the same story.

Frank and his friends had listened to most of it on his black and white radio. Sometimes Frank knew stuff before his mom and sister, and even his dad did. The Detroit broadcast was weak and full of static, maybe because they were usually sitting under the huge metal expanse of the Ambassador Bridge.

Day after day, Smooth Daddy Groove had scolded his Detroit listeners from his studio at the top of the Penobscot Building. "Why you burnin' your own homes, fools? Why you attackin' police and stoppin' firemen and ambulance drivers tryin' to save your children and old folks? Who's gonna stop this crazy jive-ass violence if you don't help 'em do their jobs? I'm lookin' down, and it looks like holy hell! You shame me, brothers and sisters. You shame our people." But even the city's most listened-to black voice on the airwaves couldn't stop the years of accumulated anger burning out of control in Detroit's streets.

"Black anger." "Black streets." That's how the newscasts described it.

The violence, sniping, looting and burning had gone on for five days and nights, and cost an estimated one hundred and fifty million dollars, his dad had reported later. Before it ended, Michigan Governor Romney called in thousands of Michigan National Guardsmen with bayonets fixed and orders to "shoot to kill if fired upon."

"Shoot to kill," Frank's mother had shaken her head. "I

never thought I'd hear those words for real directed against civilians in a neighbouring city, even if it is America."

And it got worse.

As the days of rioting in Detroit had continued, Frank's father could hardly bear to give the latest news to the family. "Four thousand and seven hundred paratroopers from the 101st Airborne are coming to help combat Negro violence."

"Actual paratroopers, Dad?" Frank's jaw had practically dropped to the floor in disbelief.

"Looks like it, son."

"Hey! Watch for the parachutes, guys!" Frank had told Larry and the gang the next day. "Could be, like, hundreds of 'em dropping into that smoke. Don't want to miss it!"

Frank had sneaked his grandfather's old duck-spotting binoculars and scanned the smoke-smudged skyline for the white blossoms of parachutes above the constant grey swirls and eddies.

Larry started coming over after supper to get the latest from Frank's dad and watch the nightly TV images. As if trapped in an unreal dream, the nervous troops with M-1 rifles, and the tanks and armoured personnel carriers mounted with big .50-calibre machine guns, patrolled the fire-gutted, devastated streets. Daring news coverage picked up the rat-tat-tat of light machine gun fire. The machine guns punctuated the growing crescendo of non-stop sirens and the occasional Whump! Whump! Whump! of the heavier machine guns that could take down a brick building. An entire building!

What a contrast that had been to the brief images Frank

caught one night: news footage revealing a lone black Baptist minister, with his wife and daughter, welcoming the newly homeless—black and white—into his church for food and shelter and relief from the chaos. Yet what had caught Frank's eye the most had been the solemn-faced black girl, the minister's daughter, who wore a complete baseball uniform with "Junior Tigers" in black letters across the front of her pinstriped white jersey. Kinda weird.

Larry hadn't been interested in such stories. "Man!" his best friend had exclaimed, with his eyes glued to the TV. "Will you look at the size of those army helicopters—like hunting 'gooks' in Vietnam or something!" Frank had winced. "Bet they're using 'em to track snipers and looters across the rooftops." Larry and the whole family had stared at the flickering screen as the heavy flying machines beat low through the sky with a sound like jackhammers and whipped up whirlwinds of greasy, grey-black smoke. "Cool!" Larry exclaimed again, and slapped his knee.

Frank elbowed his best friend . . . too late.

Frank's mother stood up and turned on Larry with a rare voice that cut through Larry's excitement like a .50-calibre machine gun.

"There are no 'gooks' in Vietnam, Larry. They are people like us, suffering through a war they never asked for. Women and children burned to death by napalm bombs or casually slaughtered like dumb animals, their fields blown up or intentionally destroyed by Agent Orange so they starve to death and worse. It is *not* cool! Think of the thousands of poor Detroit parents and children just a few miles away losing their homes and businesses. Old people left on their own, afraid, maybe trapped in apartments. No food. No water. No power. Fire and smoke all around them, and the air filled with gunshots. They must be terrified. And those firemen are risking their lives."

Larry had cowered under her words, like the image of one of those people Frank saw alone on a Detroit rooftop curled into a tight ball under the shadow of a giant helicopter gunship.

Frank's dad had finally intervened, standing and putting a hand on his mother's arm. "Enough, Laura. Larry's got the message."

Frank's mother whirled and disappeared into the kitchen. His father and Fancy, holding Mr. Nibs, trailed after her.

"You're so gross, Larry!" Fancy hissed on the way by.

"Sorry, Mrs. Phelan," Larry offered, too late.

"You should probably head home, pal," Frank said. Larry nodded and was only too eager to slip out the front door.

Still, almost as troubling to Frank at the time, was that Monday's *Detroit Free Press*, which had reported gunfire and rioting in the area of Grand River and Trumbull.

Just north of Tiger Stadium!

Could rioters end up looting and burning Frank's favorite ballpark? The one his great-grandfather Wally sweated to build? Would Frank never again sit in his favourite seat in the front row of the upper deck in right field? Never see Al Kaline crush a fastball at home plate or make an impossible, diving catch at the fence below Frank's feet?

Sweet Jesus, no!

"It's ok. The park's still there, Frank," his father had told him the next day, and Frank collapsed on the couch in relief.

"And maybe I shouldn't tell you this, but last Sunday afternoon? Seems Willie Horton left Tiger Stadium after the game, still wearing his Tigers uniform, to talk to the rioters. Stood on the top of a car and pleaded with the crowd to stop the anger, the shooting, the looting and the fires."

"Wow!" Frank had tried to imagine Horton on top of a car surrounded by a sea of angry black faces. Horton was black and lived right there in Detroit, a hometown boy.

His father had looked down and shaken his head. "They wouldn't listen, Frank. Willie Horton, and they wouldn't listen."

"Geez." Hearing this, Frank began to think about the people surrounding him on the riverbank each day, buzzing over the sights and sounds a short mile away across the water in front of him. He'd begun to recognize some of them. And they began to recognize him, nod at him. Frank nodded back, like a bobble-head doll.

The thing was: they were all white.

They'd all been pointing and talking and enjoying snacks like a crowd fascinated by the strange behaviour of exotic animals in a zoo. Yeah, and who were the animals? Blacks. Negroes. That's who. Frank looked down at the half-eaten Crispy Crunch chocolate bar in his hand and didn't want to admit it. But it was true: Frank was pointing, talking, snacking and being fascinated, along with all the rest. He looked forward, actually looked forward to seeing and hearing and smelling the violent events unfold and sharing the excitement.

Frank had remembered his mother's warning about coming down to the riverbank like this to gawk. He remembered the force of her hands gripping his head, the look of stone in her eyes, his promise. Not a promise, but a bald-faced lie.

Man, they're real people suffering over there. Mom's right.

"And I'm white and I'm here and I'm not feelin' so good," Frank said to himself.

He'd wrapped up the remains of his Crispy Crunch and stuffed them in his pocket. Mumbled an excuse he couldn't remember to Larry and his friends. Picked up his bike and pedaled home. Frank took his transistor radio with him.

Larry and the guys hadn't liked it one bit. But that was Frank's last day with them on the riverbank.

Still, Frank had that personal stake in the outcome. Every evening, after his father returned home with the latest updates from his colleagues at *The Windsor Star*, his dad first had to reassure Frank that his precious Tiger Stadium was not reduced to rubble and ash in the firestorm of anger that consumed whole neighbourhoods.

Frank could tell his dad had been worried too—about more than just the ballpark. "I'd hoped we were coming to our senses," his father had said one evening, after four days of rioting on a scale none of them could ever imagine. His dad looked exhausted.

Maybe he wasn't sleeping so good, either.

Frank was restless himself at night. Staying awake longer before sleep claimed him for a few hours. His dad took off his glasses and rubbed his eyes. "Have the people in Detroit already forgotten Martin Luther King and John F. Kennedy? So soon?"

"Two good men dead," his mother had agreed, "one black, one white. What's changed?" His parents' bleak expressions were new. It scared Frank. Unsettled him to the core.

Frank had watched his parents come together and embrace. Fancy had even spread her arms and joined them, tears streaking her cheeks. Frank wanted to open his arms, partake of the comfort, but couldn't bring himself to look weak in front of his family. His excitement over the riot, following that difficult afternoon with the Crispy Crunch on the riverbank, had steadily transformed to a sickening feeling of dread. And there it remained.

So who was right? Blacks? Whites? Everyone? No one?

By Thursday, at the end of it all, if there was an end, Frank still wasn't sure. "And I bet I'm not the only one," he remembered whispering.

There had been more. Right from the start, his mother was upset that the media kept referring to the rioters as Negroes. "This is 1967. If we are Whites, they are Blacks or African Americans." His dad said she had a point, and they all agreed to use the term Blacks in any conversation.

But in his mind's eye, Frank saw it as **BLACKS**.

thirteen

"Frank, what's wrong? Snap out of it! We're almost there!" His grandfather was shaking Frank's shoulder and staring at him from the front seat. "You have your wallet and birth certificate?"

"Uh . . . sure, no problem." Frank shook his own head and the scene in front of him snapped into focus. The Galaxie was next in line at the U.S. Customs and Immigration booth. Frank remembered that the same Michigan Governor Romney, who'd called in the National Guard with fixed bayonets and orders to "shoot to kill if fired upon," was supposed to be at this Tigers World Series game five. In just a few hours, Frank might even see the governor there in person. "Spooky," he murmured at the thought.

"Ok, here we go," his father said, "be courteous Canadians and smile when you answer the customs officer's questions." Ten seconds later, his father slid the Galaxie to a stop by the customs booth.

Frank's smile froze ice tight to his face.

Uh-oh!

The booth at the end of their long line of cars and trucks was staffed by one of the handful of female customs officers Frank had seen over the years. His few experiences had convinced Frank these women were extremely thorough and competent compared to some of their male colleagues who would blithely wave them through with little ceremony. This particular customs officer was newer to Frank's experiences at the border—female yes, but also middle-aged, large—and BLACK. Frank couldn't help the capital letters. And the sense that she was very confident and took her duties seriously. When the woman leaned forward and peered into the car, her big head and wide bouffant hairdo filled the whole window. Even Frank's dad tightened his grip on the steering wheel, impressed by her sheer physical presence. "Citizenship and destination? Nature and length of visit?"

The officer's words came like bursts from one of those .50-calibre machine guns. Frank shivered.

His dad had their birth certificates ready and handed them over. He smiled and followed his own advice. "Good morning, officer. We're all Canadians. My father and I are taking the boy to the World Series game this afternoon and coming home right after."

The woman appeared unimpressed. She leaned in farther and looked at each of them closely. Frank told his mouth to smile naturally, but it wouldn't. His face was still frigid-rigid. The officer said nothing. Instead of handing back their documents, she stepped back into her booth and consulted some kind of list or something that Frank couldn't make out. He sensed that even his grandfather, a veteran border-crosser, was tense.

Geez!

The officer finally returned to the window. "Do you have any illegal goods or contraband? Any liquor, drugs, or firearms with you in the vehicle, sir?" Frank could tell his dad was more than a bit rattled by the look of surprise on his face. They were used to these kinds of questions from Canada Customs officers on their way back from Detroit.

"Uh, no sir. Uh, I mean ma'am, none."

"Would you step out of the vehicle and open the trunk for me, sir?" Frank's father did, stumbling a bit as his feet found the asphalt. Both were soon back. *That should be it.* Frank let out a breath he didn't realize he was holding.

He was wrong. She still held the birth certificates.

"Would you show me your series tickets, sir?" *Oh no!* Now Frank felt his pulse beating a rapid tattoo at each temple. His father sputtered like a dying outboard and didn't know what to say. The silence stretched and the woman's suspicions with it.

It was his grandfather who answered, at last. "I'm sorry, officer, but our four tickets are being held for pickup at the Tiger Stadium box office."

"Four tickets, sir?"

Geez! How can we explain all that?

"Uh, yes, four, officer. You see I actually won them. On the WSMU radio contest. This last Friday."

The woman consulted his grandfather's birth certificate. Frank's heart tried to pole vault out of his chest. "What is your name again, sir?"

"It's David Edward, uh, Phelan." There was a too-long pause, until at last, the officer leaned in for a third time and took a long, very close look at his grandfather. Her head and her hair and her shoulders just about filled the front seat area. Frank could smell sweat and the cloying sweetness of her perfume. Now Frank could get no oxygen at all.

We're screwed!

"Would that be David Edward, as in Brother Edward? From the great Canadian metropolis of Peterborough?" she asked.

"Uh, I'm from near there, yes."

"The Cobb's Lake, Scheib Series Special, Smooth Daddy Groove, Double or Nothing Tough Tigers Trivia, Brother Edward?"

Frank's grandfather's face flushed fire engine red. "That would be me."

The woman pulled her big head back and stood with both her hands on her hips and shook her head. Then gave his grandfather the widest, whitest grin Frank could remember on either side of the border!

"Far-r-r out, Brother Edward! I'm proud to make your acquaintance. Our family's been Tigers fans since God kicked Adam outta the Garden but left the fool enough sense to invent baseball. Husband at work even come up with the trick answer to that jive-ass Cobb's uniform number question. My man tried phonin' and never got through. But hey, brother! That Double or Nothin' Cobb's Lake one? You were fa-a-antastic, man! Heard most of it on my radio in the booth. Congratulations!"

Before Frank knew it, the smiling customs officer handed back their identification, reached a huge arm across his father and was shaking hands with his grandfather. "Enjoy the game, now, Brother Edward. Wish I could be there. Though I'm 'fraid this might be the Tigers last roar. McLain's pitchin' arm might as well be a foot. An' that Bob Gibson throwin' for St. Louis?" She shook her head in futile denial of his pitching genius.

His grandfather nodded and smiled his relief. "Thank you. And just to keep the record straight, it was actually my wife who reminded me about the Cobb's Lake thing. Wouldn't be here if it hadn't been for her."

"Even better, Brother Edwards."

AR-R-O-O-G-G-H-A-A!

A jaw-jarring blast sounded from the air horn of a big Ford Motor Company transport truck behind them, upset at the delay. Not one second later, the smile disappeared, the head withdrew and the customs officer was stalking back to the cab of the truck, with her right hand on her black leather belt like she was about to draw her six-gun and shoot the poor fool.

Now Frank knew she was angry!

As his dad pulled away, Frank looked out the back window and saw the big woman jump right onto the running-board of the truck, rip open the door and virtually tear the impatient driver out of his cab onto the asphalt, shouting.

"Geez!" Frank said, with a loud sigh of relief.

"Amen to that," his grandfather replied.

fourteen

"And there she is, my friends."

Frank's dad pointed as they made the familiar turn, north off Porter and onto Trumbull, four blocks below Michigan Avenue and Tiger Stadium. Frank thrust himself halfway over the front seat, between his father and grandfather, and peered out through the sloped windshield. Above the roofline of the ballpark, Frank could just make out the top half of the magnificent Stars and Stripes, stiffened by a strong breeze, at the top of its unbelievable one hundred and twenty-five foot flagpole in deep centre field.

Since the Detroit race riot, no matter how many times he saw the flag, it was like the first time—a huge relief. The sight lightened Frank's mood.

Immediately, the traffic and the crowds all around them thickened into streams of excited humanity. The rollicking, raucous, colourful masses of people arriving this early surprised Frank. He found the sheer numbers filling the sidewalks and navigating around the cars in front and behind them a little daunting. It *was* the World Series. Still, he guessed it would be even busier as game time got closer. With his fingers on the window handle, he hesitated for a few seconds after they made the turn onto Trumbull.

Aw, what the hell?

Frank cranked down one and then the other window in the rear seat, and sank back with his Kaline glove. The cacophony of jubilation and anticipation spilled in from both sides and flooded the car to the rooftop. A few seconds later, his father and grandfather rolled down the front windows.

"Whoa!" Frank felt like he might drown in the joyful noise. The wind swirled in around them, and Frank pulled his Tigers ball cap down tighter on his head and inhaled the rich, urban and industrial smells of the Motor City.

Without warning, Frank's heart swelled bigger in his chest, and he laughed for joy at the return of a familiar sensation. Even after the riot, his excitement in anticipation of the game gave a welcome relief from the worst fears that sometimes haunted him, a relief, Frank discovered, he could still count on.

"You ok back there, Frank?" his grandfather asked from the front seat.

"More than ok. Thanks to you and Grandma Norah, and those incredible tickets."

For the next block on Trumbull, Frank moved from one side to the other like a human metronome, feasting his senses and letting his own excitement build.

Just then, the penetrating sound of exuberant drivers honking horns rippled up and then back down the never-ending Detroit River of cars.

R-E-E-P! R-E-E-E-P! R-E-E-E-E-P-P-P!

"Geez!" Frank exclaimed. "Now I know why they call them eardrums!" He put both hands over his ears, but still felt the sharp, penetrating beeps. His grandfather laughed and did the same, two monkeys hearing no evil.

"What about me?" Frank's father said, with his left hand on his left ear and his right hand still on the wheel. Frank and his grandfather shared a barely audible laugh and shook their handheld heads at him.

"Ok, you clowns. If I can't beat 'em, I'm gonna join 'em!" Ten seconds later, as the next wave of honking horns rolled over their Ford Galaxie, Frank's father did just that, steering with his right hand and stabbing at the horn with his left.

The decibel level in the car climbed from fun, through annoying, to unbearable. "DA-A-A-D!" Frank's plea went unheard. Then his grandfather forgot all about his eardrums and slapped out a complex rhythm on the dashboard using both hands. He swiveled his head with his eyes closed, like he was grooving to the raucous beat. Frank slammed his handheld head against the back of the seat. "Geez! Who's the teenager here, anyway?"

His father honked, his grandfather slapped and grooved.

"I SAID, WHO'S THE TEENAGER HERE?"

But they couldn't hear his question.

"At last!" Frank took his hands away from his ears. "C'mon, Dad, Grandpa, you're embarrassin' me, already."

Frank's father laughed, but had both hands back on the wheel. "Nothing like a do-or-die game in the World Series to bring out the fans!"

"And the fanfares," his grandfather said, with a low chuckle.

"And the crazies," Frank added.

His father and grandfather shared a look and a burst of laughter. "Those too, son," his dad said.

Frank was soon at the windows again. "Wow, look at all this incredible Tigers stuff! I wish ours wasn't all in the trunk."

"Yep. Should've thought of that," said his grandfather.

It looked to Frank like everyone in the crowd sported a Detroit pennant, poster, banner or jersey. All were blowing and flapping in the wind. There were small knots of St. Louis fans in Cardinals red and white, but they were swept away in the familiar rush of the orange, black and white of Tigers pride.

"Now that's what I call real home team pride!" Frank's father echoed his very thought.

Then it hit Frank like a fastball to the head—what the World Series might have done for the people of Detroit—all the people. Not only was the hometown crowd displaying the famous Detroit Tigers colours, but BLACKS were walking side by side with WHITES! Whole families chatting, laughing, comparing banners and tickets, bragging about their great seats, quoting stats and theories, full of predictions about this crucial game. Frank heard snatches of a dozen conversations through the open windows of their crawling car in a whole train of crawling cars. Each vehicle had its black heads and white heads, black arms and white arms, no capitals required, hanging out the windows and waving the same Tigers pennants, the same Detroit ball caps.

"Maybe there's still hope." Frank didn't realize he'd spoken out loud.

"For the Tigers and the city," his grandfather said.

"Amen to that," Frank's dad agreed, and they laughed with less reservation than they had for a long time. Frank felt his lifting spirits lift even higher, like a flag of good feelings working its way to the top of the pole.

Yes, the Tigers were on the ropes, and only one game away from what could be a pretty humiliating defeat. As Frank's grandfather had pointed out, teams at this level just don't come back when down three games to one in World Series play. McLain had disappointed, and the Cardinals Gibson, as well as their speedy base-stealer, Lou Brock, had shown unmistakable championship form, Hall of Famers all the way.

"I wish we could go just a little bit faster," Frank said.

"We can't, son. So just cool your jets and enjoy the experience," his dad said.

"Hear, hear!" added his grandfather. "It's not just the World Series, Frank, it's the journey, for the Tigers, for the city, for us. Now we're still plenty early and we need to find a place to park."

"Sorry, Dad. I guess I can wait a little."

"Hey, we all feel the same way," his grandfather said. "Us old guys just hide it better."

Three blocks from the stadium, Frank hung out the car window the way others were doing and let the noise and spectacle, the total experience of the World Series seep through his pores. Until one homemade poster on his left jumped out and snagged his eyeballs like he'd made the thing himself.

"Cool!" Frank murmured under all the noise.

The colourful poster showed a magnificent Tiger, in full orange, black and white colours, chowing down on a feast of helpless little red birds, screaming out, "No! No! No!" Underneath was the bold caption: "Go Cats! Bite Birds! OH YEAH!"

The artist was a black teenaged girl about Frank's age and almost as tall. She had on well-worn jeans, a Detroit ball cap and what must be a Detroit baseball jersey behind the poster she carried in front of her. The vinyl belt around her waist stood out in vivid Tigers orange, and a well-used fielder's mitt, a *blue* fielder's mitt, hung from the belt on her right hip.

The girl looked confident in the prophetic power of her artwork, as if the artistry and the words were magical—talismans against the imminent doom the Tigers were facing. Frank envied her lack of doubt, her pride in her team . . . their team.

Something about her tickled at his memory.

On impulse, Frank hung farther out of the window, waved his Kaline glove with his left hand and slapped the side of the car door repeatedly with his right.

"Hey! Hey you! With the poster!" he shouted, with all the force he could muster, and finally caught her eye, in spite of the noisy crowd and the honking horns in the slow-moving traffic.

The black girl flinched and then pointedly looked away when she realized he was yelling right at her.

"Hey! It's ok! I just wanna tell you . . . " The words dropped dead from his lips and Frank experienced terminal brain-lock. His arms were spread against the side of the car door as if he were a circus seal waiting for the trainer to toss him a dead mackerel. He stared with his mouth open and his tongue stupid. But it wasn't a dead fish Frank got. It was a weird thought.

Nah. Couldn't be. What were the odds?

Frank leaned out farther. But what could he say? He had to say something. Was it really *that* black girl?

Frank flapped his hands like clumsy flippers on the painted sheet metal. It didn't help. The black girl wouldn't look and the crowd was closing in around her.

Frank shut his mouth and forced his tongue to shift gears. "Uh, just wanted to say, uh, I like your poster! It's . . . really cool!" On impulse, Frank made the V-for-Victory sign with his right hand. "Tigers Rule!" He smiled and bobbed his head like Slippery the Seal. "TIGERS RULE!"

Without even looking, the black girl raised her right hand, extended the middle finger and flipped Frank the bird—the black bird.

It was deliberate, unexpected, shocking.

What'd I do?

But Frank hadn't done anything. No, it was something much worse. Not who he was. It was what he was: WHITE.

A moment later, a large man put a hand on the girl's shoulder and was steering her deeper into the crowd, parting it like Moses and the Red Sea, if Moses had been black.

No! Frank couldn't leave it like this. He needed to explain. To say something.

He moved forward and put his own hand on his dad's shoulder. "Dad! Speed up, please, just a little. I need to see something."

Frank's grandfather turned around in his seat. "What are you shouting about, Frank? "See what?" His grandfather glanced over his shoulder out the window. "That black girl with the Tiger on the poster?"

"Uh, I'll explain later. Just speed up a little, Dad. Try."

"That's impossible, Frank. And if we were going any slower, we'd be driving backwards."

Frank moved again to the window, but the black girl and the black man were lost from sight, somewhere up ahead of them. He put his hand on the door handle, and for one crazy moment, considered jumping out of the car and following them on foot, trying to catch her up. It was crazy. Too crazy. Frank collapsed back in the seat. "Damn!"

"What?" Frank's grandfather laid the hairy eyeball on him.

"Nothing, Grandpa. You know, just worryin' about the game, an' all."

"We all are. First, let's worry about parking."

But it wasn't nothing. Just for a moment there, when the black girl had passed them on the sidewalk and given Frank that quick look, before she'd given him the finger, he'd caught a glimpse of her right cheek. He desperately wanted to confirm what he saw. To explain himself to his father and grandfather. "Too late, now."

"What are you mumbling about?"

"Nothing, Grandpa. Nothing."

A second later, something blew by the back window. When Frank turned to look out, he saw it was someone's ball cap, a Tigers ball cap.

fifteen

"Screw it." Frank said to himself, and tried to put the whole black girl thing behind him.

The car moved closer to Michigan Avenue and Frank's attention was caught by more and more St. Louis fans decked out in Cardinals red. They looked supremely sure of themselves, eager for the World Series Championship celebration that would erupt if they won just one of the next three games. Their flying Cardinals banners and artwork appeared for a minute to overwhelm the Detroit orange, black and white.

"Well, my friends, have a look at this, will ya!" Frank's grandfather pointed through the front windshield, shook his head and began to laugh. "My oh my! The Cardinals have landed and they came in a flock."

Frank pushed between his father and grandfather for a better look. "Wow!"

"I'd say that's at least a double wow, Frank," maybe even a triple," said his dad.

"Yeah." Frank was impressed, but not in a good way. A group of six—no, seven Cardinals fans had made full-length, matching redbird costumes, from the tall crimson head-combs, feather-duster tails and big open beaks, out of which their cheering faces peered, right down to their black bird-claw feet. The seven formed a conga line weaving in and out of the traffic, stopping on cue to flap wings, shake their tail-feathers and shout Cardinals chants: "Redbirds! Redbirds! Whaddaya know? These pussycat Tigers have got to go! Redbirds! Redbirds! Whaddaya say? Win this game, go all the way!" When the seven conga'd in front of the Galaxie, Frank could see that each one had a little Detroit Tigers stuffed toy dangling by a hangman's noose from its red beak.

The Galaxie was swallowed up by a raucous mass of Cardinals red and white moving as one body. The mood in the car shifted. The honking horns paused. Tigers banners and pennants had serious competition. Now the power of the black girl's poster felt weak, diminished. These Cardinals fans had their magic too, and the overwhelming force of their confidence belittled Frank's own.

Frank's grandfather broke the spell with his familiar plea. "I think we better find that parking place as soon we can, Norm. I don't believe we can get to our usual spot. Frank, keep an eye out left, I'll watch right."

At every intersection, there were at least two Detroit policemen, beside their white Harley-Davidsons, directing traffic and trying to keep cars and pedestrians from any sort of dangerous encounter. But the effort was futile. Open beer and liquor bottles were everywhere, easily visible. Dozens of fans, Tigers and Cardinals, were already drunk and staggering. Frank saw more than one cop wrestling down reeling and abusive revelers, to cuff them and shove them into squad cars and paddy wagons parked at alley entrances and in every commercial loading zone. It was barely eleven o'clock.

Now, less than two blocks from the stadium, fans were getting dangerously thick. Mounted police on tall horses, and with batons and bullhorns, warned them on and broke them up by prodding batons on backs and shoulders. At least two of the mounted cops held long riot guns with the stocks resting on the fronts of their saddles. More than a few red or black-capped heads were cracked in the policing process. The police were not having a good day, but keeping the lid on things as much as possible, trying to manage the chaotic ebb and flow of the crowd.

"Man, check out how they're wearing those guns." Frank was never more conscious of weapons, big silver pistols worn so openly on the cops' hips in police-issue, breakaway holsters. "Geez!"

This wasn't Canada anymore.

Frank figured all the guns were a leftover effect of the riot.

"I don't believe it! There! Over there!" Frank's grandfather pointed to an asphalt lot between two warehouses. A pole-thin black youth with a wide Afro and a big flashlight was trying to wave cars in. A hand-lettered sign advertised "Series Parking $10." The lot was already half full. When Frank's father's intention was clear, the kid stepped boldly into the pedestrian traffic on the sidewalk and stopped the flow to let his dad turn the car in. Once on the lot, the young man came over to collect the fee. Frank saw his grandfather had a U.S. ten-dollar bill ready to hand over.

"You be here jus' for the game or longer?" the guy asked.

"Just for the game, thanks," his grandfather said, offering the bill.

"Ok, muh man. That be twenty dollar."

"What?" his dad exclaimed in disbelief. "Your sign says ten-dollar parking!"

"That right, muh man. Ten dollars gets you the space. But we gotsta charge for security too, dangerous neighbourhood like this. All these crowds an' drunks. You doan want no fool to be messin' wit' your vehicle." Frank's dad gritted his teeth in disgust, but his grandfather put a hand on his arm and replied politely.

"Maybe we'll try another spot. Thank you."

The young man curled both fists and snarled like an animal.

He was suddenly BLACK. And Frank and his father and grandfather were very, very WHITE. A chill of apprehension rippled over Frank.

"Then haul-ass off muh space, ya dumb Canucks, before I bang on this hunka junk muhself!" He began to pound on the left fender as Frank's dad looked frantically around for some way to reverse out through the sidewalk crowds and back into the line of cars on the street.

Frank cringed back as his mind flooded with TV images of last year's race riot.

Geez! How could they handle this jerk and get away?

The banging sounded like muffled explosions to Frank and seemed to go on forever. Until it was over-ridden by the revving of a motorcycle engine, a police motorcycle engine.

Frank saw a flash of the white Harley-Davidson's fuel tank and a leather jacket as the black rider practically ran over the angry black youth, revving the motorcycle until Frank thought it would explode. Wide-eyed, Frank winced as the cop drew his baton and brought it down hard on the young black guy's forearm. The pain, outrage and curses that followed were scary. "Back OFF! NOW!" the policeman ordered.

The black youth retreated, throwing insults over his shoulder. "You an Uncle Tom! You a white nigger! You a goddamned Stepin Fetchit!"

Frank was stunned. He got the Uncle Tom, and even the Stepin Fetchit TV character. But a white nigger?

Frank's father and grandfather were speechless. Frank hunched down in the backseat. When the cop maneuvered his motorcycle around to talk to his father, Frank was reassured by the black officer and sat up straight, giving him a wide smile of gratitude.

"You folks just follow me. Don't let that street trash ruin your day." The black police officer seemed about the same age as the punk who was threatening them and handled the big police Harley like a kid's scooter. He took them right, one block along Bagley, and then south on Lincoln and east again on Larosse, using his siren twice to open traffic.

The cop stopped at Holy Trinity Elementary School, where the staff parking and playground areas had been turned into a series parking lot. Four bearded giants operated the expanded space. Each one was dressed in a colourful jacket and baggy pants in electric limes, reds, oranges and blues, flapping in the wind. All wielded huge scimitars and sported ornate fezzes with long tassels. "Shriners!" His father let out an audible sigh of relief.

"Yo, Rocky!" the policeman shouted. "Take good care of

our Canadian friends here. They got caught out by some street hustler tried to stiff 'em for some fast cash."

"Hey, Lawrence! No problem. Keep 'em coming." A large sidewalk sandwich board announced:

PARK HERE!
$8.00
SHRINER FUNDRAISING
ALL PROCEEDS TOWARD
CHILDREN'S BURN HOSPITAL

"Will do, Rock."

"Thanks for your help, officer," Frank's father said, "we appreciate it." The policeman waved once and roared back to duty.

"Wow!" Frank said.

"That'll be eight dollars for the parking, sir," Rocky said.

David reached across and handed the tall Shriner two American bills. "Make it twenty dollars. For the kids," David said.

"Why thank you, my friend! Most generous! Just follow Brother Sylvester here." Brother Sylvester had squeezed himself into a little red clown-car convertible and quickly led them to a wide space against the wall of the school on the far side of the staff parking area. It was close by an exit so they could be one of the first cars out after the game. They still had to walk five blocks to the stadium, but the peace of mind was worth it. The three Phelans distributed a big umbrella, seat cushions, pennants, Tigers blankets and jackets among themselves, and joined the jostling mass of fans back on Trumbull. They were soon heading north again, into the brisk wind, toward the looming stadium. By the time they reached the area around the ticket windows, Frank had re-captured the infectious enthusiasm of the crowd.

The drunks and ticket hustlers were actually far fewer than Frank expected, and the majority of the crowd, black and white, were good-natured and considerate, with the antics of even the more boisterous fans still keeping it positive and fun. These people were dedicated followers of the sport. People of all ages, all walks of life, all colours and both sexes were here to see a crucial game in the one and only World Series of baseball. Each looked ready to live or die with the fortunes of their respective teams.

Maybe this was part of the magic of baseball, more powerful than even Frank realized. It was a heartening thought.

sixteen

"You get our programs, Frank, and then wait here with your father while I pick up the tickets," his grandfather told them, and then turned toward the shortest of the long lines at the ticket windows.

"Ok, but try and hurry, Grandpa," Frank urged. "Batting practice will be starting, and . . . "

"Frank! I am not going to tell you again to cool it!" his father said. "There's a line-up. So give me your stuff, get the programs and be ready to move as soon as your grandfather has the tickets. Now scoot!"

Scooting was out of the question. Frank made his way carefully through the crowd, heading for a fat, jovial-looking man standing in a kiosk that barely contained his girth. It did raise him three feet over the heads of the crowd of people, where he waved a big fan of programs in each fist with enough energy to take off and fly. "Heya! Heya! Willy has your official souvenir programs he-ah! Get your series program he-ah! Hur-ry! Hurry! Slip me a buck, buy the Tigers some luck!"

Frank took a couple minutes to work his way to Willy and hold up his American five-dollar bill. Willy reminded Frank of the Pillsbury Doughboy. What he might look like if he'd been slow-baking in the late season sun and was done to a beautiful brick red.

"Three, please, sir."

"You got it, man!" Willy handed him down the programs and his two dollars change. Frank took only the programs.

"Keep the change. The Tigers need all the luck they can get."

"Crazy, man!" Willy saluted, and his smile cracked even wider.

Frank clutched the programs to his chest and worked his way back to the ticket area that was even more crowded than before. It took him a while to spot his father. Frank and his grandfather, one with the programs and the other with the four miracle tickets, reached his dad about the same time.

"Ok, I got the tickets." His grandfather handed out one each of the precious cardboard rectangles. Frank could hardly believe what he was holding in his hand. One of his life's finest moments! He scrutinized every aspect of the ticket, memorizing its whole form and content, loving the grinning orange and black Tiger-head logo. The ticket would soon be torn and become a stub, but a special stub—one Frank planned to keep for the rest of his life. To Frank, this World Series ticket stub was every bit as valuable as a hard-to-find Topps baseball rookie card.

"Cool!"

Frank's father and grandfather must have caught some of

his emotion, because all three, in the midst of the noise and crowd, shared a private look. His grandfather squeezed Frank's shoulder. Did the same with his father. "Thanks a lot, Grandpa," Frank said.

"You're most welcome, Frank. Now I have some business to conduct, so you and your dad find our seats, and I'll join you shortly. We're on the third baseline, a few rows back from the field, behind the Tigers dugout. Maybe walk around and go in off Cochrane Avenue. Norm, you might want to get us some hot dogs and beer and whatever Frank wants before the crowd really packs the concessions. Frank, you're still going to try and catch the batting practice?"

"Are you kidding, Grandpa? You know the Tigers always sign autographs and stuff right there behind the batting cage." Frank's father and grandfather shared a quick look above his head, and Frank felt his optimism fade. They both knew he'd done this dozens of times before during regular season games. But Frank could never get through the crowds of kids and older fans and be lucky enough to be one of the few autograph hopefuls a player chose for the honour. Kaline was especially popular and hard to reach.

Frank knew they didn't want him to be disappointed again and maybe have it take away from his enjoyment of this special game. "It's the World Series," he reminded them.

"True enough," said his father. "A guy's gotta try. Ok, let's go. Good luck with selling the ticket, David. No St. Louis fan though, eh!"

"Never!" And Frank's grandfather headed back to the bustling ticket area.

Frank twigged. "Hey! Grandpa's gonna scalp the other ticket. Right?"

His dad paused and said: "He's just going to try and sell it, Frank. So another Tigers fan can enjoy the game from a good seat."

"Yeah! But is he gonna sell it for the ticket price or more?"

"Son, it's better if we don't ask. After all, these tickets are your grandfather's to do with as he sees fit."

"Sounds like scalping to me, Dad." Frank knew he was making it one of those difficult father-son moments, but couldn't resist. His dad was so straight about things like this.

His dad took the parent's familiar way out. "Your grandfather knows best. So just leave it. Understood?"

"Sure Dad, anything you say." Frank smiled as his father turned a lovely shade of parental-embarrassment-red, also familiar.

In fact, Frank enjoyed watching the fast-talking gaggle of scalpers that hung out around the ballpark, wheeling and dealing tickets. He'd been present earlier in the season when the police on duty had dragged away a slippery-looking guy, with a stingy-brim fedora and a fistful of tickets, protesting all the way: "Come on, man! I'm doin' the fans a favour. These are great seats, for a great Yankees match-up. The price is amazing!" The officers were unimpressed.

"Yeah, one of your 'favoured' customers just informed us," the officer applying the handcuffs said, "great seats for a Yankees game played two months ago."

Frank knew that as a scalper's customer you were a little fish swimming into the teeth of an experienced shark, trying to steal a morsel of baseball. If you were not super-careful, a scalper could ruin the whole experience of a team match-up and ballgame you'd looked forward to for weeks. Frank suddenly worried about his grandfather.

"Ok, let's find our seats." His dad put a hand on his shoulder and steered Frank through the crowd toward Cochrane Avenue. Each juggled his share of the programs, cushions, two pairs of binoculars, lucky Tigers pennants from other victories, a team blanket in case the wind and weather turned harsh, and the big Tigers umbrella to huddle under in any rain. Frank looked up into the grey sky and hoped no rain would fall. Driven sideways by the periodic gusts of wind, the umbrella might not do much good.

The trek to their seats was a further quarter-hour's struggle, but worth it. Frank arranged all their stuff, while his dad went back to the nearest concession booth for hot dogs and beer. Frank let out a satisfied sigh and sat for a minute to take it all in.

Frank's stomach was jumping with excitement, and he felt as if he couldn't eat a thing, not even his usual Hershey bar with almonds. Frank was in his very own seat, live at the 1968 World Series, and what could well be the decisive game for both teams. "So all right! Get a grip and enjoy the vibes, man!" He relaxed on the wooden seat and ground his fist into the smooth pocket of the autographed Kaline glove.

Wish you were here, Fancy.

Frank tipped his ball cap to the stadium. "Thank you for dusting us with diamonds, Mr. Scheib. You too, Smooth Daddy."

Their prize seats were three rows back from the field, opposite third base, with a good view of all the action: the plate and the batter; the on-deck circle; the Tigers players, coaches, and manager, Mayo Smith, entering and leaving the dug-out; and the pitchers already warming up in the bullpen farther down the foul line. And, straining a little, they could still see the plays at first base.

The stadium capacity was fifty-three thousand. Frank was surprised, based on his impression of the crowds outside, that even with close to two hours before game time, the good seats around him were still sparsely occupied, as were other areas of the stadium. This was the World Series!

In regular season games, in the years since Frank had been coming with his father and grandfather, they had gotten the best seats they could afford. So at one time or another, Frank had been seated in most sections of Tiger Stadium. But in these last few years, since Al Kaline became his favourite player, Frank had always done the same thing. At some time during the game, no matter where they were sitting, Frank would make his way to an empty seat in the front row of the right-field, second-deck bleachers, if he was lucky enough to find one open.

This second-deck location was unique in American ballpark design because it over-hung the lower deck by a good ten feet, giving a wonderful, fan's-eye view of the outfield plays. So after confirming that the empty seat was not taken, Frank would eagerly install himself above right field and watch his favourite Tigers player fielding just below him.

Kaline was a consistent all-star choice in right field since his first time in the All-Star Summer Classic in 1955. In Frank's admittedly biased opinion, Al Kaline patrolled his defensive position to perfection. Frank was always learning something that improved his play in the Junior Leagues at home.

But right now, Frank's attention was attracted to the big scoreboard on the left-field fence, where it had been moved in 1961. "See, Frank," his father had said. "There were three players—Charlie Maxwell, Norm Cash, and Al Kaline—who complained that in its original position at the four hundred and forty foot mark in dead centre field, it interfered with their view of the pitch and hurt their success at the plate." Frank devoured every tidbit of that kind of baseball lore from his dad and grandfather, and was always hungry for more.

While Frank and the other early-arriving fans watched, the scoreboard flashed the starting line-ups for the Cardinals and Tigers. Frank dutifully filled in the players' names on his program in preparation for the game. He was pleased that Mayo Smith had maintained Kaline as the starting right fielder. Mickey Lolich was on the mound for Detroit and would have to pitch the game of his life if Detroit was to stay alive. "Man, talk about pressure!" Frank tried to imagine it and couldn't.

"Ok, batting practice, man! At the World Series!" Frank checked his watch and looked to his right, to home plate. The groundskeepers had not quite rolled out the batting cage. Still, it was almost time. He closed his eyes, leaned forward in the seat and let anticipation of the World Series experience to come energize every atom of his being.

seventeen

Frank heard the rumble and squeak as the Tiger Stadium groundskeepers began to roll the heavy batting cage toward home plate. His eyes snapped open. "Damn!" How could he be sitting here when he needed to be down there?

Frank took only his Kaline glove and made his way right along the rows and tall stairs to join the fringes of the group of people already waiting, seated or gathered at the fence, to take in the pre-game batting practice. Frank was already late, forced to sit on the aisle, four rows back, and forced to watch over their heads while the batting cage and pitching mound screen were carefully positioned and locked down, anticipating the players to come. No wonder the stands nearby seemed empty! Everybody was here.

"Damn!" he said, again, upset with himself.

It looked as if more than a couple hundred fans would soon be clamouring for the attentions of their heroes: shouting, waving autograph books, programs, Tigers ball caps and more.

There was a healthy sprinkling of red-and-white-wearing, St. Louis Cardinals fans too. They broke into lusty cheers as the Cardinals batters emerged from the dressing room to take their batting practice before the home team. It didn't take a brainiac to tell their confidence was super-high. Who could blame them? Already St. Louis fans were pushing roughly through the Tigers fans and shouting for the attentions of speedy Lou Brock, the Cardinals ace base-stealer and hitter.

Maybe Frank could still work his way down to the fence when Al Kaline and the Tigers came out to practice later.

Yeah, right.

Energy draining, Frank slumped on the hard wooden seat, discouraged at the sight of such competition for the star players, even if they were Cardinals. And yeah, the World Series made his chances even more hopeless. Al Kaline would never add his personal, face-on-face endorsement to Frank's hard-earned new glove or ball cap. Frank would be disappointed. Again.

The autograph crowd was a good mix of adults, teenagers and kids, male and female, with about equal numbers of blacks and whites. It was hard to tell in the raucous crush and tumble. The guy that caught Frank's eye was an ambitious black fan, tall and skinny and maybe a little older than him, steadily working his way to the fence with a combination of "excuse me's," toothy smiles and snake-like agility.

Frank noticed right away that the kid's faded junior team jersey had the number 13 on the back. "Man, what was the guy thinking?" he murmured. Maybe the kid wasn't superstitious, but it made Frank thankful again that Kaline's number was a nice, neutral 6. "No way for that bad-luck, mean 13!" Why risk tempting the gods of baseball to give you a royal screwing?

Frank thought once more of the many times he'd asked his grandfather to tell him the story of Ty Cobb and "Li'l Rastus," whenever they got onto baseball superstitions and the head game, while waiting for a contest to start. Knowing and recalling the story made it easier to see why blacks might be feeling odd, like second-class citizens, and even in a mood to riot decades later, hence: "DETROIT BURNS!"

Frank's grandfather had told him that in Ty Cobb's day, and even before the turn of the century, besides the lucky number 7 "made in heaven" or "mean 13" on jerseys, players used various charms and odd trinkets to bring them luck. In 1928, Yankees star pitcher, Waite Hoyt, claimed he won an impressive twenty-three games through the simple but powerful expedient of sticking a wad of Black Jack chewing gum to the button on top of his ball cap.

"But here's the bizarre thing, Frank," his grandfather had said, "players, teams and even baseball writers, also made use of living icons: black boys, white boys, greyhound dogs, dwarfs, hunchbacks and more, as good luck charms. Believed rubbing a black boy's hair or a hunchback's hump would improve your bat-work, enlarge your glove, put fire in your fastball and wings on your feet, to beat out those throws to first."

"Actual hunchbacks? No way, Grandpa!" Frank said, the first time he heard the stories. He and Larry had watched Anthony Quinn, as Quasimodo, in a re-run of the old *Hunchback of Notre Dame* movie on television. The sight of the deformity made them both uncomfortable, even though it was only an actor in a movie. But these baseball mascots were real people.

"Every way, Frank," said his grandfather. "But remember, the turn of the century was very different in terms of racial attitudes and just general respect for people with disabilities or differences."

Yet, with the riots last year and all, Frank wasn't so sure. Did the ghost of the young black mascot, Li'l Rastus, still haunt the Tigers and the city of Detroit? Frank felt more than a little guilty that, nonetheless, this remained his favourite Ty Cobb and superstition story.

"You see, Frank, Ty Cobb was a Southerner, the Georgia Peach, with many of the prejudices of that time and place. Anyway, in 1908, Cobb came across a black boy called Li'l Rastus, and he kept him around the clubhouse as the Tigers team mascot. Cobb actually believed Rastus had brought his Tigers the good luck every team needs at some point in their seasons, but especially in the World Series."

Like now? Frank caught himself, guiltily wondering if the Tigers couldn't use a mascot to change their luck in this World Series game, sixty years later.

Don't go there, man.

"For a while," his grandfather had recounted, "the magic truly seemed to work. The Tigers were having a pretty good season. But then things like bats and balls, gloves and pieces of uniform began to disappear from the clubhouse. And at the same time, the Tigers went into a scoring slump. So that was it for the magic. Cobb suspected Li'l Rastus. Supposedly, he'd been keeping Li'l Rastus generally hidden from the public eye, but he kicked him out of the locker room when the season went bad and the equipment went missing."

"So what happened, Grandpa?" Frank's grandfather had

laughed and taken a swallow from his tall paper cup of Tiger Stadium Stroh's beer.

"What happened was, Li'l Rastus got his revenge on old Cobb. He went over to the Chicago Cubs for the World Series, later that year. And would you believe it? The Cubs did beat the Tigers in the Fall Classic."

"Wow! Bummer."

"With a capital B. Anyway, Cobb, still wanting every edge, turns right around and brings Rastus back to the Tigers the following year. This time, so the story goes, Cobb kept him under his bunk!"

"What? And you believe that, Grandpa?"

"Hey, this is what I heard, Frank. Just as Cobb hoped, the magic returned with the mascot too, or so the Tigers believed. This was because the Tigers pitcher, George Mullin, stole Rastus away from under Cobb's bunk, installed him under his own bunk and pitched a solid shut-out the next day, while getting three hits at the plate."

"And?"

"And nothing. If Li'l Rastus had 'the power,' it didn't last into the post-season. Rastus didn't do for the Tigers what he'd done for the Cubs. Cobb's team lost the 1909 World Series to the Pittsburgh Pirates."

"What does that stuff all mean, then?" Frank had really needed to know. His grandfather drained the rest of his beer in one long swallow.

"Well, in that case, racial prejudice and the superstition of the time for sure. But right up until 1967, as far as I know, only the three players—Blue Moon Odom, Steve Barber and Turk

Farrell, all pitchers—were brave or reckless enough to take the mound wearing mean 13 and have some success."

"Geez!" Frank had flopped back in his seat as wary and confused as ever.

His grandfather's stories were from more than a few years ago. Since then, and as now, Frank took these events with a grain of salt, as cautionary tales. But Frank wasn't sure how big that grain actually was.

And these days, to tell the truth, Frank was deathly afraid to risk dismissing the power of superstition. This summer, when Frank's team had played the Hellcats in the Windsor Junior League championship final, Larry had ragged him during the seventh inning stretch. Frank, even more particular than usual, had religiously avoided any of the chalk lines and kept up his whispered, play-by-play patter in the outfield. In spite of all that, the Hellcats had beaten the Werewolves by a single run, and now the Hellcats wore the championship crests Frank and Larry so desperately coveted.

His best friend had been merciless. "We lost, Frank. So now don't try and tell me the chalk line or the rap thing means dick, bud," Larry said, when the teams shook hands after the closely fought game.

And what could Frank say? He'd gone 4-0 at the plate, the damned captain of the team! It had never happened during the season when his bat had been a regular contributor to the Werewolves victories.

Dejected and down on himself, Frank had later asked his

father and grandfather about the whole superstition thing, at home, when he could finally talk about it.

They only shrugged.

"We all accept the head game is a real phenomenon," his dad had said, finally. "It can give an edge, put a player in the right space. But how and what it will do, and when it will do it, is part of baseball's mystery, son."

"If it was predictable and everybody could do it," his grandfather had added, "the game would be the poorer for it. Some of the magic would be lost."

"Your grandfather's right, there, Frank. Each player has to decide for himself. Remember, Larry only bugged you about the chalk lines and talking to yourself when the Werewolves didn't win this important game. Yet, when you'd been doing all that, and winning all your regular season games, Larry only mentioned it the couple times you told me about. Right?"

"I guess."

"And Larry was never elected the Werewolves captain," reminded his grandfather. "Your teammates chose you. And your coach, Butch Cassidy, agreed."

Frank had nodded his acceptance of that, but didn't really feel it. The championship loss was too bitter and recent. After the final out, he remembered his dad reaching out and adjusting his ball cap more squarely on his head. Frank could see his own pain reflected in his father's eyes. "Now get over there and shake hands with the Hellcats, son. You're the captain and your teammates need to see you have the pride I know you have for your Werewolves and the game of baseball. There'll be other seasons."

Frank had done that, yet it was a bitter memory, especially

now, with his beloved Tigers on the edge of defeat in a World Series.

Lucky numbers, unlucky numbers, Li'l Rastus, avoiding chalk lines, rapping to yourself, game magic—a guy could go crazy!

Not even the amazing Tyrus Raymond Cobb had mastered the subtleties.

Still, Frank was glad he had his Kaline stuff for this World Series game. And he hoped that when Al Kaline took the field, he too would avoid the chalk.

Down at field level, the St. Louis players began to take practice as the Cardinals pitching coach threw balls from behind the wire screen on the mound and assessed his starting players. "Screw off, boy!" Frank watched with more than casual interest as the tall black kid, mean 13, got roughly pushed to the deck when he tried to slip by an oversized white kid, with freckles and bright red hair, to get to the fence.

Was this the real mean? Black and white?

Man! Frank ground his fist into his Kaline glove and felt the tension in his gut.

eighteen

"Mind if I join you? Your grandfather's not back from selling the ticket yet."

Frank moved one seat to his left and gave the aisle seat to his dad. "Maybe the cops arrested him for scalping." His father raised a finger in warning. Frank and Larry had decided long ago that it was part of their duty as teenagers to bug their parents like this, kinda keep 'em a bit off balance.

Don't wanna let down the side.

Frank's dad held up a fresh Hershey bar with almonds and a large root beer, on a paper tray, along with his own Stroh's and a hot dog. "So, do you want the chocolate bar and root beer, or should I go back to our seats and offer them to the next polite teenaged fan I see?

It took only a moment for Frank to decide that junk food was the better part of impudence. "I'll take 'em."

But his dad still held them out of reach. "And the scalping lamp is out, now and for the rest of the day?"

"It's out," Frank said. He realized he really was starving. Probably still not recovered from all those weeks of junk food deprivation while he'd saved his money to pay for the Kaline glove.

"Then feed your face and grow your zits like a good teenager."

"Yeah, my zits are kinda hungry." They both laughed and Frank's father handed him his rations and took a sip of the Stroh's and a bite from the hot dog.

Frank figured that now, while they watched the Cardinals practice, they had some time for the serious Tigers talk they'd been avoiding in the car on the trip over. He took a bite of Hershey chocolate and a deep breath. He tried not to sound whiney.

"What happened to the Tigers, Dad? They won the American League Pennant by twelve games this season. Twelve games! So what happened?"

"True, son. Best finish since New York's thirteen-and-a-half-game win in 1943."

"Then, what?"

"Well, remember those *Detroit Free Press* articles we read?" Frank nodded. "So, what did Red Shoendienst say about pitching in this series, Frank?"

Frank remembered exactly what the Cardinals manager had said. "Schoendienst said the difference would be the pitchers. It would be eighty percent of the series."

"And so far he was right, ok? Gibson's been unbeatable and McLain has lost it. And remember, the Cardinals are coming off their big '67 World Series win over Boston. So this year St.

Louis is a 3-2, odds-on favourite. Right?" Frank thought about it some more.

"Maybe Mayo shouldn't have shifted Mickey Stanley from his regular position at centre field to short stop. Not a week before the series. Even some Detroit sports guys said he was nuts."

It was partly true. George Cantor, a much-read Detroit sports writer, was so moved as to call Smith's decision one of "legendary" significance. "The boldest ever made by a manager entering the World Series."

Frank's father looked at him in some surprise. "Hey! Weren't you the guy punching holes in the air like Muhammad Ali a few weeks ago shouting, 'Kaline's in! Kaline's in!' till your mother had to order you to sit down for dinner?" Frank shrugged and took another bite of chocolate. "Smith made the move to get Al Kaline's bat in the lineup. Now here you are waiting for your baseball idol to take batting practice, and about to try for his autograph. It's Mayo's move that has made it possible."

"I know, Dad, really," Frank said. "And 'try' is the word. Just look at this buncha autograph hounds."

His father glanced down at the fans milling along the fence behind the batting cage, standing in the aisle and occupying more rows in front of them. If anything, the mob looked even bigger now.

"True, they do love their teams and players. And they want that special autograph just as badly as you do."

"Yeah, that's what I mean."

"Guy's gotta try," his dad reminded him.

Frank turned red. "Yeah, I will, Dad."

His father took a long swallow. "And speaking of guys trying, who's the only Tiger since Ty Cobb that has a chance to reach the three thousand hit mark?" Frank felt even more stupid. Maybe his dad was getting even for the scalping thing. But he knew his dad wasn't like that.

"Kaline," Frank admitted.

"Right. Your grandfather thinks he'll do it, too."

"Yeah, you're right, Dad." Still an' all, parents must have a knack for reminding their kids of what they already knew—and making them feel like dumb kids because of it. The Cardinals finished practice and signed a good number of autographs before heading off for their warm-up stretches, jogging or fielding drills. A few lucky St. Louis fans did get Brock's signature on a cap or program. And, Frank noted, some of them were Tigers fans! It felt like betrayal to him.

Frank wanted to get another issue out. See what his father would say. "I guess Brock's looking pretty good. Even our own fans think so."

"Well, you have to respect him, Frank. He's already a World Series champion." His father elbowed his biceps. "But here comes another champion, right?" Frank and his father watched as the Detroit Tigers, lead by Kaline, Freehan, Cash and even Mickey Lolich, the Tigers left-handed starting pitcher, took over the batting cage from the Cardinals.

Below them, the many Tigers fans waiting at the fence and above it erupted with a long burst of cheering and hand clapping. Then the chanting began.

"KA-LINE! KA-LINE! KA-LINE!"

Frank and his father put down their drinks, jumped to their feet, and began clapping and chanting with the rest. "KA-LINE! KA-LINE!" They carried on for more than a minute.

It felt right, both of them cheering together, in the stadium his great-grandfather Wally helped build.

Frank watched a strong gust of wind ruffle his idol's hair as Kaline tipped his ball cap to the chanting crowd. "Kaline looks pretty calm," Frank said, and looked at his dad. This was really a question. His father knew Frank was looking for some reassurance.

"Well, son, looking calm may mean he's feeling confident."

Frank took it. "Yeah, maybe . . . "

But damn! Would it be enough?

nineteen

The chanting and clapping for Kaline and the Tigers stopped. Frank and his dad sat back down with their food. Enough other fans did the same so they had a good view of the batting cage action.

"How do the rest of the Tigers look to you, Dad?"

Frank's father waited and watched awhile before answering. "They look like a serious group of close-knit professionals. Professionals who know their business and are going about it like they've gone about it hundreds of times before."

That was an adult's answer. "Yeah. I guess."

But how do they feel? Confident?

The Tigers Mickey Lolich went to the pitching screen and picked up some practice balls to begin throwing to the Tigers fourth-spot cleanup hitter, Norm Cash, at the plate. Kaline and catcher Bill Freehan stood talking behind the batting cage. Then Frank noticed Kaline and Freehan abruptly stop talking and look out toward third base. Frank and his father, and the other players and fans looked too.

A lone Cardinals player in crisp red and white sprinted like a greyhound toward the bag from second base. Fifteen feet from the bag, the speedy runner went smoothly down on the dirt and executed the most perfect hook slide Frank had ever seen in his life. The toe of the player's extended left spikes just kissed the bag, but somehow stuck, with the left hand to follow, and both avoided the tag of the imaginary third baseman.

"Wow!" It was his dad who said it, but Frank was thinking it, and more. *Double Wow!* The crowd at the fence, now mostly Tigers fans, couldn't help but applaud. Frank had to hold himself stiff to stop doing the same. It was the showy Lou Brock, the best base-stealer in the league. "Have to give it to Brock too," his father observed. "Man really knows how to send the Tigers a message."

Yeah. Another part of the head game, Frank realized, but didn't say aloud.

A noticeable wind began to gust toward home plate from the outfield. It stiffened the Tiger Stadium pennants and blew the cloud of dust raised by Brock's slide toward Kaline and Freehan, momentarily enveloping them. Brock gave the two Tigers a confident smile and a wave that Freehan and Kaline returned. But Frank, even at a distance, could feel it was a tense moment.

Bill Freehan spit deliberately into the dirt at his feet. The duel between Brock and the Tigers catcher would be decided in the dust of home plate. Frank remembered Freehan's comment in the *Detroit Free Press.* "I gotta get Brock. I'm gonna step on his toe."

Frank saw Brock and teammate Curt Flood heading toward the outfield fence to run wind sprints, but keeping an eye out to avoid any Tigers practice balls that might be hit their way.

"You know, Frank," said his father, "maybe there's one other thing that might make a big difference in this series." He spoke into his empty beer cup.

"You mean Brock's bad fielding record?" Frank hardly noticed as he ate the whole Hershey bar and drank most of his root beer.

His dad shook his head. "REVENGE." His father said it like the word was a newspaper headline.

"Revenge?" Frank echoed. His father took a bite of his hot dog while Frank figured it out. "Oh, yeah! 1934? What Grandpa said about Dizzy Dean?"

"Yep. This World Series between the Detroit Tigers and the St. Louis Cardinals has already been played—thirty-four years ago."

"Wow!" Frank suddenly realized. "That matchup between the two numbers thirty-four: the year 1934 and the year 1968, thirty-four years later is pretty spooky. Like fate or destiny. Like the same game has come around again."

"H-m-m-m. Don't know much about fate or destiny, but I agree the numbers do seem suggestive when you add them all up."

"So, what do you think it means, Dad?"

His father laughed and wiped mustard from the side of his mouth with a napkin.

"Could mean nothing. Could mean something. Could mean everything," he said. "It's another mystery, Frank. But if you remember what your grandfather told us, you can bet Mayo

Smith and every Tigers player out there today will be thinking about what happened to the old Tigers in that 1934 World Series against the Cardinals, too."

"But it was so long ago."

"Not so long. But unique," Frank's dad maintained. "I was only two years old, of course. But your grandfather always said he and your great-grandfather Wally thought those seven games in 1934 made for one of the wildest and most closely fought World Series championships, before or since. An absolute stunner of a series."

"Yeah, Grandpa does still talk about The 'Gashouse Gang' from St. Louis," Frank said.

"More than that, son. He even has half a dozen incredible photos of St. Louis pitchers 'Dizzy' and 'Daffy' Dean, and of both those old teams, in his collection."

Frank couldn't believe it. Photos of the enemy! "But I've never seen them!"

"I know. And don't tell your grandfather I told you. Promise? The memory's painful and he keeps them well out of sight."

"If I can have a hot dog and another root beer, later?"

"Sounds like a deal. But more importantly, Frank, your grandfather still talks, in particular, about the Dean brothers, Jerome Hanna and Paul Dee, with both of us. Right?"

Frank thought he understood that. "I can't believe they let themselves be called Dizzy and Daffy. Or that the St. Louis team was nicknamed The Gashouse Gang." Frank smiled at the thought. "But Dizzy Dean?"

"Well, Dizzy Dean was maybe the most colourful pitcher in the majors in his time," said his father. "From '32 to '36, Dean simply dominated on the mound and did it with outrageous style. His antics might have been dizzy, but his arm was deadly. People just called him Diz. He was that well known."

"I guess."

"No guessing about it, Frank."

It was a weirdly familiar feeling. The Gashouse Gang's whole season had ridden on one game, the seventh and final game of the '34 Series, with the Tigers favoured. St. Louis had needed one final installment of Dizzy Dean's magic on the mound. Now, thirty-four years later, the Tigers hopes were riding on this one game in the 1968 Series.

Frank's father wiped his mouth a final time with the napkin and stuffed it into the empty beer cup. "Thing of it was, Frank, no one thought Dean could even start game seven.

"Yeah, I remember, now."

"Dean was hit on the head by a ball and knocked unconscious the game before," his father continued. "So, as they say, the whole United States, an anxious nation, held its breath and waited."

"I guess I can't really imagine something like that now."

Except maybe the Detroit race riot. But that was different, wasn't it?

"Anyway, son, Dizzy's head was finally X-rayed. So The Gashouse Gang, the Cardinals fans and his brother Daffy, not to mention the Tigers fans like your grandfather and great-grandfather Wally here, waited on pins and needles for the results."

"Yeah, this I do remember, Dad."

It was Dizzy himself who had relayed the infamous diagnosis that became instant baseball lore and legend: "They X-rayed my head today. Nothing was found."

There was a game seven. The Diz would be back!

"I guess the only way we can imagine the tension in that final game in 1934, Frank, is to take the tension we feel right now for the Tigers and maybe multiply it by ten."

Frank recalled this too. The Gashouse Gang had destroyed the Tigers pitchers with an almost unheard of seventeen hits. On the mound, Dizzy Dean was as good as his word, dominating Detroit batters and winning the 1934 Baseball World Championship with an embarrassing 11-0 shutout of the favoured Tigers from the Motor City. Dizzy's "nothing" was everything he'd needed to ensure his own, well-deserved place as one of the truly great characters of major league baseball.

"And you remember the famous photograph?" Frank's father asked him, stuffing Frank's Hershey bar wrapper into the cups with his napkin.

"I think so. Grandpa told me about it but I've never seen it. After the game, didn't Dean twist the tail off a toy tiger in front of all the sports guys?"

"That he did, son."

The image reminded Frank of this morning's conga line of giant red Cardinals with little Tigers dangling from their beaks. It was another not good memory.

"Well, Frank," his father stretched as he spoke, "you think about that and don't be so down in the mouth. Revenge can be a powerful motivator, even after thirty-four years. You can bet Al Kaline and the Tigers are looking for some payback. Now I better get back to your grandfather. And remember, son . . . "

"Uh-huh, Dad. A guy's gotta try."

Frank's father squeezed his shoulder and left. Frank moved back to the aisle seat and did think about it.

Had being the odds-makers' favourites way back in 1934

jinxed the Tigers? And yeah, the positions might be reversed, but it was Kaline and the Tigers, not the Cardinals, who seemed jinxed in this series. Was revenge more powerful than a jinx? As powerful as Dizzy Dean in that long-ago series?

Frank wished he knew.

part two

FRANK AND ELLIE

twenty

Frank

"GO! GO! GO!"

"RUN FOR IT!"

"HAUL BUTT!"

Frank stood up and moved into the wide aisle by sheer instinct, snapped out of his thoughts by the sight and excited yells of dozens of kids and adults, charging right for him in a boiling mass of bodies that seemed intent on stomping him into the cement like human chewing gum.

"What the hell?"

Frank panicked, tensed and froze into a half-crouch. He looked wildly around him. Too late! No place to run. How had he become the object of a stampeding mob?

One big kid, older than Frank, red hair like curled wire and face a rash of orange freckles, came straight for him. The fat dude had a crazy intent look on his face, lips drawn back and teeth like dirty Chiclets. Red shouldered aside other kids and even some adult fans with curses and flying elbows. Frank felt like a naked ten-pin in the middle of an alley about to be bowled over. He could do nothing. "Geez!"

In the final moments before impending death, Frank unfroze and dropped down to the cement and tried to cover up, still no wiser about the reason for his imminent doom.

Why me? What have I done?

"GET IT! GET IT! GO ON!"

The yells and pounding feet assaulted his ears on all sides. "NO-O-O-O!" Frank yelled his denial.

"OUTTA MY WAY, DICKWAD!"

Big Red kicked Frank hard, with an impact that drove him sideways onto the unyielding cement. Frank's head hit with a sickening impact that shook loose his ball cap and rattled his brains. "A-a-a-h-h-h!"

Stunned and disoriented, Frank couldn't make sense of the shouts of the mob of fans still streaming past him on both sides. Headed where?

Slow seconds later, Frank fought his way up and back over to his aisle seat with a moan. He probed the hurt on the right side of his head and examined his fingers. No blood so far.

Where's my ball cap?

Frank's blurred vision barely allowed him to locate the cap at the edge of the aisle a few feet away. "Just great!" He could feel that the cap was dirty and stomped flat by the rushing crowd. Frank began to brush off the dust and grime.

Only then did Frank think to turn around in his seat and look behind him. It took time for his addled brain to figure it out. "Oh, no! NO!" he moaned, and it wasn't just the pain from his bruised head. When Frank swung around forward again and looked down at the Tigers batting cage through watery eyes, the whole of his dread was confirmed.

"Well damn! DAMN IT!"

Frank picked up the Kaline mitt and slapped it against his thigh, and the knot of pain deep in his head exploded like buried dynamite.

Whoever the Tigers batter in the cage was, the out-of-focus figure must have hit a foul ball straight up to the leading edge of the top of the batting cage. The ball's spin and impact had propelled it back, over Frank's head, and high into the seats behind him. "No!"

Denying it didn't matter one bit. Frank had been the closest person to the ball. The precious World Series souvenir could have been his. His!

Frank got shakily to his feet and looked behind him, up into the stands. Sure enough, the elusive prize ball was now bouncing erratically in and out of his sight, pursued by the manic horde of surging fans. The ball disappeared from Frank's view somewhere in front of Big Red and the scrambling mass—

Until a high-pitched shout of triumph announced the end of the quest for the super-precious World Series baseball and Tigers souvenir: "E-e-e-e-YAH!"

"Aw, damn!"

"Too late!"

"Forget it!"

The other pursuers looked on in envy and then slowly turned to trickle back down the aisle and rejoin the crowd of autograph-seekers at the backstop. The receding wave continued past Frank, until finally, the lucky prizewinner stood revealed.

Frank was beyond stunned. "No way! There's no freakin' way!"

"E-e-e-e-YAH!" a proud black girl yelled again, holding the World Series ball high above her head in triumph and jumping up and down like a demented pogo stick.

"JUNIOR TIGERS!"

The words came clearer and jumped out at Frank from the front of her white pinstriped jersey. She was unmistakable. The teenaged black girl waving the ball was the Tigers fan from Trumbull Avenue who had carried the cool, Go Cats! Bite Birds! OH YEAH! poster. The fan Frank had tried to exchange victory signs with from their slow-moving car. The girl who'd refused to look at him. And when Frank kept at it, trying to communicate his pleasure and pride in her poster and its sentiments, trying to communicate his solidarity with her as Tigers fans together, had given Frank the bird, the black bird.

Frank's shock and hurt came rushing back, and with it, a ton of resentment—first at the finger, and now, at the fact that she, not he, held the precious World Series souvenir.

The joyful expression on her face was the exact opposite of the bitter, fleeting glance she'd given him on Trumbull.

"Well hell! Hell!" Frank was pissed at himself.

What a pathetic freakin' loser, I am!

Frank's seat in the stands had indeed been closest to the foul ball hit so shortly after his dad had left. The prize had easily been his for the taking. But again, his thoughts were elsewhere, on Dizzy Dean and the revenge thing, not on getting a souvenir ball, much less Al Kaline's autograph.

Frank's luck was as bad as the Tigers in 1934, but there was no Li'l Rastus in the mix. He had no one to blame but himself. "Great!"

I should just take poison and die right here.

In his disgust, Frank slapped himself right in the face with his Kaline glove. Then he slapped himself again. The pain from the bruise on the side of his head glowed with sullen fire.

Above him, Frank couldn't help but stare at the Junior Tiger examining the ball closely, the awe on her face still shining clear as her amazing luck sank all the way in. She shot up a sudden fist in the black power salute.

Frank took a calming breath and looked down at his feet. He tried to forget the bird she'd flipped him and put aside any feelings of, what? He didn't want to say "prejudice."

But the word popped into his head with a life of its own. And why not? It was so easy to, well, to hate.

So, hate yourself, man!

Frank thought of his mother and was ashamed. Black or white wasn't the issue here. Still, it felt complicated. The fact was: the black girl got the ball that could've been his because he blew it. Frank felt a massive, World Series-sized headache settling in and gritted his teeth against the steady jolts of major league pain.

He slumped down in his seat again, leaned back and put his battered ball cap over his face. It was so tempting to just dive deep into the pity pool and wallow there. Why couldn't he be even a little glad for her? "Why not?" he asked the inside of his ball cap.

Forget the dirty bird, the black-white thing.

She was clearly an enthusiastic and loyal supporter of the Detroit Tigers they both loved. The Tigers series souvenir was fairly recovered and, yeah, justly deserved. Frank almost considered telling her so, considered swallowing his disappointment, ignoring her actions on Trumbull and actually congratulating her.

That is, until he heard a familiar name being shouted by the fans around the batting cage below him.

Just at that moment, the fickle gods of baseball sent a gust of wind to lift the ball cap off Frank's face. After catching it, Frank looked down at home plate—and wished he hadn't. He rubbed moisture from his eyes. How could he have missed seeing it the first time? How could he! The big number 6 from the back of the hitter's jersey flew into focus and blew Frank's eyes out.

"Kaline?"

KALINE!

The gods of baseball had practically put an Al Kaline foul ball into Frank's Kaline glove! And he hadn't realized. It was all a sick, sick joke. The gods of baseball, at whose altar Frank worshipped, were laughing at him like satanic jackasses. But Frank was the jackass.

Could it get any worse?

Once again, Frank lay back in his seat and covered his face with his Tigers ball cap to block out the world. Talk about depressing.

Now Frank shifted forward with his elbows on his knees and rubbed the stiff cotton of the cap against his face. He felt the wet pressure starting behind his eyes. The beginning tears made him angry. He was fourteen. Fourteen! Still, how would he ever live with this memory? Frank decided right there to shove the memory down deep, bury it in an unmarked grave and forget it.

"No-o-o! NO-O-O-O!"

What? What now?

Frank ignored the sounds and breathed through the cap held against his face.

"No! IT'S MINE! MINE!"

"Geez and double geez! What is that?" The defiant words jagged down through the chilly air and split the back of Frank's aching head like the baseball gods' lightning. It made Frank angry.

"YOU'LL HAVE TO KILL ME!

"What the hell, now?" Frank lowered the ball cap. It hurt to even turn his head and look back over his shoulder for the source of the irritating noise. Frank's vision was almost clear. Something tall and bulky came into soft focus. It was more than a dozen rows up, at the seven-foot face of the wide cement access that led to the higher bench seats. "Wha-at?" Frank shook his head once to try and bring the sight clearer.

The strident protests were joined by a deeper voice that overrode the denials. Whoever it was sounded pissed. Really pissed.

Frank stood jerkily up, put his cap on his head and rubbed carefully at his eyes.

Big Red?

There was a moving flash of white pinstripes behind the hulking redheaded kid. Someone was waving a baseball in the air.

A baseball!

Frank took awkward steps sideways into the aisle for a better angle. There was no one else around him. The season's ticket holders in this reserved seating area could afford to arrive last.

Sure enough: the black girl!

Big Red was in some kind of argument with the black teenager. No look of joyous triumph on her face now. The Junior Tiger was shaking her head and setting herself against the threat. Red advanced on her. His bulk soon hid her from Frank's view again. Frank wasn't sure what was going on, but it didn't look good for the Detroit Junior Tiger with the Kaline ball.

Again the black girl shouted, "JUST TRY IT!" Now her voice was heavy with challenge. Red must have her backed against the cement section wall behind them. She probably couldn't move.

"Hell!" Frank felt the blood pulsing behind his eyes. He stood swaying on his feet, legs like rotten matchsticks. Looked desperately for help again. But with the noise and crowd around the batting cage, no one noticed what was happening that high in the stands. It was still too early.

"Yeah? TRY IT!" The sound of the girl's voice was unyielding.

"Damn it!" Frank swore. Before he could think about it, he'd started up the cement steps, two at a time. His legs crumbled underneath him, and his right shin hit the edge of the cement step and delivered more pain straight to his brain. "A-a-a-h-h-h!"

In spite of the hurt, Frank heard Big Red's deeper voice like an approaching storm. The words were too low to understand, but the menace was clear. Once more Frank pushed himself to his feet and started up. His Keds squeaked on the cement as, this time, he made sure of each step, still moving like a wooden Pinocchio before the Blue Fairy did her thing.

A one-legged blind man could move faster.

It felt like a year before Frank reached the top of the section, his breath coming in rapid pants. He turned right and stepped warily down the wide walkway between the last row of seats and the vertical cement section wall. The Junior Tiger was holding the ball behind her back and shaking her head at Big Red, defiant. Red had both his hands planted flat against the wall on either side of her. He was speaking intensely, in low tones. Frank couldn't hear it all clearly, but it didn't take R. Wayne Dipstick to figure out what was happening.

" . . . about time I returned the favour, you nigger bitch."

Then Frank did understand. Too well. It made him shiver. The pit of his stomach turned to ice. Yeah, no doubt and just as he dreaded, this wasn't only about the ball. The words had never loomed so large in Frank's imagination: BLACK and WHITE, in screaming high capitals.

"Well hell! Why me?" Now Frank's Keds were frozen to the cement. His left hand was sweaty in the Kaline glove. He'd almost forgotten he still wore it. The black girl was head low, looking daggers into Red's eyes. Frank's brain filled with blossoming dread. "Damn it! Do I really want to go up against this guy?" Frank still felt Big Red's kick from a few minutes before and again spoke his doubt aloud. "Do I?"

It was Kaline's ball. How could he not?

In spite of the dizziness, in spite of the white points of pain ricocheting around his skull, the next words tumbled out of Frank's mouth from nowhere, and he was making it all up as he went along.

"Hey? Junior Tiger! Congrats on getting the ball! Any Tigers fan would die for a Kaline foul tip." Frank's feet unfroze and he moved closer. "I'd really like a look at your ball. Just hold it once in my own hands—if you wouldn't mind? I'm kinda into Kaline. Got his number and glove. I'll give it right back. Promise . . . "

The black teen ignored Frank.

"Geez!" Frank smiled stiffly and gave her the same V-for-Victory sign he'd flashed on Trumbull. "Go Cats! Bite Birds! Tigers rule, right?"

And that's when Frank saw it all: first, the Junior Tigers logo; then, the blue glove from Trumble Avenue; then, high on her black cheek, the pinkish-grey scar from Blondie's steel-cleated baseball shoe.

Another moment of involuntary brain-lock.

Frank flashed back to the image of the sliding black girl; to the blonde third-baseman bringing his steel-shod foot around; to the spike to the face; to the cry of pain and the bright flow of blood down the girl's cheek. And one more thing—

"Ellie. It's Ellie, isn't it?"

The redhead finally turned toward Frank, but kept his hands pressed to the cement wall on either side of the determined black teenager.

"Hey? Piss-off, pinhead!" Red warned. "The nigger bitch is gonna give me the ball. She owes me. Right, bitch?" Big Red rolled his shoulders to show Frank the dangerous potential of his bulk. The black girl flinched at the word nigger.

Frank felt ashamed. And then angry. What could he do?

"Tigers! Right, Ellie? They rule!" Frank repeated and nodded encouragement. "Right, Ellie?"

Frank could tell the exact moment when realization lit on the black girl's face—and then quick calculation.

"I said, piss-off, before I take you apart." Red reached out a meaty hand to push Frank back. Frank was in no mood to be pushed. No way he'd let the Kaline ball fall into the sweaty hands of this king-sized jerk.

In a blur, in spite of the pain, Frank put up his own flattened hand and chopped Red's arm aside. "I don't think so, fat-boy!"

Frank saw Red's disbelief at this unexpected challenge. His heavily freckled face ballooned with angry blood, red on Red. Red couldn't decide whether to stay with the girl or risk beating the bejesus out of Frank.

"Ok. Have a look," the black girl shot back at Frank.

In a heartbeat, the Junior Tiger made a sharp, underhand toss of Kaline's ball. Frank's eye was on Red, not on the ball. But Frank's hand was quicker than his eye. When he looked down, miraculously, the Kaline ball was in the Kaline glove.

Sweet!

"Hey, 'at's my ball!" Red protested and moved toward Frank with hulking menace. It was enough. The black girl slipped down and away from the bully, snatched her ball from Frank's glove and sped off down the steps with her words thrown over a shoulder.

"Move your bootie, white boy!"

twenty-one

Frank

Frank again sat four rows behind the autograph crowd at the fence, this time a few seats off the aisle, rubbing both temples to relieve the jackhammer ache in his head. After the confrontation with Big Red and the black girl, when the adrenalin rush was over, he'd felt as useless as a sack full of dog dirt. He lightly explored the damage with his fingers and thought he could already feel the swelling. *Jesus, it hurt.*

"This seat taken, white boy?"

"Wha-a-t?" Frank didn't open his eyes or look around.

"I said, is this seat taken, white boy?"

Frank opened one eye and groaned at the new impact of pain. He wasn't sure if it was his throbbing head, his aching shin or the sight of the black girl at the end of the row. She pointed to one of the seats near him with the hand that still held the Kaline ball.

Seeing the prize in her hand, Frank felt even worse.

Kinda stupid since I just helped her keep it.

"Hey, please, just leave me alone, will ya? You got your ball, Red's screwed off and everything's cool, right?"

"You look like crap, white boy."

"Dog dirt, actually."

"What happened to your head? That bruise?" she persisted.

"Jesus! I just wish someone else was wearin' it, ok? You can't help with that, so please, go away."

"O-o-o-h, sorry, white boy. Can't do that."

Now Frank slammed the armrest with his Kaline glove and looked at her. "Will you once and for all, for pity's sake, please stop calling me that?"

The black girl ignored him and plopped herself down one seat away. "Call you what, white boy?"

"Call me that," Frank replied.

"You look white, white boy."

"Geez! And you look black. But I don't call you . . . black girl."

Frank caught himself.

But isn't that how I think of her?

"But I am black, white boy."

"Double geez! That's it!" Frank slammed his Kaline glove once more and stood to leave, and take his sorry head with him.

The teenaged black girl was up before he could turn away, grabbed his arm and held on. Frank was surprised at the strength in her grip.

"Ok, ma-a-a-n," she drew the word out teasingly.

Frank shook off her hand. "Ok, man, what?"

"We need to discuss it."

"Holy weeping Jesus! Discuss what?"

"Well, see, ma-a-a-n, I read about these old-timey

knight-dudes, but I never, like, met one, especially a white knight dude. And all those old-timey, flat-bootie damsels-in-distress? Definitely flat-bootie white damsels." The girl laughed at her own joke.

"Hey look. I'm white but I'm no knight."

"No. You look, m-a-a-a-n. I'm black, but I'm no damsel. Least not in the old-timey, fairy tale way."

"Yeah, I figured out that much." Frank checked around again for Big Red. No sign of him. Now he just wanted to leave the area.

And what about my Kaline autograph?

"Hey, but I guess I was in distress, m-a-a-a-n. Like, being threatened by an evil red anus," the black girl laughed again.

"No kidding," Frank agreed.

"So it hurts like hemorrhoids, m-a-a-a-n, but thanks, uh, white knight or whoever you are.

Wasn't that "hurts like hemorrhoids" thing a Smooth Daddy Groove line?

"Jesus weeping sledgehammer Christ! I'm Frank. Frank Phelan, ok. And, yeah, it does hurt like hemorrhoids, but don't mention it. Good-bye, so long, farewell, adios, and have a nice life." Frank turned and began to move off down the row.

But once more, the black girl grabbed his arm. "Ok, ok, Fr-a-a-a-nk. But I still gotta know."

"Ok, I'll bite. Gotta know what?"

"Du-u-h-h! Dude, you knew my name was Ellie! So I'm, like, ok, so I do remember you from the car on Trumbull, but my name?

"Du-u-h-h! And do you remember giving me the finger Ell-ie-ie-ie?"

"Yeah, well, kind of a habit thing. Before I, like, knew the white knight bit. So c'mon, Frank, my name?"

"Look, uh, Ellie, my head hurts and it's a long story."

Ellie looked down to where Kaline was still batting at the plate. "So, just give me the headline, dude."

"No, look, Ellie, really I . . . "

From the batter's cage, the air split with a tremendous K-R-ACK-K!

Frank had only heard it at Tiger Stadium a few times before. But he knew instantly what it was. It was the special sound made by the seasoned ash of a Louisville Slugger, swung strongly by an experienced big-league hitter, and connecting squarely with a hard-thrown fastball in a marriage of physics and sweet spots that meant a towering, out-of-the-ballpark drive that would capture all ears and all eyes, in any stadium anywhere, and bring thousands of fans to their feet in wonder.

Frank forgot all about his headache. "Hot damn!"

Frank was a young but experienced hitter and outfielder himself. In spite of his head injury, his focus sharpened and he quickly picked out the speeding ball and followed its progress in silent awe, along with Kaline and the rest of the fans. The bullet drive rose up and up into the wide space above far centre field and was on its way to the North Star, somewhere over Cherry and Trumbull Streets.

But the ball never made it.

In an occurrence that was even more rare and unusual than such an incredible blast from a major league bat, Kaline's ball hit near the top of the feature that made Tiger Stadium unique among all big league baseball parks. That one hundred and twenty-five foot tall flagpole, in fair play, that rises straight up in the middle of deep centre field and is the focus of all proud American players and fans during every singing of the national anthem at the start of the game.

"Damn! I can't see it! I can't see the ball, man!" A frustrated Ellie tugged on the sleeve of Frank's jersey.

"It's there," Frank pointed, "at the top of the flagpole."

He was almost right.

The white ball was clearly visible, suspended against the background of the stiffly streaming Stars and Stripes . . . then disappeared completely from the view of Kaline and the excited fans below. The flag appeared to collapse in on itself, its red, white and blue shape crumbling against the grey sky.

"What the hell?" Frank managed. And he and Ellie looked at each other in dismay. Kaline and the rest of the Tigers hitters and fans below them did the same. Thousands of straining eyes watched from all over the steadily filling stadium.

A strong gust of wind caught the big flag, buoyed it up and open again to display its familiar red, white and blue pattern, at the same time releasing the ball. It fell back into centre field and landed at the very feet of a surprised Lou Brock.

The crowd, holding its collective breath, exhaled a long-drawn-out "A-A-A-A-H-H!" of appreciation and sheer amazement. For a few moments, Kaline's fly ball had wrapped itself in Old Glory.

"Man, was that cool, or what?" Ellie exclaimed.

Frank felt the hair prickle under his cap and along with everyone else experienced an uncanny shiver of excitement. Something miraculous had just occurred, although Frank wasn't sure exactly what. He absently massaged his temples and wondered where the pain had retreated.

For Frank, the white ball lying at the feet of Lou Brock on the green outfield grass was charged with crackling kinetic energy. Brock must have sensed some of this strangeness, too. He and Kaline, and Frank and Ellie, and all the other fans and players looked at it intently, as if a small meteor on a fantastic voyage had come home at last to Earth.

Brock squatted down for a closer look, as if he'd never seen a baseball before in his life. Then the Cardinals outfielder shrugged, smiled and picked it up from the short grass, as if it were, after all, just a baseball. Frank saw that Brock was undecided for a few seconds, but made up his mind and began to trot in from centre field toward the batter's cage, leaving teammate Curt Flood shaking his head behind him.

"Very cool!" Frank finally answered Ellie's question.

They both watched Brock hand the ball back to Kaline at the plate. The St. Louis player said something, smiled once more and then headed into the Cardinals dugout along the first baseline. Kaline held the ball gingerly, as if he hadn't just seen it and sent it on its way only a minute before. Frank thought the Tigers all-star hitter looked uncertain about what to make of its brief odyssey, and what to do with it now that the ball had unexpectedly come home to his hand.

Ellie suddenly laughed and pounded her own Kaline ball into her mitt. Before he knew it, Frank did the same with his fist, his empty fist.

They both stared as Kaline held up the "magic" ball for starting pitcher, Mickey Lolich, whose arm had delivered what must have been a fastball and provided some of the energy that powered Kaline's exceptional drive. Frank knew Lolich would normally have taken all his warm-ups in the bullpen, under the watchful eye of the pitching coach. But as a ballplayer himself, Frank understood this might be the left-hander's last game in the World Series. Maybe Lolich had a superstitious need to join batting practice with his teammates and the other players in the starting lineup, a need to be close with them before trotting over to join the rest of the pitchers. The head game again. Frank guessed that Lolich must have gradually increased the speed of his pitches near the end of Kaline's practice. Frank was sure Lolich had never seen his fastball hit quite that hard.

Good for Kaline, but maybe a bad sign for a starting pitcher in a must-win game, probably the biggest in his career.

"That was some weird happening, white knight," Ellie said.

Before he knew it, Frank replied, "Call me just Frank. Ok?"

"Ok, just Frank."

Man! What's with this girl?

Below them, Lolich pointed to the bicep of his pitching arm and struck a classic, Charles Atlas muscleman pose. Frank loved it when first Cash, and then McAuliffe, Northrup, Wert, Price, and the other Tigers held their noses, as if avoiding a bad smell, and booed Lolich loudly with slapstick over-acting.

"Yea-a-a-h!" Ellie cheered beside Frank. Someone, somewhere began to clap. Frank and Ellie freed their hands and quickly did the same. Soon every Tigers fan in the whole stadium must have joined in. The happy applause relieved some of Frank's doubt about Lolich.

"Lolich looks ok," Ellie said.

"Yeah, he does. Kaline too."

It was a good Tigers team moment. Frank sensed the Tigers

tensions dissipate in the shared comedy and camaraderie of the exchange.

Frank stood, deciding to leave at last. Ellie pulled him back hard and he collapsed into the seat next to her. "Jesus!"

"I thought it was Frank? But, ok, Son of God, give me the gospel 'bout my name, already."

"Ok. Then it's quits, alright?"

"You're the messiah."

Didn't this girl ever stop with the lame jokes?

"Ok. Almost two months ago, right? That exhibition game you played in Windsor? Against the Hellcats? I was a spectator there. I saw you. Heard the crowd call your name when you came in to pitch."

Ellie turned completely around in her seat and grabbed Frank's arm. Hard. "Are you jivin' me, Jesus?"

Frank pulled his arm loose and held his palm up to take the oath. "Swear to God my Father and hope to die."

"That is so messed up, man!"

"No black girl. What is so messed up is Blondie's privates. After you pounded the piss out of them with that baseball at home plate when he tried to spike you again. Guy'll need a monster miracle from God my Father if he ever hopes to have kids."

Ellie flopped back in her seat, stared at Frank and said nothing.

A miracle?

Frank stood up once more. But he had a question of his own. "The redheaded fat-boy back there?"

"Yeah?"

"What'd he mean when he said you 'owed' him?"

Ellie's black face closed like a door slamming shut. She stared out over the stadium, maybe watching the Stars and Stripes streaming in the wind from the flagpole in centre field. She didn't look at him.

"You're not from around here are you, Frank?" Still watching the flag.

"I told you. I'm Canadian. From Windsor. So I guess not."

"Then you might not understand."

Frank understood that black was back and that he felt like a dork just standing there. The headache returned big time. He sat down again, but one seat away from the black girl. "Try me."

Ellie hesitated for long seconds and then nodded, more to herself than to him.

"So, you hear what the red anus called me?" She still looked away.

Man, do I really wanna go there?

"I heard." More seconds passed.

"You can say it."

"Nigger." Frank could, but it didn't mean it was easy.

"Wasn't the first time." Now the black teenager looked right at Frank. "A couple of weeks before we came to Windsor, I pitched for the Junior Tigers in the Eastern Junior League Championship semi-final, against Red's team, all palefaces. He played first base. I got two hits. Both of 'em were singles. Both times, when I was on first, when he thought no one was looking, he grabbed at me and called me a nigger ho."

Frank had known it was coming, but still flinched at the bald statement from her lips.

"Later, after we lost to the big anus and his team, before

we were supposed to shake hands and he was joking with his buddies near his bench?"

Frank nodded for her to go on.

I slipped over behind him, picked up a barrel of that new Gatorade and dumped it on his fat red head.

"No way!" Frank tried to imagine it.

"Yeah, but unlike this scar on my cheek, that scar is harder to see. Just a nigger ho."

Frank sensed Ellie wanted to look away again. But the black girl didn't. It was Frank who dropped his eyes.

twenty-two

Frank

Geez! Why don't I just leave?

What amazed Frank was how bad Ellie's story made him feel, even when it wasn't his fault. And would those rogue elephants ever stop stampeding around his skull?

"Uh, ok. I really should go. Congratulations on the Kaline ball."

This time, Ellie didn't grab him as he stood up. "Wait, man . . . please." Frank sensed the last word took real effort. "That true what you said before about being into Kaline?" Ellie pointed at the big number 6, still in the batting cage hitting a few last balls.

"It's true."

"That the new Kaline model glove?"

"Yeah."

Why should I get into this?

But Frank's mouth got ahead of him. "I guess Kaline personally autographed fifty of them. Besides the mass-produced stamped signature, I mean. Only ten for Canada. I got one of 'em." Even now, Frank couldn't help feeling proud.

Yeah, at least I have the glove.

"You jivin' me? Ten gloves for the whole of Canada and you just happened to get one of 'em?"

"Geez, no! Didn't 'just happen.' I worked like holy hell for a month to earn it." Frank decided not to explain his mother and grandmother's role. That's when he saw the envy in the black girl's eyes.

Maybe the Kaline ball wasn't everything.

"But, hey, when you went out to pitch that day you got spiked, you had a Kaline model glove too."

"Oh, yeah? How would you know?"

"I just know, alright?"

"Yeah, ok. But it's an older one. My dad's. Practically an antique. And really special to him. I don't get the chance to use it much. But this is my regular glove, and I'm proud to own it too."

"I've never seen a blue glove," Frank said.

Ellie laughed and held it out to him. "It's the Willie Horton model."

"Hey, cool! I get it." Willie Horton was the Tigers hard-hitting, hard-throwing black outfielder. The blue Wilson A2145 Autograph Model was very similar to Frank's glove. Horton's stamped autograph was in silver, and it had the same Grip-Tite pocket and other features, as well. Frank didn't know if he should mention Willie Horton standing on top of a car that Sunday the riot broke out, wearing his Tigers uniform, yet still failing to stop the burning and looting. But the glove made sense.

"He lives here in Detroit, so he's local," Ellie said. "And

when he was just sixteen, he played an all-city high school game right here in Tiger Stadium and hit a home run over the fence."

"Very cool!" Frank hadn't known *that.*

"But your father gave you the old Kaline glove that day."

"I knew he had it with him. I wanted it for luck. Because we'd never played in Canada before and stuff."

"The head game," Frank suggested.

"You know about that?"

Frank resented her apparent surprise. "Duh! Of course I do? You think I don't play seriously? That's why I had to have the Kaline glove. Because he signed it personally, added some magic, if you believe."

"Course I believe."

Now the look on the black girl's face . . .

Man! Why do I keep calling her that? No wonder I feel guilty.

The look on *Ellie's* face, turned hopeful. Before Frank knew it, Ellie moved into the seat beside him and stuck out her right hand. "Cool! Shake on it, man!"

Frank hesitated.

He didn't intend to. Not at all. But he did. Worse, Frank could see in Ellie's eyes that it wasn't unexpected. The BLACK-WHITE thing. And the capitals were back in heavy black. Something drained out of Ellie's expression and lay dying on the cement between them.

Who's the anus, now?

But Ellie kept her hand out and gave him time to decide. It took a hell of a lot of guts Frank realized. And in front of a guy she hardly knew, too. Yeah, guts, but pride, as well. And not just black pride, her pride.

Ellie's hand was still out. Frank took it, held it firmly and solemnly shook it. She was warm to the touch.

"I'm pleased to meet you, Ellie."

After a few seconds, Ellie let him go and pointed to his hand.

"See, man, it doesn't rub off." Now Frank was ashamed again and looked away.

"I didn't, uh . . . "

"Hey, white knight?" she continued. "Gimme the low-five." Now Frank was embarrassed and confused. Ellie laughed, took his hand and positioned it palm up just behind his back. "Like this. Low-five!" She slapped his palm with her own. "All ri-i-ght! Now you." Ellie turned half-around, held her hand low until Frank slapped it, weakly. Then shook her head. "You're really not from around here, are you?"

"Like I said. I'm a Canuck. But hey, that 'hurts like hemorrhoids' bit? I bet we both listen to the Smooth Daddy Groove show."

"Dude! You listen to 'the Dad with the Bad on the Rad,' too? Then who knows, maybe there's hope for you yet, white knight. So what's Phelan?"

"My name?" Frank watched Ellie roll her eyes.

"Duh! Yeah, but what is it?"

"Oh. It's, uh, Irish. Black Irish, actually. Geez! I mean . . . "

"Dude! You mean the white rubs off? And underneath, you're *Black Like Me*? Like that white dude who painted himself black in the south? And wrote that book about all the racism that got dumped on him because of it. Wow, man!"

Geez, how can I even talk to this girl?

"Ok, what I said sounds pretty stupid. It just means stuff

like dark hair and features." Frank didn't want to say skin. Ellie giggled. Frank felt as dumb as he sounded.

"Hey, dude, I'm Ellie *Fitzgerald*. Like the jazz singer. Because my dad really digs her. Fitzgerald is Irish too, right man? So I'm the real Black Irish—Watusi branch, from darkest Africa—like, do the Wah-Watusi!" Ellie stood and put her glove and ball on the seat. She began to snap her fingers and sway back and forth from one foot to the other in a comic imitation of the popular dance from teen TV shows like Dick Clark's *American Bandstand.*

Frank was at a total loss. His mouth was full of marbles and his head pounded to Ellie's Motown beat.

"I said do the Wah-Watusi, Frank! Loosen up, man! Get with 'the beat on the street.'" Before he could say a word, Ellie pulled Frank to his feet. "Wah-Watusi!"

She was crazy. Ellie snapped her fingers, waved her arms and twirled around and around. Frank noticed some of the fans below them looking on in amazement. His head continued to pound. He closed both eyes and wanted to sink down through the cement to the centre of the earth.

But Ellie pulled the Kaline glove off his hand and threw it onto the seat with her own. "Do the Wah-Watusi, white knight!" When Frank continued to stand there, Ellie grabbed his arms, lifted them above his head with hers and began to sway them back and forth. What was that expression his Grandma Norah always used at times like this? Oh yeah. *"I'm mortified. I'm freakin' mortified."*

Below them, people were pointing up and laughing at their dancing.

"Aw, what the hell." Frank freed his arms from Ellie, waved them back and forth, snapped his fingers and twirled in unison with her. He shouted down at the gawking fans. "Hey! We're doin' the Wah-Watusi! Can you dig it?" The watchers shook their heads, like there was no hope for two dorky kids embarrassing themselves in public.

Finally Frank and Ellie collapsed back into their seats, side by side, laughing at their own antics in front of the bewildered baseball audience.

"Low-fives!" Frank leaned forward with his hand down, palm open.

"Low-fives!" Ellie agreed. She slapped his palm and Frank felt her hold her hand against his. Black and white together. No capitals required. "Thanks for this, Frank Phelan, Black Irish dude from Canada."

Frank knew she was talking about more than her Kaline ball.

"You're welcome, Ellie Fitzgerald, Black Irish Watusi from Detroit."

twenty-three

Frank

Frank was still getting used to this new relationship.

He and Ellie watched together as Kaline finished his practice and stood chatting behind the batting cage with the other Tigers in the starting line-up. The insect buzz of hundreds of excited conversations began to vibrate the cool October air around them. Soon it would be tens of thousands, not to mention tens of millions watching or listening to the broadcast play-by-play on televisions and radios across the U.S. and Canada, and even the wider world.

Frank guessed it was more than an hour and a quarter until the national anthem and the opening pitch. The stadium in front of them was filling steadily, except for the season's ticketholder seats immediately around them. The crowd looked to Frank to be about evenly split between black and white fans, and, to his relief, they were mixing, smiling, chatting. Baseball fans together, and the only colours that mattered were their Detroit Tigers orange, black and white.

The men wore dark suit-jackets, white shirts and narrow ties, many with wide-brimmed hats pulled low. The women or girls wore multi-coloured coats and dresses, like falls of bright autumn leaves descending on the stadium. And many had equally colourful scarves tied round their heads against the late season breezes. The men's preference for sombre blacks and greys and browns rendered them almost invisible, a duller background in vivid contrast to the splashes of bright blues, reds, greens, and the more distinct pinks or yellows of the women and the groups of younger fans in evidence. It was a school day. Yet Frank could see that many hundreds, maybe thousands of students, had played hooky like Frank and Ellie to experience this once-in-a-lifetime major league contest in person.

And the colourful dress wasn't the only thing to make an impact on his eyes. Frank's spirits buoyed and the pain in his head receded to dullness, as he saw that more people than he could ever remember had, indeed, brought a bright orange Tigers pennant or other colourful, home-team souvenir, already waving as they flowed in steady streams through the many entrances beyond and around him. Soon the Tigers orange, black and white colours would overwhelm all others, as they did the red and white of the less numerous Cardinals fans.

If only his Tigers and Al Kaline could do the same on the field.

Frank didn't say it out loud to Ellie, for fear of jinxing their chances. And yeah, there were significant pockets of Cardinals red and white too, where St. Louis fans moved to their seats and enthusiastically waved their own banners with a confident enthusiasm that unnerved Frank. Sure enough, far off to his left, like his worst fears made feathers, Frank saw the spectacular group of giant Cardinals redbirds dancing in the aisles and working up their nearby supporters into cheering explosions of excitement. Those fans were all smiling and laughing and shouting out with the unwavering faith of true believers. Frank told himself it was to be expected, but it didn't help his nerves.

Gotta believe in the old orange, black and white, man! Just gotta!

Fitful gusts of wind swirled the dust at home plate and along the baselines. The gusts had a chill edge and Frank was glad he'd worn his long-sleeved sweatshirt under his number 6 Kaline jersey. Once again he pulled down his own Tigers ball cap tighter on his head.

Electronic static sounds and crackles like crushing tinfoil came from the loudspeakers high up behind Frank and Ellie as the sportscasters got ready to broadcast this crucial game to the stadium and the world. Frank reminded himself to keep a lookout for the Michigan governor. How did it feel to be the governor of a state or the mayor of a city that almost burned itself out with the fires of racial hate that raged for almost a week last year?

Frank noticed Ellie had her eye on his Kaline glove. "So, Frank Phelan, can I have a look? An' you want, you can check out my ball?" Now Frank's envy was almost impossible to restrain. It was the World Series, and Ellie's Al Kaline baseball was exactly the personal souvenir from his baseball idol he'd wished for as long as he could remember. Even so, the cool thing was, with Ellie now he was sure he didn't have to hide it. Still, this longing for a hands-on Kaline memento remained an aching, physical pressure that almost burst through his chest. First his head, and now his heart. If the Tigers lost this game, Frank imagined his whole body would disintegrate in an explosion of crushed tinfoil and teenaged hope.

"You can try my glove on, sure." Frank passed over the golden glove and took her prized ball in return. With one finger, Ellie traced Kaline's handwritten signature in black Sharpie on the smooth yellow cowhide. Frank held her Kaline ball like it, too, was gold from a god.

Ellie looked back at him, and her face did seem to glow with appreciation. "It's so damn beautiful, Frank. I bet this glove is magic. Feels like I could reach it right out and snag a falling star."

"Yeah, that's why I just had to have it when I saw it shining in the window of the sports shop back home." Frank fingered Ellie's Kaline ball and brushed his thumb across the dark smudge where his idol's bat had marked it. "You know, if this were my ball, Ellie, I wouldn't sell it for a million bucks."

She nodded. "Hey, I know, man! This ball's, like, my greatest treasure now. The only way that big red anus would have got it out of my hands was if I was, like, dead."

With an undeniable reluctance, Frank made himself put the Kaline ball firmly back in Ellie's hand. At least he'd touched it. She passed him his Kaline glove.

Frank nodded back. "Too right. The only thing cooler, would be if Kaline personally autographed it for you." Ellie's eyes grew wider as she considered it.

As one, both Tigers fans looked down at the man himself, long finished his practice swings and still standing behind the batting cage chatting with the other Tigers.

Tigers fans gotta try! Why not?

"So let's do it, Ellie. Let's just freakin' do it!

"You mean . . . ?

"Hell yeah! Let's Wah-Watusi down there and get the man's name on the man's ball. You game for the game?"

"You serious, man?"

Frank stood up, waved his Kaline glove in the air and danced around like Dick Clark's worst nightmare from *American Bandstand.* He pulled Ellie to her feet beside him and put both hands on her shoulders. "I sure as hell am. Like, Dick Clark, Smooth Daddy Groove, double dog dare you, serious."

Ellie left his hands where they were, but took a long look down at the clamouring group of avid autograph hunters that grew by the second with the rest of the crowd. Frank followed her gaze and saw no sign of Big Red.

"So c'mon, Ellie. Screw the crowd, screw Blondie the eunuch, screw the big red anus. Tigers fans together, right?"

"Ok, why not?" Ellie shrugged, but with less enthusiasm than Frank had hoped for. Until she abruptly brightened. "Hey! Maybe you'll be lucky too, Frank. Get Kaline to sign your ball cap to go with the autograph on your glove or something."

Lucky! Lucky! Lucky!

Frank wished she hadn't brought up his luck.

"What's the problem, white knight?"

"Well, I haven't been so far. Lucky, I mean," he admitted. "And I've been trying for Kaline's autograph a long time."

"Well, you were lucky for me, white knight. So God bless Canada!"

"Thanks."

"And at least you're here to see Kaline play the biggest game of his life in the one and only World Series. That's pretty lucky."

"Yeah. My grandfather won tickets for me and my dad on the Smooth Daddy Groove Show—with some unexpected coaching from my grandmother. She was, like, amazing! My grandfather brought us over today."

"You jivin' me, man? That hurts like hemorrhoids thing? The Scheib Series Special? All those Tough Tigers Trivia questions?"

Frank nodded. "The Double or Nothing Big Bonus Question, too. So we got four tickets." Now Ellie was looking at him with major league skepticism. Frank did a bobble-head.

Ellie shook her head in wonder. "I'd say you're very lucky, Frank Phelan." His unexpected friend stared at him for a long time, until he shrugged and gave her a half-smile. It took Frank a moment to recognize the strange feeling creeping around the edges of his emotions, seeping into the corners of his heart, filling up some of that aching hole.

Could it be hope?

"Then let's Wah-Watusi!" Frank urged. "So, come on. Kaline's out of the batting cage. Let's go for that autograph. 'No lyin' or die tryin.'"

Frank took Ellie's hand and squeezed it for a few seconds before letting it go. But not before he caught the pleasure and the relief this simple action gave her. Frank knew without a doubt that Ellie truly wanted him to be lucky with Kaline too.

Maybe it would make a difference.

twenty-four

Frank

The area around and above Frank and his new partner was still relatively empty. Frank knew the concession areas underneath would be jammed and slow. And these seats would be reserved for Tigers season ticket holders who could afford to arrive so late for the best seats in the stadium. He and Ellie stood up from their seats in the fourth row and then climbed up onto them to better see over the crowd of fans waiting expectantly for Kaline and the other Tigers at the fence below.

Big number 6 had joined his teammates kidding Lolich, but now seemed uncertain about what to do with that special ball from the flag. Catcher Bill Freehan brought over an empty equipment bag, punched Kaline on the arm and said a few words. Kaline shook his head, laughed and carefully dropped the ball into the bag. He next added the bat that had launched it on its unusual journey and tightly cinched the rope tie.

"He's keeping that ball," Ellie observed. "Good idea."

"Yeah, I'd feel a little weird about it too," Frank agreed.

"Not want to throw away, you know, whatever magic it might have now." Ellie nodded as if she understood. She probably did, Frank thought. That made her a real ballplayer. He considered once more how it must be for the only girl playing on a team with all guys. Frank guessed she'd have to prove herself every game, again and again, or be labeled "just a girl."

Kaline took off the old, sweat-stained practice ball cap he'd worn beneath the batting helmet and stuffed it under his belt, then seemed to change his mind. He re-opened the equipment bag and put in the practice cap too. Black outfielder, Willie Horton, number 23, came over, took the protective plastic batting helmet from him and handed Kaline what must be his special World Series game cap.

Frank felt time slipping away. The big Longines clock above the scoreboard showed a bit more than an hour before the game. The grounds-keepers were on the field, beginning their grooming of each base, the pitching rubber, the chalk baselines and home plate. The big stadium looked about half full.

Yeah, Kaline's game cap!

Frank knew from interviews in the *Detroit Free Press* that his hero had begun wearing the new ball cap to mark the beginning of his first World Series. It had taken Kaline sixteen long seasons to get here, a huge milestone in his career. Frank could sympathize. Kaline's game cap was a symbol of that milestone. Each time Kaline came out of the Tigers dugout, to bat or to take the field, he would view the series from under the bill of this brand new ball cap. Frank guessed that it was crucial to Kaline's head game, literally, not to break the routine in this game five, especially with the Tigers down so badly. Who knew what jinx would befall his hero and the team if he took the field wearing anything else?

Kaline motioned to Willie Horton and shortstop Mickey Stanley. Then he reached into his pocket and held up a small cylinder in bright paper colours. Horton and Stanley reached into their pockets and did the same.

"What are those things, dude?" Ellie asked.

"I'm not sure."

The players worked at the small objects in their hands.

"Life Savers!" Frank murmured. "Gotta be." It looked like each player gave the others not one, but two of the fruit loop candies.

"Life Savers, yeah, I get it. Maybe it'll help," Ellie said.

With great ceremony, Kaline, Horton and Stanley popped them into their mouths, and smiled.

"Wow! So when did they start this, Frank?"

"I'm not sure. It's usually gum, if anything. But my grandfather said it used to be chewing tobacco. For the nicotine edge. Players kept a wad of it in their cheeks to stay sharp. And they spit out that brown guck all over the field."

"Yuck!" Ellie made a sour face. "Gum or Life Savers are an improvement."

"Let's hope so."

Abruptly, in growing alarm, Frank and Ellie watched as Kaline tipped his game cap to his teammates and turned and headed for the Tigers dressing room and his private preparations for the start of the game. The equipment bag with the magic baseball dangled from his right hand.

"Oh, no!" Frank moaned. "Kaline's heading for the dugout. We'll never get that autograph now. . . ."

"HEY, AL! AL! OVER HERE! PLE-EASE! OVER HERE!"

The voices of Kaline's young fans blended together and carried over the infield with the emphatic tones of desperate hope. Standing on their seats, Frank and Ellie's voices were only two among many dozens.

"We're screwed, dude."

Frank was about to agree, the new resolution fading fast, and the aching pressure in his head returning. Kaline stopped in mid-stride. The Tigers outfielder turned, dipped his head and held up one finger in the wait signal.

"Alri-i-i-ght!" Ellie exclaimed, and she and Frank cheered with the rest when Kaline turned and jogged easily through a couple of brown dust-devils the breeze had kicked up, pushing his game cap back on his head in a boyish gesture. He laid the equipment bag against the boards of the fence nearby and greeted his adoring fans with a wide smile.

Frank fought it, but felt the old doubt, the inevitable disappointment blossom once more. There were just so many people between him and his hero. Kaline said a first few words to a fan Frank could barely see and signed a precious autograph with the usual black Sharpie. Frank estimated there must be way more than a hundred fans with the same idea, all jammed up in front of him and Ellie.

Frank watched the chosen kid jump high in the air in his ecstasy, before starting to push through the crowd behind and move toward the steps, waving his autographed program. *Geez!* Frank recognized the number on his back: mean 13! It was the skinny black guy from before, the one with the agility of a snake who'd survived his own brush with Big Red and earned his Kaline souvenir. Another dozen fans scrambled to take his place. *Geez!* What happened to unlucky 13?

Ellie seemed to share the same sinking feeling. "I don't know, dude. Doesn't look so good anymore."

Frank stood silent beside her. What could he say? They watched as the minutes slipped by and more fans received Kaline's signature on programs, small souvenir bats, replica Tigers ball caps, and even ticket stubs. The wind carried only fragments of Kaline's comments up to them, and they strained to hear.

" . . . toughest game . . . play my best . . . times doesn't work out . . . Yeah, Lou Brock is . . . "

"At least I have his baseball," Ellie said, finally. "And you got his autograph, sort of." Frank saw his new friend's shoulders slump, and then number 13 ran past them up the aisle, his face alight with pleasure..

Something erupted in Frank's brain. "Geez, Ellie!" He grabbed her arm and almost pulled her off balance.

"Whoa! What, man?"

"Double geez!"

This time it wasn't a sudden brainwave, or impulse, or spur of the moment thing. This time Frank saw the process complete in his mind's eye, like following a ball leaving the pitcher's fingers, seeing it curve toward him, knowing where his bat would be, about to crush it. He was already there.

As Frank watched Kaline slowly begin to withdraw from the forest of proffered programs and caps, the plan shone like a small sun, orange-Tigers bright in his imagination. It was actually pretty simple. Simple but not easy. Frank had done the thing dozens of times before in contests with his friends on the playing field at J.E. Benson Junior High School, back home in Windsor.

"We have to let him know, Ellie! We have to let Kaline know," Frank declared, looking straight into her eyes.

"Dude! Know what?"

"Know you have his ball. Make him see you with the ball." Frank jumped down to the cement, pulled Ellie off her seat and into the aisle after him. Looked down, looked up, and calculated. "Gotta get higher, though." Frank led her away from the crowd, up three more tall rows. Stopped, looked, climbed three more rows, then a little way along the tenth row seats, near a wide metal pillar that blocked the aisle on their left. Now they were virtually alone: no fans nearby, and the autograph hunters, the Tigers players still crowding the fence below them, yet all within shouting distance.

Frank intended to make some noise!

"But we're getting farther away, man?" Ellie looked at Frank like he was bonkers.

"Yeah! Exactly where we need to be! Just do what I tell you to, Ellie. There's not much time. So hop up."

"What are you sayin', man?"

"Make like a bunny and hop it. Get up on my shoulders. Quick!"

"Dude! That's insane!"

"Totally insane!" Frank cackled like a chicken on bad drugs. "That's the whole idea. But just do it, Ellie. You want that Kaline autograph? DO IT!"

Frank ignored the pressure in his head, the pain from his shin, and got down in the aisle. He put aside his Tigers cap and the Kaline glove and motioned for Ellie to climb up on the nearest seat and then up onto his shoulders. Crouched like this, Frank lost sight of Kaline and the crowd below.

"Dude!" Ellie hesitated and shook her head no, even as she was getting up on the seat and gauging the further technique and effort required to reach Frank's shoulders. "It's insane, man!"

"Do it, Ellie! Do it! Do it! DO IT!"

"O-o-o-h-h, man!"

But Ellie bent her knees and launched herself onto his waiting shoulders.

This was pretty insane, Frank silently agreed. Pretty far-out. The whole thing! The World Series. Meeting Ellie. Her being black. Him being white. The big red anus so, well, big and red! Saving Ellie's Kaline ball. Doing the Wah-Watusi. Exchanging low-fives. Now ordering Ellie to get on his shoulders like a game of schoolyard pull-off. All of it.

Too insane! So take your own advice and just do it, man!

Frank braced himself under Ellie's added weight. "Ungh! Ok! Ok! I've got you, Ellie. Hold on to my head . . . no, don't cover my eyes . . . the forehead . . . that's it . . . I'm gonna stand up . . . ready?"

"Whoa, man! Almost dropped the ball! I'm scared, Frank!"

"Me too. Here goes." Frank tried to stand up in a single fluid motion. But Ellie was heavier than she looked. He overbalanced and came close to pitching them both forward into the seats below.

Geez!

"Who-oa!" Ellie screamed a second time, grabbing around

his eyes again. Frank recovered his balance and straightened up but, like, blindfolded. He tried not to panic.

"Alright! Alright! I got you, Ellie. We're ok. My eyes, remember? One arm around my forehead . . . yeah, that's it. And just hook your legs behind and squeeze. I got your feet. You won't fall."

"I don't like this, Frank. Some autograph hunters are starting to look at us like we're some really weird monkeys."

"That's good. We want 'em to look. We wanna be weird monkeys. Now let Kaline know. Wave the ball around. Tell 'im, Ellie! Tell 'im!"

"But what do I say, man?"

Ellie was starting to get heavier already.

"Call Kaline's name! Tell 'im it's his ball. You want him to sign it? Do it! Geez, you're Ellie *Fitzgerald*, remember?"

Frank felt Ellie tense her jeans-clad thighs around his neck. Heard her suck in a breath. Give forth in a rich alto voice like a performer on stage at Detroit's Cobo Hall Auditorium, which in a way, she was. Even with his ears mostly muffled by her thighs, Frank was impressed. Ellie's father sure knew what he was doing when he'd named her after that jazz singer.

"MR. KALINE! UP HERE, SIR! I GOT YOUR BALL! YOUR FOUL TIP! PLEASE SIGN IT! IT'S YOUR BALL! PLEASE!"

Frank could feel the frantic efforts when Ellie stretched high and waved the ball back and forth, back and forth. He spread his feet wider in risky steps, teetering slightly, trying to maintain his balance. Ellie was sure heavy. And with that wiggling around, man!

The October wind blew suddenly cold on Frank's face. Yet

a bead of sweat squeezed from his forehead where Ellie gripped him and tracked down the side of his nose, driving him nuts with an itch. One he couldn't risk scratching.

"MR. KALINE? YOU HIT IT! PLEASE! SIGN YOUR BALL!"

Too late!

Frank could just see that Al Kaline had begun to turn away from the anxious fans, getting ready again to head for the dressing room. The number 6 stood out from his back and began to recede. Frank felt Ellie's desperation. Her growing disappointment, on top of his own, added even greater weight to his shoulders. Frank groaned with strain and frustration.

"MR. KALINE! PLEASE, SIR! IT'S YOUR BALL! PLE-E-E-A-S-E!"

Frank was angry with himself. Angry with the baseball gods he worshipped in vain, gods who'd turned their backs on Frank and his Werewolves at their championship final. Even angry with Al Kaline who, at the moment, did the same to him. It was all insane.

Could he lower Ellie without killing them both?

Frank began to sag downward. Ellie squeezed his head harder. He felt the blood stop flowing to his tinfoil brain. She covered his eyes again. Frank thought he might be swaying back and forth, farther and farther each time. His wooden Pinocchio legs splintered underneath him.

"FRA-A-A-N-K!"

twenty-five

Ellie

Where was Frank?

"Whoa, man!" Ellie's head was a buzz of white noise when she managed to push up from the cold cement and stand. Her legs belonged to some other girl. It took an age before her feet agreed to shift even a few inches. A tentative examination revealed that she hadn't actually hit her head. But sharp arrows of pain radiated from her right shoulder, side and arm, and her right knee began to throb. "Wha-at?"

Ellie put out a hand to the seatback in front of her to steady herself. Looked down to the fence from where a new noise of rolling confusion seemed to originate. Then looked again. "Whoa!" A fresh, slow-rising shock of reality zapped her brain and made what voice she could command unsteady as a shy child's. "Wha-at?" Her mind worked to process the foreign noise into words.

"OK, KID! COME ON DOWN!"

"HE'S HERE WAITIN'!"

"GET A MOVE ON!"

Then Ellie wilted under the growing realization that a hundred strange faces and eyes were looking up only at her. The mouths were smiling. The arms were beckoning. The whole crowd seemed to be waiting for . . . what?

Was it someone else who held up a baseball and spoke in a voice so pure and clear that even her idol, Al Kaline, now back at the fence and looking right at her, seemed to hear? "Uh, . . . I got your ball, Mr. Kaline, sir."

And then Kaline, and then Denny McLain, and Dick Tracewski, and Roy Oyler, and Mickey Lolich and a horde of enthusiastic fans were frantically waving at Ellie, calling out to her to "bring the ball" and "come right down."

Down!

Ellie looked down at Frank beside her.

Her Canadian friend didn't look good. Frank was curled on his side like a wounded animal, hugging himself and panting with exhaustion. In spite of the cool breeze, his Kaline jersey was dark with sweat at the shoulders where she'd sat. Frank moved only one hand, the fingers gingerly exploring his right forehead. Before Ellie's eyes, an angry black bruise expanded its size like an ink stain, then split and bled. The blood changed colour as the seeping wound formed a lipstick crimson pool on the cement beneath.

The sight of her new friend's running blood brought Ellie back to herself. She shook her head once more to clear it and dropped to her knee beside him. "Frank! Your head. You're really bleedin', man." Below Ellie, the strident voices continued to entreat her, impatient now, spiraling upward in pitch and volume, as more fans joined in. She raised her head and risked a quick look over the seat backs.

The voice Ellie heard next emanated from the religious realms of the baseball gods. Gods in whom Ellie had placed her faith from the first moment she'd slipped on a baseball glove and begun her fervent worship at the high altar of big league baseball, the Mount Olympus of her childhood dreams.

"Ok. Let's give her some room, folks. Let's make it happen. I think she's earned it." And that was it: her god had spoken. Just a few magic words from the deep, resonant voice of Al Kaline, and a ragged seam began to open up in the sympathetic crowd of fans, parting the orange, black and white sea of Tigers colours only for her. The way to the altar of her gods was open and big number 6, in all his magnificent glory, awaited her coming. Albert William Kaline, Mr. Tiger, stood right at the fence and waved his famous, all-star right arm at only her, at Ellie Jane Fitzgerald!

Albert William Kaline. He was The One. The Only.

Yet Ellie, even now, even as every cell in her body yearned toward her idol like iron filings drawn to a powerful magnetic force, was torn, hesitant to follow the attraction, especially by herself.

Beside her, Frank had not moved.

Ellie reached out a hand to his shoulder. "How you feelin', Frank? You're hurt. You're still bleedin', man." Frank was stunned and groggy. His mouth opened and closed like that wounded animal's to take in as much air as it could.

"Geez." Frank managed, at last, like he wanted only to stay alive, to keep conscious, and no breath to spare for talk.

"COME ON DOWN! COME ON DOWN *NOW*!" The hundred voices entreated with growing urgency.

Torn and frantic, Ellie pulled out a white handkerchief from her pocket, knelt closer and pressed it against the bloody bruise and cut. "Take it, man. You gotta take it." Frank groaned, but she guided his hand to replace hers at his forehead. "It worked, man! Your crazy plan worked. The weird monkeys. Al Kaline saw us. He wants us. We can go down together, like you said. Get his autograph on my ball. Get his autograph in person on your glove or your cap, right?"

The crowd below sounded too impatient now. Ellie peered over the backs of the seats again. The two of them were keeping Al Kaline waiting. Al Kaline!

Ellie wasn't sure Frank understood the entreaties, but he shook his head slightly and then pushed her away when she tried to help him up. It was clear: her wounded white knight couldn't do it. Not in time. Frank was just too weak, too unsteady.

Ellie watched him make it to an elbow and try to shape his mouth into an encouraging smile before he pushed her away again. Frank didn't speak, just pushed her a third time, harder.

Ellie looked down at Kaline's beckoning arm, took a deep breath and decided.

"Ok, white knight. I'll go. But I'll be back. Now you're the one who needs rescuing." Ellie stooped lower over Frank again, her right leg still aching but working, and dropped a wad of Kleenex tissues from the other pocket of her jeans into his lap. "There's a lot of blood, man. Use these too. And take it easy, man. I won't be long."

"Go. Go, Ellie. I'll be . . . ok," Frank said, weakly.

Ellie didn't believe him. "I'm still scared, man."

"Tigers fans, remember? Go for both of us. Get . . . get the damn autograph."

"Low-fives, man!"

Frank tried to smile, but it was a sick smile. "Geez, later, already."

"Ok, man."

Ellie squeezed her ball tight and started down the opened path to Al Kaline.

"Man, I wish you were with me, white knight."

Ellie talked to herself and worked her way down and through the mob of fans. She didn't move fast, afraid of losing her feet, and winced at the stabs of pain from her side and right leg. Voices all around praised her effort in getting the Kaline foul tip. A dozen strange hands patted her sore shoulder, pushed her forward, and she hated it, wanting to shake them off. She looked up just once, and almost stumbled, still not convinced the real Al Kaline, Mr. Tiger, waited at the fence just for her, just for Ellie Fitzgerald. The last fans moved politely back as big number 6 motioned Ellie forward the final few feet to the fence.

He was big! And intimidating.

"Well, hi there, young lady," the Tigers all-star said.

Up close, Kaline was too big, too unreal. Ellie kept her eyes lowered. Of course she'd watched him from the stands. But her most recent images of him were smaller, television-sized impressions from their new colour TV and those first World Series games. And Kaline smelled faintly of sweat and leather and playing-field dust, with a hint of fruit candy. It wasn't unpleasant or anything, only unexpected.

Ellie still didn't look up into his face, and instead, stared at the black Detroit team 𝔇 on his jersey. And Kaline's voice, even those few words, really shook her. Not its deepness, which seemed right for a man of his size. Or its loudness, because it was pleasant and even inviting. But the fact that Al Kaline was speaking to her, to Ellie Jane Fitzgerald, was, like, too scary. The fans around her began to snigger at her shyness, and Ellie hated that too. It wasn't like her.

"Maybe I could autograph this ball for you? That be ok?" Kaline at last reached out and placed one finger gently under her chin, tried to get Ellie to raise her head and eyes, to look at him.

You're fourteen, already. Deal with it!

His soft touch and friendly manner finally shrunk him in Ellie's imagination, and she found her voice at last. "Uh, yes, sir. Signing it, that's what we hoped."

"Happy to." McLain offered his teammate a fresh black Sharpie, and Kaline took it and then carefully extracted the ball from Ellie's grip. He held the pen poised over the sweet spot. "That your friend up there?" He glanced briefly up at the stands behind her.

Ellie's attention split again between worry for Frank and the autograph from Kaline. She had the urge to look back, but guessed the guilt would make her feel worse than she already did, that blood an' all. "Uh, yes, sir." Just those few words took concentration.

"Looks like you guys would make a pretty good pair of outfielders, way he was holding you up so high," Kaline said. "Like no ball hit could get past you two. Your partner all right?"

With that, Ellie did turn and look up at Frank, now leaned

back in a seat with his eyes closed and her white handkerchief and Kleenex held to his forehead. She turned around front again—and found herself looking right into Al Kaline's eyes. *Man!*

The eyes were alert and inquiring, the forehead above wrinkled with concern. The force of Kaline's Gorgon spell on her broke. Frank looked to be upright, at least, and Mr. Kaline's face was actually human and, like, nice!

"Well, Mr. Kaline, Frank uh, he has a bump on his head from our fall. And there was some blood. But he really wanted me to come down and get your autograph. It was his idea an' all."

Kaline smiled once more and pushed his cap farther back on his head. That boyish gesture again. Still, up close, he looked older than she thought. But Ellie really liked his eyes. Below the tan mark of his cap, the eyes were surrounded by dozens of small lines. Ellie figured they were the kind of lines etched into the skin of all big league outfielders. It was the years of squinting into the sky and sun above big league ballparks, tracking fly balls into their gloves. Sure, charcoal smears under the eyes and the wearing of sunglasses helped reduce some of the strain. She did that herself. But even Ellie could see that Kaline's sixteen major league seasons were all right there, indelibly recorded by these marks. The crinkles were friendly though, and the other lines around his mouth all turned up, as if he smiled a lot.

Ellie began to smile too.

"So the autograph would be my pleasure, young lady. What's your name?"

"It's Ellie, Ellie Fitzgerald."

"Hey, like the jazz singer, right? Kaline guessed.

"Yeah. My dad, ya know?"

"Well, you've got quite a voice all right." Kaline was just about to write her name on the ball when Ellie surprised them both and interrupted politely.

"Uh, sir? My friend Frank, could you put his name on your ball too, please? Without his help, I wouldn't have the ball or even have made it down here. He's from over in Canada, but you're his favourite player. He has a lot of your stuff, an' all."

"Canada, eh? No problem, Ellie. And I'm glad to hear it." Kaline wrote carefully for Ellie to see, speaking the words as he did:

"To Ellie and Frank from Al Kaline
1968 World Series"

"How's that?" Kaline handed back the ball.

"Thank you, sir. This is the best present I ever got! The best!" Kaline and the other players laughed, enjoying her enthusiasm.

"Well, I'm very happy I could give it to you, Ellie Fitzgerald. It's fans like you guys that make the game worth playing. I'm glad you came out. Enjoy the game now."

And Al Kaline raised a hand and waved one last time in recognition of the other fans. The cheering rose in volume and Ellie waved her magic ball and added her own shouts of encouragement. Then Kaline turned away once more, to follow the other players walking to the Tigers dugout and dressing room.

twenty-six

Ellie

The loudspeakers came alive with the rousing strains of *Hold That Tiger!* from the old *Tigers Rag* song. The biggest game in Kaline's career was three-quarters of an hour or so away according to the scoreboard clock. The fans around Ellie continued to applaud the retreating Tigers. Ellie, holding the dream ball in her hand, was seized again with the desire to let Kaline know that no matter what happened to the Tigers or to him, he would always be a winner with her. And with her Black Irish, white knight, Frank Phelan, from Canada, too.

The anger at Blondie's racism and spike, at Big Red's hurtful label and attempted theft, would still be there. But like the scar, Ellie knew they would fade. She squeezed the autographed ball between her thighs and cupped her free hands around her mouth and gave voice to her pride in the Tigers, in Kaline, in Frank, in herself.

"GOOD LUCK, AL! YOU'RE A GREAT PLAYER!

ONE OF THE GREATEST! WE'RE ROOTIN' FOR YA! ALL THE WAY!"

Still only a few yards from the fence, Kaline must have just heard her voice through all the other applause and cheering, and over the sounds of the stadium loudspeakers. Ellie watched as he looked back over his shoulder to give her a confident smile and a big thumbs-up, one that Ellie and dozens of other fans returned with a roar of approval.

Ellie turned away and held up the autographed ball for Frank to see, waved it back and forth in triumph. "Frank! I got it! I got the autograph!"

Frank waved briefly with the bloody wad of her handkerchief and Kleenex tissues, and sat up straighter. The bruise on his forehead stood out like a red and black badge, still angry-looking, but no longer bleeding. Frank returned her wave a second time, then leaned back in the seat again, closed his eyes and held his ball cap against his face. Relieved and still glowing from her achievement, Ellie turned for another glimpse of her hero.

Yet instead of continuing on to the dressing room, Kaline stopped abruptly. He looked around him for a moment, at a loss, and then shook his head, and began jogging back, straight toward Ellie! *What?* He had a crooked smile on his face as he reached down for his equipment bag leaning against the fence a few feet away from her. "Can't forget this."

KR-A-A-CK!

Ellie thought the unexpected sound came from behind Al Kaline, somewhere out in centre field. A batter she couldn't see must have hit a baseball very hard.

No. Couldn't be.

It wasn't. Beyond Ellie, beyond the stooping Kaline, high out in centre field, the softly rippling red, white and blue fabric of the stadium flag snapped straight out to rigid attention with a loud crack of heavy cloth. Ellie looked up at the tall pole to see the flag held cardboard-stiff by the force of a powerful gust of wind, rushing down from the northwest and across the playing field toward home plate, and her. "Wow!"

The fast-moving air reached the other Tigers players halfway to the dugout. The wind tore at their uniforms, halted their conversations, turned their heads away with its carriage of dust and paper field debris. They held their ball caps and snorted in surprise.

Ellie slitted her eyes and turned partly aside in anticipation of the irritating grit the wind would deliver. The swirling gust hit Kaline just as he was turning around with the equipment bag. The impact teared and grained his eyes, and forced him to reach up to clutch at the bill of his precious game cap—too late.

Ellie could just see the swelling current catch his game cap first, grabbing it by the bill and flipping it backward off of his head. The wind held the cap in the mid-air and buoyed it up with invisible, helicopter force. Ellie's hand was already holding the bill of her own ball cap.

"What the . . . ?" Ellie barely caught Kaline's words as the wind ransacked her jersey like a cold-fingered thief.

Dropping the equipment bag and knuckling his eyes, Kaline turned and watched helplessly as the wild air lifted his cap higher and spun it away.

Ellie let go of her cap, turned and jumped for it. . . . But the Kaline cap was just out of reach above her head and the heads of the other reaching fans. "Damn!"

The fence and the rising slope of the stands forced the wind upward in a cresting wave, and the Kaline cap with it. Ellie and the handful of other fans squinted through the cloud of dust to point at the flying cap, and then matched Kaline's alarm with inarticulate cries of their own.

The Detroit Tigers ball cap continued to spin: away from Kaline, away from Ellie, away from the fence, just over the shouting mouths and outstretched hands of a dozen willing young fans, like a foul ball sailing out of reach.

Freaky!

Kaline now pressed against the fence a few feet away from Ellie, still keeping his eye on the cap, and shouting for the fans to pursue and retrieve it.

Behind Kaline, the other Tigers players had stopped and turned to take in the excitement.

Ellie thought Norm Cash must have said something funny, because the whole group began to laugh at their teammate's strange predicament. Lolich, particularly, was running comically in a drunken circle, head up, arms outstretched and yelling for an imaginary cap to "Come back! Come back!" in a cartoon voice as high-pitched as Ellie's own. The other players doubled over with laughter, pointing at the distressed Kaline. "Hold that Ti-i-ger! Hold that Ti-i-ger!" Lolich took up the loudspeakers' refrain.

But Ellie saw that Al Kaline was desperately concerned for his game cap. She put her head down, and for a few steps, joined another charge of fans in screaming pursuit . . . when it all stopped: the raucous appeals, the running feet, the voice of Mr. Kaline himself. And Ellie heard once more the disappointed "Ah-h-hs" and the admissions of "Too late!" and "Forget it!"

Ellie wasn't sure what had happened. Above her, as before when she'd secured her Kaline ball, the fans all turned back and were again dispersing to wherever in the stadium they had their seats.

At the fence, the face of Al Kaline showed immense relief. What could he see from his angle? Behind him, the other Tigers players also turned away chuckling and continued on toward the dugout and dressing room. The excitement was obviously over. Kaline was smiling hugely, pointing and waving at Ellie to come down to the fence again.

Me?

She went back down, but it took her only a few moments to figure out that Kaline wasn't waving to her at all. She turned around to look. And then Ellie broke into a big grin herself.

It *was* freaky!

"Frank! Frank! FRA-A-N-N-K!" she yelled up.

twenty-seven

Frank

"Man, what's all that shouting about now?"

The noise from the loudspeaker on the deck above him drilled into Frank's ears. The elephants continued their unbridled charge round and round the inside of Frank's skull. His cap covering his face had no answer. "Geez!" The yelling went on and Frank thought he caught Ellie's high-pitched voice riding over top of the sounds of the stadium. "She callin' me? Again?"

Frank lifted the bill of his cap to look down. It was a mistake. "Damn!" The chill gust of wind, dust and small debris invaded his eyes, nose and mouth. He hunched forward with the cap in front of his face, spitting and swearing. Turning away, Frank used the end of the wadded handkerchief to clear his eyes of the irritating grit and then blew his nose into the Kleenex tissue and wiped his mouth with it, spitting out the grainy bits. The wind died down and Frank risked putting his cap back on his head, careful of the sensitive, pulsating bruise and cut.

When Frank looked down, Ellie was back at the fence, almost

alone save for a handful of fans moving away and . . . was that Al Kaline just a few feet behind her?

Weird.

Even weirder, both Ellie and Kaline seemed to be pointing up. At him? Just trying to figure it out caused the herd in Frank's head to speed up the stampede. "Wha-at?"

Frank tried to lever himself up onto shaky legs, decided it was too painful and settled for leaning farther forward. Ellie's shouting rose to a soprano pitch.

"It's right beside you, Frank! RIGHT BESIDE YOU!"

Beside me?

At last, Frank dropped his eyes and looked to either side. On a seat just three feet to his right lay an alien object that might as well have dropped down from the planet Mars for all he could figure out. "What the hell?" A Tigers ball cap? From, like, nowhere? The cap from outer space sat alone and pretty on the painted wood. For a second, Frank's addled brain thought it was his. But even through the pain, he felt the familiar grip of his own cap on his head and looked closer at the alien interloper. *Weirder.* Down at the fence, Ellie and Kaline both nodded and smiled, dipping their heads in a duet of agreement.

"Geez." Frank pushed himself up again, and in spite of the protests from his head and wooden legs, managed to reach over and pick up the cap in both hands.

"Weird, man." He stood up carefully, a hand on the seat back in front of him. The ball cap was undoubtedly official, but something more. Frank massaged his right temple beside the painful bruise and did his best to sharpen his vision and focus. The ball cap's workmanship was beautiful: rich black material, inviting texture, pristine colour, perfect blocking and shape, and apparently, hardly worn.

Frank's own Tigers ball cap was also official, bought early last year from the licensed, American League sales shop under the stands of Tiger Stadium. Yet Frank's eyes and exploring fingers told him that his cap was in no way the equal of this cap and never would be. Ever. "Really weird." The cap was just too perfect, looked way too professional for any common tourist or baseball fan like him. The white Detroit 𝔇 raised on the stiffened material of the front crown was invisibly but perfectly stitched and centred, as if this was the cap Frank's own cap was meant to be, the original, the mold, the ideal, not his workman-like, mass-produced copy.

Ellie yelled something from the bottom of the steps below and gave him a big thumbs-up. Frank looked beyond her, to the bareheaded Tigers outfielder smiling and waving at him from the fence. That was all it took. A sudden, atomic-fueled depth charge detonated in the middle of Frank's brain and rained down painful chunks of wild elephant. "Jesus Christ!" He winced and squeezed his eyes shut, swayed alarmingly and began to sink down. Frank groped one hand forward again, found the back of the seat and just managed to stay afloat. "Geez!"

Frank took a steadying breath and cracked one eye open. Then he opened his other eye and, sure enough, he, Frank David Phelan, Canadian Junior League ballplayer, newly elected captain of his Windsor Werewolves, and Detroit Tigers super-fan forever, held the big league baseball cap of Albert William Kaline in his own two hands. Three words slipped out between Frank's lips like a distant echo from a former life.

"Lucky! Lucky! Lucky!"

From the soles of Frank's Keds to the top of his head, and everywhere in between, pleasure and excitement warred with the pain. The joyous feelings won the battle, at least for the time being. The gods of baseball worked in mysterious ways, their wonders to perform: Al Kaline's World Series game cap!

It was a wonder, a certified, official, no-shit-Sherlock wonder. And now Frank alone and after, like, whole years of disappointment, would have the chance to return the holy treasure, actually meet the man himself, talk to him, tell him—whatever! "Wow!" The residual ache from his fresh bruise receded farther. This was the antidote!

And then, like a traitorous bolt from the most forbidden depths of his imagination, the urge hit Frank. Hit Frank hard. A temptation so powerful, because it was so foreign to his thinking, so unexpected.

The cap could be his! Frank's own head game. Literally! At least for a few seconds.

"Oh, ma-a-a-n!" Frank had to gather all available energies to resist, had to fight the urge to observe his hands like Frankenstein body parts attached to the ends of someone else's arms. Frank warred with himself to stop those traitor arms from bringing up those guilty hands, taking off his Tigers ball cap and slipping Al Kaline's miraculous game cap onto his very own head, just for a few precious seconds. The impulse was so immediate, so overwhelming, yet, he argued against himself, so natural, really. To experience the once-in-a-lifetime specialness, the Walt Disney, Fantasyland magic Frank knew he would feel, to be able to remember the beauty of it, the weight of it, the texture of it, to imagine the look of it, always. . . .

He didn't do it.

It seemed like a year had passed, but time had slowed, and when he came to himself, it was only a few life-changing seconds.

Frank looked down at Ellie, and Kaline, now standing just behind her, waiting, expectant. Frank raised his right arm high, waved the Kaline cap in acknowledgement and turned toward the aisle steps with his thoughts running true.

It wasn't like handing back the Kaline ball that Ellie had won fair and square. That was right and just. This was bigger than right. Frank was a ballplayer in love with the long traditions of his sport. He respected this one.

This was Al Kaline's game cap, World Series game cap. The cap he wore at home plate, wore in the outfield and when he ran the bases. To wear another player's ball cap, use his equipment, sit or stand in his place or interfere with his pre-game rituals was to hazard dulling his edge, destroying his magic, ruining his play, changing the game's outcome, the season, even the World Series, this World Series. The head game. It wasn't superstition; it was faith. Frank believed. And here, in 1968, in game five, Al Kaline and his beloved Tigers had this last shot to extend the series and come back for a game six, even a game seven. Even, the baseball gods willing, a World Series title and the sacred, engraved series rings that would immortalize the players forever.

Frank paused only to turn back, reach down to the seat beside him and retrieve his golden Kaline glove. He looked down and flushed with heart-filling heat at seeing Kaline's welcoming wave, the pure pleasure and pride that lit Ellie's face. Frank reached the aisle steps and deliberately paused to look again at his greatest baseball hero, waiting at the fence below.

Hold That Tiger! continued to play. And Frank decided he was holding something just as precious and rare as any tiger.

At least he would have this memory, Frank consoled himself.

But now Ellie was jumping up and down, frantically screaming and pointing up at him again with a look of stark horror contorting her dark features. Frank was too intent, too preoccupied with returning Al Kaline's wonderful game cap to really process the change.

twenty-eight

Frank

THUN-K-K!

Big Red's sledgehammer fist caught Frank full on the side of his head just as he turned into the aisle. The sky and the stadium tilted crazy around him. The force of the unexpected impact knocked him stumble-stepping sideways to spin counter-clockwise between the rows of seats with arms weakly flailing, hands grabbing nothing but empty air. "Ah-h-h-a-a!"

Frank crash-landed on the cold cement.

The blow enlarged and re-opened the head wound, and sent his ball cap flying. Stunned and confused, Frank brought his knees up and his arms down, to cradle his ailing head, and lay sideways on the cement. The elephants returned with justifiable vengeance, and Frank gave himself over to the jungle-thick shadows at the edge of consciousness to escape being trampled.

A few centuries or a few seconds later, Frank imagined he heard a girl screaming beneath the lively music and squeezed his head tighter in a futile attempt to stop the growing irritation. It didn't help. The shrill, air-raid siren hysterics were too penetrating. Until another voice entirely overrode them.

"I'll take that cap ya nigger-lovin' bastard!"

"Wha-at?" Frank's mind barely processed the promise of new menace in the tone of the rough voice, but it was enough to lighten the jungle darkness, in spite of his burden of hurt. Frank curled further into the fetal ball and clung fiercely to this new awareness. Some deep instinct for survival prodded him to keep conscious.

"Let go of it, nigger-lover! Ya cost me my baseball from that nigger ho, so the Kaline cap is mine. Give it up, or I'll kick the livin' crap right outta ya!" The coarse voice was familiar, disturbing. A second later, the brutal kick to Frank's kidneys made it clear enough whose it was.

"A-h-h-h!" Frank's nervous system didn't know which point or variety of pain to deal with first. He groaned in agony when a second heavy kick jarred the middle of his spine and radiated outward along every nerve in his back. The third kick took Frank right between his shoulder blades. "Ungh!"

Could the torture get any worse? And would that stupid girl never stop screaming?

The same deep instinct prodded Frank to tighten his grip and to shift his hands to protect the back of his head from the inevitable kick to come.

"'At's better, dickwad. Now give it up!"

The kicks appeared to stop. Frank dared to be relieved in the midst of an overwhelming agony. He felt a tugging at his hands covering the back of his head. *Wha-at?* Frank tightened his grip further and tugged back. There was a reason he had to hold on, if he could just manage to remember it.

"I said let go of it, bozo!"

New wetness collected beneath Frank's head. He smelled his sweat, cold and dank as the cement beneath him. The elephants had broken out of his head and were rampaging up and down his spine on blunt feet. Frank tried to arch his back and shake them off, but his brain didn't deliver the message. He held on to consciousness and something else too. Frank felt both of them slipping beyond his grasp. And that stupid girl was still screaming at him.

What have I done wrong?

twenty-nine

Ellie

The stadium loudspeakers roared out the Tigers theme song, pumping up the crowd. Ellie, with Al Kaline at the fence below, watched it all unfold with growing alarm.

Like the looming return of Ellie's worst nightmare, as soon as Frank picked up Kaline's flying cap, Big Red emerged from the shadow of a nearby exit behind her friend and started to move. His fat face glowed with hate like bad sunburn.

Ellie figured Big Red must have spied on her and Frank for some time, pissed off and seething with frustrated anger, calculating his revenge. Yet Ellie had forgotten him in the crazy effort to get Kaline's attention and then in the excitement of actually doing it. Incredible, since Red had just threatened her with the most vile physical damage a short while before.

Ellie watched from below in her own agony as Red stalked Frank from behind. She tried her best to shout a warning. But Frank appeared not to register her alarm, too caught up in the wild and unexpected drama of the blaring speakers, the rising wind and the unbelievable ball cap. In a million years and a thousand games, who could have guessed at such a bizarre mix of events?

It was happening too fast. Ellie's brain was teeming with possibilities and sick with dread. The reserve section was only sparsely occupied.

Too far away, she began to jump up and down in her helpless frustration and growing anger. "No! No! NO-O-O!" she screamed again and bent forward in the effort to break through to Frank and alert him to the impending attack. Ellie knew from her argument over her Kaline ball that Big Red could get out of control. The look of sadistic anticipation that now twisted his expression, even at a distance, told Ellie it would be far worse for her friend then it had been for her. Who knew what Red was capable of after Frank had so cleverly outwitted and humiliated him? Now her friend's decision to intervene and help a complete stranger was going to cost him unbelievable pain. And it was her fault. Ellie felt wholly responsible for whatever disaster was unfolding above her.

Damn! It was up to her to . . . what?

Before Ellie's mind sorted the thoughts and her resolve solidified into purpose, Ellie's feet moved. Ten long high rows. Ten! Ellie had to get up those tall rows, like, yesterday.

Ellie registered Kaline's yell from behind, something deep and strident, but could spare no attention to process it into meaningful words. Instead, Ellie seized on the emotion, used Kaline's alarm and desperate need to further fuel hers. Adrenaline poured into Ellie's legs like high-octane gasoline. Her feet hit the cement with the piston pounding force of a

Detroit Speedway dragster. Ellie risked a quick glance upward and screamed her shrillest warning. Still in vain.

Big Red checked the empty seats around him. Chose his moment. Drew his right fist back and delivered a half-hidden but vicious blow to the side of Frank's head.

The surprise was total. The blow spun Frank half around and pushed him sideways. He crumpled out of sight between the seats by the metal pillar. It took only seconds.

There were still no spectators near enough to notice Frank hidden between the curving rows of seats or Red ducked so low over him. The wide metal pillar hid them both on one side, the curve of the seats on the other. All attention was on the flashing images on the big scoreboard screen or on the groundskeepers working on the pitching mound and smoothing the area around home plate.

At six rows to go, another glance, and Ellie screamed out her rage once more. Big Red kept low, braced himself on the seat backs beside him, drew back his right leg and delivered a punishing kick to the hidden Frank. Ellie didn't have to see the kick land to know that her new friend was in deep trouble.

Ellie drove upward with her arms churning, gave her legs all the gas she could muster.

Five rows. Another glance and Red was barely visible, speaking down at Frank in words Ellie couldn't make out. It didn't matter. The message was clear.

"No-o-o! Ellie protested in vain when the crouching Red kicked Frank again! And again! Didn't anyone else see it? Didn't anyone realize what was happening to Frank on the cement between the curving seats?

Two more rows. "STOP I-I-T!" Ellie screamed again, arms

and legs on fire with the effort. She had to distract Red. Get the bully's attention. Let him know!

The loudspeakers continued blasting the Tigers theme song.

"Too long. Too long. Too long." Ellie chanted. Her legs worked. Her breath came in rasps.

It was an age, but Ellie was there, at the end of the fateful row.

The Junior Tiger recoiled in horror when she saw the angry mass of Big Red bent almost double with the effort of revenge, looming low over the huddled Frank like an enraged animal, no longer human. Saw him try to pull Frank's hands apart over his head. Wrest away the Kaline cap. Saw Frank resist and Red fail.

How could Frank do it? How could he hold out against that kind of punishment? Part of Ellie was amazed. "I said, NO-O-O-O!" she screamed.

So intent was Red on his attack, he didn't register her outrage above the speakers' noise. Ellie was panting, frantic.

Then Red swore and did stop!

Red kept low and renewed his grip on the seat backs on either side. In an instant Ellie knew he was about to draw back his thick right leg again to deliver the final, decisive kick. The kick that would damage her friend forever—a calculated, hot-blooded message of agony to the back of Frank's head.

Frustrated and livid, Ellie squeezed the autographed Kaline ball: saw again Frank's name and hers written across it in indelible black marker by the hand of the hero they revered; felt its white cowhide perfection, its solidity, its potential.

The ball!

That's all it took. A single second and Ellie was in the game deep, overflowing with a rage so monumental she could not contain it. Energy crackled around her.

Ellie was a Junior Tigers pitcher. The solid concrete beneath her feet was her mound. She knew exactly what she had to do.

Ellie took just the single, short moment needed to plant her feet firmly on the cement. She gripped Kaline's ball, fresh with his aura of power, by all four seams. She put her eye on the strike zone and saw nothing else in the stands, in the stadium, in the world. She wound up in a muscular flow of motion and drew her arm back. Paused at the peak of her windup to gather all the energy coiled in her game-hardened body. Let the pitch erupt, forward and away from the tips of her fingers. Ellie put all of the combustive force of her outrage behind the Kaline ball and delivered her own personal message to Big Red with a loud grunt of effort: "UGH-H-H!"

Denny McLain?

Bob Gibson?

Ellie Fitzgerald!

Hunched over Frank, inarticulate with frustration and with his thick leg in motion to land his most paralyzing kick, Big Red didn't disappoint. Ellie's cannonball pitch exploded through the strike zone, and Red received the souvenir Al Kaline baseball with shattering impact on the sweat-covered sweet spot behind his left ear.

BONK!

Red's half-delivered kick missed Frank's head completely.

"YEAH-H-H!" exclaimed Ellie, punching the air with her fist. "Ya wanted my Kaline ball so bad, ya got it, fatboy!"

Stunned and thrown off-balance by the force of the impact, Red twisted fully around on his left leg. Fell flat out, face-first to the cement deck, splitting open his chin and rattling his dirty teeth.

It was the pitch of her life!

Ellie's athletic frame brimmed with the power and elation of her triumph. She'd done it! The damsel in distress, a black damsel, rewrote the fairy tale and rescued the white knight. Magilla Gorilla was down and out of the game. "Ye-a-a-h!"

Ellie's triumph was short-lived.

To her disbelieving eyes, Big Red groaned low, drew back and gathered his arms under him. He began to push his wide body up onto his hands and knees, his face a study in confusion. Red shook his heavy head from side to side, opened his mouth in further groans and drooled saliva in a steady runnel onto the cement below him. Drops of blood from his split chin added gory detail.

"Jesus!" Ellie was amazed—but not finished. Not yet. She and her dad had also taken in a lot of Detroit Lions football games. Ellie knew all about kickoffs.

"Ya like to kick guys when they're down? Eat this, fatboy!" Now Ellie held the seatbacks, drew her right leg back and delivered a hard kick to Red's pug-nosed face. The toe of her hard rubber sneaker hit squarely between the uprights of his ears and split the base of his nose with a satisfying crunch of cartilage, a burst of blood following. Red went right down this time. His chin and nose leaked steady scarlet ribbons onto the dirty cement.

Ellie still had to get to Frank, who lay curled and motionless in his tight protective ball, his Kaline jersey scuffed with dirt from Big Red's kicks. Yet Red was blocking the entire aisle, out of it, but breathing noisily from a broken nose, burbling low saliva sounds.

A few spectators were looking over her way, still no one near enough to help.

Ellie didn't think twice. She jumped onto his back with both feet then wide-walked down the prone length of his body.

It was a mistake.

Somehow, Red reared up on his knees, turned and leered in challenge. Ellie flailed her arms, cried out and pitched forward across Frank. Before she could react, Ellie felt herself gripped by both ankles and dragged backward along the cement, scraping her own chin.

"Now I . . . gotcha . . . ya nigger bitch!"

thirty

Ellie

"I'm gonna freakin' kill ya!"

Ellie believed it.

Could no one see what was going on between the curving seats? Was it the metal pillar?

Red kept low, checked the area around him, ducked down and smiled through the blood and snot. He grunted, levered Ellie over onto her back, straddled her body with his knees tight on either side in the narrow space between the rows, hunched forward and clamped both hands around Ellie's throat. She twisted and strained and beat at his looming head and stiff arms with one bare fist and her blue Horton glove. Red let out a manic giggle and welcomed it all. His thumbs dug into the soft flesh of her neck so hard, Ellie's attempts to cry out her distress were squeezed back and extinguished, and she feared she would never breathe again.

Where were the other fans? The attendants?

Ellie's eyes expanded whitely, while Red's blood dripped

onto her face in a steady rhythm. Ellie needed to blink away the sticky flow, but it pooled around both eyes until she saw through a red haze. The disgusting blur and sensation triggered a frantic effort. Ellie let her glove drop to form both hands into desperate claws and scratched at the crazy eyes in the wide face. She thought she felt skin collect under her nails but could no longer see the effect. She scratched and scraped again and again. It did no good.

And what about Frank?

Ellie's efforts grew feeble, pathetic. Red swore and squeezed and dripped. Ellie felt the weight of her flesh lifting up and away, her spirit expanding and lightening. She closed her eyes and broke free of her body, free of the strangling pain, and drifted in what felt like the welcoming grace of God. "Angels' breath," her father called it in his sermons. Her father was right. The feeling was heavenly. She glowed with born-again life, the peace and promise of faith. It was bliss. . . .

Until God spoke—

"LET HER GO! LET HER GO NOW!"

Ellie knew His voice. The meaning remained a mystery, yet the tone did not sound inviting. Ellie continued in limbo. The promise of heaven's peace beckoned. Ellie brushed at her eyes with fingers she couldn't feel. The lids cracked open.

"Ah-h-h-h!" The crushing weight of reality returned. A white figure loomed above the dense mass that pinned her. Ellie felt the grip on her throat loosen. Her airway opened enough to entice a part lungful of air to revive her. The white figure loomed clearer. *Her guardian angel?* But the angel was nothing like the otherworldly, near-feminine figures in the stained glass windows of her father's Baptist church. It wasn't an angel, but the effect was almost as heavenly.

The face slipped into rough focus. It was . . . Mr. Kaline! *But how?*

With irresistible force and finality, Kaline jerked Big Red's hands fully away from Ellie's throat, wrenched his arms around his back, held them there and pulled upward, drawing an angry gasp of pain. The blunt upward pressure levered Big Red off Ellie and back onto unsteady feet.

"ENOUGH! IT'S FINISHED! THIS ENDS NOW! YOU HEAR ME, BOY?"

At last, over the tops of the rows above her, Ellie could just make out the heads and shoulders of approaching fans, attracted by the commotion, and by the unexpected sight of Al Kaline in the stands. The Tigers theme song ended with raucous cheers from the hometown crowd. The speakers crackled with static and began an Earl Scheib commercial at a lower volume.

Ellie ventured a deeper breath, but almost stifled it when her throat rebelled at the raw agony of the effort. Above and beyond her, Big Red sputtered and howled in animal outrage. He gave forth a spitting stream of obscenities Ellie's brain couldn't yet translate. Instead, she concentrated on the pure pleasure of air, painful though the process of inhaling it was.

Ellie did watch in awe when Kaline snaked a muscular forearm between Red's right arm and head, at the shoulder, forcing him forward and down from the waist. Red was no match for the Tiger. Kaline kept him in an immobilizing, wrestler's half nelson. "Enough, I said!"

Ellie rolled onto her side, forced herself half-up and rested against a seatback behind her. She put a hand to her throat and probed. "A-h-h-h." Like she'd gargled gasoline. Five feet away, Ellie thought she heard a low moan from Frank, but wasn't yet able to summon the energy to go to him. She could only observe the drama unfold between Kaline and Red.

"Lemme go, man! You're breakin' my arm!" the big kid protested. "I'll sue ya! I'll freakin' sue ya!" Red continued to threaten Kaline, adding a saliva stream of curses and invective that would make a major league manager blush.

Ellie pulled her knees up and continued to breathe and grimace at the searing effect of the effort. She watched Kaline use his athlete's strength and leverage to force Red back into the aisle, bent like an angry question mark. Kaline spun him around, released the half nelson and drove his flattened hand between the punk's shoulder blades with a sudden straight-arm. Red stumbled, clumsy and stupid. Lurched around like the frustrated ape he'd become to face the Tigers right fielder.

His nose and chin still dripped slow blood and one shoulder hung low. His angry mouth sputtered and erupted in more pink saliva sprays of obscenities and threats. Kaline nodded, unmoved, like he expected nothing else. His demeanour was as hard and unyielding as the concrete beneath his feet.

Now there were a dozen fans around them, buzzing with excitement and dismay, yet keeping their distance, unsure of what to do as Kaline continued to speak with unshakeable certainty, ignoring the filth. "You listen to me, boy. If there's any suing to be done, it'll be you who's sued, for attacking these two fans. I've alerted stadium security. They're right behind you. And believe me, we'll get this sorted out with your parents and the police. If you've given them any lasting injuries, you'll pay for it. I promise you that."

Red paused when the idea of parents and police penetrated his skull. Ellie saw him check quickly behind him, and then stiffen. Sure enough, Ellie glimpsed the heads and shoulders of two uniformed Tiger Stadium attendants coming swiftly down from the upper level toward them. One of them was speaking into a walkie-talkie.

"Screw you, Kaline!" Red turned back and hissed. "The Tigers are losers and so are you. So, screw you!" At the end of the aisle, Red gave Kaline the finger. Ellie continued her rasping breaths and strained to see farther over the seats. Red bulled through the wary fans, shaking off the weak attempts to detain him. He ran as fast as his fat legs could carry him, clumping and swearing down the steps, all the way to the fence. He elbowed the remaining autograph seekers aside, cleared a space and threw a leg over the padded wood. His scramble onto the field wasn't pretty, almost comic. Red trundled down the third baseline to a point where he could get back over the fence once more.

Ellie went limp with relief when he disappeared into a crowded entranceway and the bowels of Tiger Stadium.

"What a dick!" she rasped.

Now the rows around them were filling with eager spectators. Most were juggling Tigers pennants with their drinks and hot dogs and snacks from the concession stands below—all staring, all asking questions. Kaline, Ellie and Frank were an island in a sea of curiosity. But Kaline's powerful presence was such that they kept a respectful distance.

Kaline turned and bent toward Ellie. She'd forgotten just

how impressive he was. "You ok, young lady? That guy do any permanent damage? Here, let's get you seated and checked out. Got help on the way." In contrast to Red, Kaline gently maneuvered Ellie up and into a seat. Her first strained words were not for herself.

"Frank? Help Frank. Got your cap. Guy was . . . kickin' him." Ellie didn't recognize the sandpaper voice that scraped from her throat.

Kaline almost smiled but took the order calmly and squeezed her shoulder. "Ok. Sit tight. I'm getting to him right now," he said over his left shoulder as he started for Frank. His bare head looked strange without the ball cap she was used to, the tan line just visible bisecting the broad forehead.

Ellie wheezed a small sigh of relief yet couldn't still the apprehension when Kaline knelt beside her friend's huddled form. Was Frank even conscious? Ellie thought she remembered a moan.

Frank flinched and gave out a low gasp at the ballplayer's first touch. It took Kaline almost a minute, speaking quiet words of reassurance, to coax Frank's clenched hands away from his head, where he still tried to protect himself.

"Ah-h-h-h!" Ellie uttered her own groan as she moved two seats closer to Frank for a better vantage point.

Her white knight looked like St. George might have if a dragon had kicked his holy butt. Frank's chin was cut and seeping red. Blood from the re-opened head wound stained the side of his face in ugly smears right down to the jaw-line. At least her friend appeared conscious, though, and now groaned from the pain. Mr. Kaline asked the question Ellie was desperate to answer herself.

"You ok, son? You hurt somewhere I can't see?"

The two security men forced the spectators farther back around them and stood poised for action at the end of their row. They reminded Ellie of the comic strip characters her dad used to chuckle over. One tall and gangly like "Mutt," the other short and stubby like "Jeff." Mr. Kaline asked Mutt to sit with her, and asked Jeff to use his walkie-talkie to request the aid of the team doctor. Ellie shook her head and waved off Mutt's enquiring glance at her.

The doctor request shocked Ellie. Was Frank headed to a hospital? Was she? No way she vowed! She'd die before she missed this game. Frank would too, Ellie was sure of it.

Kaline began to speak so quietly to Frank that Ellie could just manage to hear the words. "I see you've got my ball cap there. Frank, isn't it? So I want to thank you for that." Frank's eyes were squeezed shut. Kaline reached for the cap and tried to persuade it from his white-knuckled grasp. Ellie saw Frank continue to resist, tightening his hold to a death grip. What a way to describe it!

"No-o! Kaline's game cap. Gotta save it for him," Frank mumbled his first intelligible words.

Kaline squeezed her friend's shoulder. "You did save my ball cap, son. I'm sorry that punk made you suffer for it."

Frank's eyes fluttered open, and Ellie could breathe a little easier. "Wha-at?"

"I said you did it, Frank," the Tigers player continued. "You held on and saved my game cap for me just like you said. Thank you." It took an anxious few seconds, but Frank's eyes cleared and began to focus. "You know me? I see you're wearing my number 6 jersey. Looks like you have my glove there too. Your partner Ellie tells me you're over from Canada. That right?"

"Al . . . Kaline?"

"Very pleased to meet you, Frank. Wish the circumstances were different."

"Mr. Kaline?" Frank ventured. Ellie saw the Tigers player's grin of relief at that. Kaline nodded once at Frank. "Uh, I think I got your game cap, sir."

"You certainly do, Frank. And I'm very grateful." Kaline finally freed the cap when Frank relaxed his rigid grip. Ellie saw Frank flex his stiff fingers, twist and arch his bruised back, gasping at the pain. The dirty scuff marks from Red's kicks stood out on his Kaline jersey, stark evidence of the viciousness of the attack.

Ellie recognized an unexpected look of embarrassment steal over Frank's tight features. Embarrassed?

He shouldn't be. Not after what he did. What he did for both of us.

Now Frank tried to roll to his knees, groaning again at the hurt and effort. Ellie hoped nothing was broken or anything. Kaline put a strong hand under Frank's arm and guided him up by slow degrees. He was wobbly, and didn't resist as the big man steered him into a seat one away from her, drawing a series of explosive gasps when his bruised back made contact with the seatback.

At last, Ellie could look at her friend from Canada. Pride and relief suffused her mind and body with purring warmth, a miracle medicine no doctor could prescribe.

Under Mr. Kaline's arm, Frank looked back at Ellie, and in spite of the whole crazy ordeal—her ball, the cap, the attacks—smiled weakly into her eyes. Black and blue, came the strange thought, just like the bruises they shared. Ellie let out a painful breath and returned the smile with the brilliance of a Tiger Stadium arc light.

She raised her right hand and flashed Frank a small V-for-Victory sign, his own signal to her from another lifetime. Frank nodded, relieved, and just managed a stiff thumbs-up in return.

"Low-fives later," Ellie croaked.

thirty-one

Frank

Geez! I've survived! Frank thought.

Ellie too. Just barely. What a sorry pair! And what must Al Kaline think, now wearing his game cap and a serious look on his face, and waiting at the end of the aisle?

Every time Frank took a breath, his back about killed him. Frank had more Kleenex tissues from Ellie, like she owned the factory or something. He pressed them against the insistent wound on his forehead. Was there ever a time when he wasn't in pain? He could feel the blood sticking to the tissue as his body tried to heal the damage. Frank fought down a ripple of nausea and put his head back for relief.

He tried to hold focus when Kaline waved at the doctor in a funereal black suit and white shirt. They made his Tigers orange tie look ridiculous to Frank and clashed with the grave expression on his face. "Grave," did Frank call it? *Now who was ridiculous?* A few moments later, the grave man opened his black medical bag and began to examine Ellie. Frank watched him use a bit of alcohol and gauze to clear the sticky blood from her eyes.

Frank himself was clear-headed enough to feel extremely self-conscious in the presence of Al Kaline. His idol now stood in the aisle below, watching the doctor, but glancing down at the Tigers dugout too. Kaline was a little taller, but they were almost at eye level. Frank felt a persistent guilt as well. He forced himself more upright in the seat, summoned what courage he could and pointed to the game cap sitting exactly where it belonged. "Uh, it's pretty messed up, sir."

Number 6 seemed to consider this when he reached up to remove the cap, shook it out and straightened it to restore the shape to near-perfection. Kaline brushed back his flattened hair with a practiced sweep of his left hand and put the cap solemnly back on his head, checking and squaring it into proper position. He let a smile widen his expression, and to Frank's eyes, reveal a hint of the younger player pictured for all time on Frank's super-rare Kaline rookie cards. Frank knew without knowing that this was the image of Kaline he would recall best when whatever happened next, happened.

"Messed up?" Kaline echoed in a thoughtful masculine voice. "On the contrary, Frank. The cap means as much to me as ever. Maybe more."

Frank didn't get that, but had to go along. "Well, I know it's your game cap, an' all. And that's really important."

"Yeah. Got this one special for the series. We're not doing so great, but I wouldn't feel the same out there today with any other cap but this one. You know?"

"Uh huh," Frank said, and warmed to the familiar subject, some self-consciousness leaving with it. "I got your glove an' stuff for the same reason. When I play right field or second base, I know it feels right."

"Then you already know more than most people. And not just about baseball. Thanks, Frank. I owe you."

Kaline leaned closer to Frank and Ellie, and held out his right hand! The top hand when he gripped his bat at the plate. The one that picked hard-hit baseballs out of his glove and hurled them with uncanny sharpshooter accuracy from right field, to throw an opposing player out or force him back to a base.

Frank watched in awe as his own hand reached out and was shaken warmly by his hero's. Frank felt the fifteen years of major league calluses and the sure athletic strength in the fingers. For those moments, Frank could ignore the nagging hurt in his head, the aching stiffness along his spine.

"Sure, Mr. Kaline. Any time."

"And thank you, too, Ellie. That was some pitch you threw there to help your Canadian friend." Number 6 reached over and shook her hand just as warmly.

"You're . . . welcome, sir." Ellie strained to get the words out, but her face glowed with pleasure.

Kaline nodded, glanced down at the Tigers dugout again, and then spoke quickly, taking in him and Ellie with his look. "Frank? Ellie? I'd like you two to be my special guests today and sit in the Tigers reserved seats, right beside our dugout. That way you'll both be together in the same place and the doctor will be nearby. What do you say, doc?"

The doctor took a full minute to examine Frank's head, ask him about the clarity of his vision and have him stand to probe his back. Frank did his best not to cry out. The doc took another minute to further examine Ellie's neck and look down her throat. He had her force down two pills with water from a flask. Only then did the team doctor shrug his approval while Kaline waited expectantly.

Frank looked at Ellie and Ellie looked at Frank. "Uh, we'd be proud to sit in those seats, sir," Frank said, while Ellie smiled in agreement.

"Good. Pride's what it's all about. Ok, guys, the doc and the attendants will explain to your parents and show you to the seats. And listen, because this is important. I want to see both of you field-side before the national anthem. I'll come to the end of the dugout."

Only then did the nearest fans around them smile, and a few clap hands.

Kaline smiled back, touched his game cap and was gone.

For a few moments, Frank and Ellie sat gingerly back in their seats and took in the colourful, bustling cacophony of activity generated by an excited, expectant crowd of Tigers and Cardinals fans. Frank was certain the crucial importance of this game would ensure Tiger Stadium filled to its fifty-three thousand capacity.

"Wow!" Frank said for both of them.

"Double wow . . . white knight!" Ellie managed, and held up her right hand, palm open toward Frank.

"What?"

Ellie laughed hoarsely and maneuvered Frank's right hand into the same position, then slapped his palm with her own. "High-fives!" she rasped.

Frank laughed through his aches. "High-fives!" and returned the favour.

The doctor insisted on one more brisk but thorough check of Frank, front and back, head and eyes. Frank winced at the sting of alcohol on his bruised forehead, but held still, as instructed, when the doctor applied a wide adhesive dressing. From his bag, the doctor produced the small flask of water and made Frank swallow two aspirin.

"Right, young man," the doctor said, "you have a nasty cut and contusion on your forehead, but your eyes are clear and appear to be focusing, right?" The doctor waited. Frank winced but nodded. "Yes, I know it's painful, but there's probably no concussion." He began to pack away his bag. "Now, that bruising on your back is bad, but no cracked ribs or lasting damage there either, as far as I can tell. Some bruising over the kidneys, so it may be painful to urinate."

Geez! Frank was embarrassed about Ellie hearing this stuff. "So I want you to watch for blood in the urine. That would be very serious. You inform me or your parents, and see your own doctor immediately." Even blushing felt painful, but Frank nodded agreement again.

"And you, young lady, that throat is badly bruised. I've given you something to reduce the swelling and the analgesic will help with the pain. Luckily, there appears to be no permanent damage. For now, try not to talk more than you have to, and drink water to keep the tissues lubricated." The doctor held up one finger, and included Frank in his look. "But, you must both promise to see your own doctors no later than tomorrow. That clear? Frank shrugged and Ellie rasped her consent. "Then here is my card for each of you, just in case." They slipped the cards into pockets.

Attendant Mutt stepped forward. "Anyone here named Ellie or Frank?" When they just looked at each other blankly for a moment, then back at the attendant, he turned serious. "No? Then I guess I'll just have to give this to some other young fans."

Frank would have laughed but it hurt too much. Ellie's face showed confusion, then surprise, then sheepishness, as the attendant revealed her autographed, Al Kaline baseball and put it into her hands.

"Our parents," Ellie rasped then.

Frank knew it was a question, and not an easy one. "Yeah, like Kaline said, let the doc explain we're good for the game first. We'll fill in the necessary details and I'll meet you in the new Kaline seats. High-fives!" Frank held up his palm and Ellie slapped it hard. He pointed to third base on their left and gave her his seat location.

"See you . . . soon, white knight."

"Definitely . . . *black* knight."

Ellie shook her head in wonder and the pride shone from her eyes.

thirty-two

Frank

Above Frank and his father and grandfather, above the doctor and the tall attendant, the stadium P.A. system hissed and crackled to life once more as the announcer, Curt Gowdy, began the opening commentary for the fifth and possibly deciding game of the 1968 World Series.

When Frank winced and struggled through the crowds of fans to get back to his family's prize seats, his head and back felt like they'd been worked over by a Louisville Slugger. The doctor and attendant were right behind him. As soon as Frank saw his grandfather's tall cup of Stroh's beer, he couldn't help but think of the doctor's warning, about his yellow urine pissing away his own blood. *Geez!* Frank was immediately wary and thirsty, yet decided to avoid his usual root beer as long as he could.

Now Frank stood in the aisle with the doctor, the attendant, and his father and grandfather. The season's ticketholders had begun to arrive and fill their reserved seats to the right of them, behind home plate. The crowd moved in a steadier flow up and down the aisle around them, and drink vendors shouted out their wares.

It took Frank a few tense minutes, but he managed to give his father and grandfather just the highlights of his story and respond to their expected questions. The doctor nodded reassurance. It was barely enough. The Phelan men looked at each other and then at the doctor, and wanted to look more closely at Frank's forehead and back. Frank set his face, stifled his impatience and complied. He could tell the white patch of head bandage really freaked them, and that his back couldn't be pretty with its growing rainbow of bruised colours.

"That everything, Frank?" His grandfather shook his head gravely when Frank finished the show and tell. David looked once more at the tall attendant, waiting a few steps behind the doctor, his face expressionless. The attendant said nothing, yet his tapping right foot made it clear he was impatient to get on with his job. "I mean, Frank," his grandfather continued, "it's just such an, an unbelievable story. But I guess you've got the bruises to prove it. Still . . . " At last, the attendant joined the doctor, nodding confirmation.

Frank was exasperated, anxious to get it over with and join Ellie in those special Kaline seats. "Geez, Grandpa! You think I did this to myself?" Frank pointed to his head, and then turned half-around to raise his jersey and sweatshirt to give them another quick look at the angry bruises on his back. And didn't they realize the doctor and attendant were waiting?

Frank's father was still reluctant. "But are you certain you're well enough to sit by yourself, son? If your mother were here, we'd all have some explaining to do. I'm sure not looking forward to facing her when we get home."

"Double geez, Dad!" I said already. I won't be alone. And mom's not here. And I'll survive. I promise."

"What do you think, doctor?" his grandfather finally asked out loud.

"Well, Frank did take quite a beating, no question. But he seems determined. The girl too. How be we let them move down to the Tigers reserved seats, and I'll check on them both at the end of the third inning and report back to you?"

Frank could see the hesitation in his father's expression.

"Please, Dad. It's Al Kaline."

Just at that crucial moment, Ellie arrived with the imposing black man in the white collar who had to be her father, and with them, Jeff, the short attendant. Frank flashed back two months, to Windsor's Atkinson Field, and to the last time he'd seen the man. Frank saw again Ellie's dramatic spiking and the near-riot that followed her amazing courage when she delivered the painful retribution the blonde punk deserved. And here now was the same big black man in that white collar. What courage he, too, had demonstrated in the midst of the chaos, raising his arms, turning slowly and displaying the peace symbol with the first fingers of both hands.

Geez! Could the man, the minister, bring the same sense of calm to this situation?

Both Frank's father and grandfather tried to hide their surprise, but didn't succeed completely. Frank was stunned to remember he had not told them Ellie was black! It didn't matter anymore—to him. And why should it matter ever again, to anyone? He knew his dad and grandfather would be cool.

Frank gave Ellie a quick thumbs-up to try and reassure her. Still, she looked apprehensive, even with her dad beside her, and hung back a bit. Some of the fans moving around them were annoyed at their unexpected obstruction, like finding a big snag in the middle of a growing river they were trying to navigate. After a few awkward seconds, it was Ellie's dad who took the initiative and introduced himself in a resonant preacher's voice.

"Gillespie Fitzgerald, sirs. And my daughter, Ellie. Pleased to meet you all." Ellie risked a slight smile and nodded, but didn't try to speak. Even Frank was momentarily taken aback by the full impact of the tall black man's immediate presence, his white collar and black minister's shirt. Until his mother's good manners took over.

"Uh, I'm Frank, Mr. Fitzgerald. And this is my father, Norm Phelan, and my grandfather, David Phelan." That snapped them out of it. All three Phelans shook the offered hand. The Fitzgeralds' presence confirmed Frank's story and reassured his family. Now there was no hesitation on the faces of Frank's father and grandfather.

Thank God!

Frank's grandfather paused to examine the poster Ellie was holding. "Hey! 'Go Cats! Bite Birds!'" David exclaimed and then considered Ellie's Junior Tigers jersey. "Yeah. You were on Trumble when we drove by earlier." Ellie again looked shy and embarrassed, or maybe it was her painful throat, and only dipped her head. "We're very happy to meet you too, Ellie." Frank's grandfather didn't force her to shake hands. He turned back to Mr. Fitzgerald. "And should we call you *Reverend* Fitzgerald, sir?"

Ellie's father laughed a rich, deep-chested laugh and shook his head. His friendly manner was engaging and Frank relaxed further.

"My presence here today is unofficial—although I may ask the Lord to bless Lolich's fastball." Reverend Fitzgerald put his hands together and looked briefly heavenward, his lips moving in mock-serious pantomime. "So, please, call me by my nickname, 'Dizzy.'" Frank watched the adults pause and then explode with laughter, and felt the formality between them dissolve. Ellie nodded at Frank and her smile widened.

Frank understood. No black. No white. Tigers fans together.

"Gentlemen, I really must be going," the doctor broke in. "The attendants will take your decision." He threaded his way down the crowded steps, through a field gate guarded by another attendant, and then moved toward the Tigers dugout and the entrance to their dressing room.

"Dizzy Gillespie? Like the trumpet player?" Frank's father said.

"Yes. I do play that instrument, poorly," Reverend Fitzgerald admitted. "And Ellie is the youngest member of our choir at Harriet Beecher Stowe Baptist Church. The nickname Dizzy is a bit embarrassing for a Baptist minister at times, but kind of a family tradition, and it seems to have stuck."

"Dizzy it is, if you'll call us David and Norm," his dad said.

"Will do. And thank you, sirs."

Even after hearing their whole story about Big Red's threats and the attack involving Kaline's ball, his autograph and game cap, Frank could tell the three parents remained a touch apprehensive about letting the teens out of their sights. Reverend Fitzgerald was definitely uncertain about the proposed seating arrangements. Ellie had a hard time even speaking, and Frank had to admit his bandage and injuries didn't look reassuring.

It was up to Frank. "C'mon. Please? The attendants are waiting."

It was his grandfather who made another proposal.

"Ah, Dizzy, I think we're all more than a little overwhelmed and understandably anxious at these turns of events. Maybe a compromise is in order to give us some peace of mind. I propose that Frank and Ellie can go, as the doctor suggests, but only if you, Dizzy, would consent to join us sitting here, in Frank's place. We can keep an eye on them together, and the doctor can get to us all quickly if there's any kind of emergency." David pointed over to Frank's soon-to-be empty seat.

Ellie's father laughed and nodded. "Thank you, again, David. That is most generous and very sensible. The Lord approves of cheerful giving, and I respect the gift of compromise."

"Low-fives!" Frank said. Ellie smiled widely as he reached down and slapped her hand. The adults erupted in friendly laughter and began to move down the row and take their seats.

At last!

A few seconds later, Frank and Ellie followed the attendants down to what must be the two best seats in the whole of Tiger Stadium. Sure enough, the seats were right at the corner of the Tigers dugout. "Cool!" Frank said.

"Very cool!" Ellie managed to croak.

thirty-three

Frank

Tiger Stadium was now filled to the cloud-scattered sky with the disparate colours, sounds, textures and smells of fifty-three thousand baseball fans, most of them anxious, some of them confident, all of them expectant. Frank felt like he was sitting inside the picture tube of a giant colour TV rippling with Tigers orange, black and white, mixing with splashes of Cardinals red and white. A TV with the volume spiraling up and up and out of control until all his senses vibrated with crackling energy and anticipation. Frank was still surprised at the number of men in formal suits, ties and white shirts, waving their wide-brimmed hats, with the women in long-sleeved dresses that looked like Sunday best beside them. Some of the women actually wore lacy veils. Almost all carried fluttering, triangular Tigers pennants.

Frank suddenly realized that the periodic wind gusts had died down. Now, there was only a cool breeze coming in from left centre field. When he looked up at the big stadium flag, it was placidly streaming its red, white and blue patriotic message, looking perfectly normal. Frank didn't know quite what to think.

Just spooky, man.

Ellie nudged him and they watched the St. Louis Cardinals and then the Detroit Tigers players fill up their dugouts. The crowd stood and applauded their entrances, and he and Ellie stood with them, Frank still uncomfortably. The attractive woman on Frank's left, wearing a shiny Tigers warm-up jacket and Detroit ball cap, was particularly enthusiastic at the entrance of the Tigers players. She held her team pennant high and proud. Yeah, there were a good number of Cardinals red and white banners among the crowd, Frank had to acknowledge, but overwhelmingly, the moving colours were his Detroit Tigers. Moving in both senses of the word.

"TI-GERS! TI-GERS! TI-GERS!"

The crowd remained standing and roared its approval, long and loud. Frank took Ellie's hand and raised it high in the air with his own. His stiff back and wounded head rebelled and punished the effort with spikes of pain, but he could ignore them. Maybe it was the aspirin, but maybe it was the thrill of being in the only place in the entire universe Frank wanted to be right at that moment: the World Series of baseball.

Frank knew he was cheering, but couldn't hear his own voice above the peoples' celebration. Even through the solid concrete, Frank could feel the whole stadium shake and vibrate as the fans stamped their feet. Many began to slam the fold-up seats of their chairs up and down, up and down, like volleys of gunfire in salute to the occasion.

Frank knew again this was the only kind of riot he wanted to be part of, blacks and whites, Tigers and Cardinals.

Then Al Kaline was there at the fence in front of Frank and Ellie. He leaned over close and motioned them forward so he could speak into their ears. Frank heard him perfectly and didn't wonder at it.

"Frank and Ellie, this lovely lady next you is my wife, Louise. I had one of the attendants fill her in on what happened, and she'll keep an eye on you both. Any problem and you let her know right away. She'll see you get the help you need."

Frank knew his mouth was hanging open like some kind of clueless dork, but he couldn't help it.

"I'm very pleased to meet such true-orange Tigers fans." The woman with the kind face under the Tigers ball cap solemnly shook hands with Frank and then Ellie. Frank flushed with embarrassment at her description of them and sensed Ellie felt it too.

"Uh, we were happy to be of service," he finally got out.

"Nonetheless, you suffered for it, and that deserves respect," Mrs. Kaline replied.

"Thanks," was all Frank could manage, while Ellie voiced her hoarse agreement.

"Here you go, Frank," Al Kaline said, holding out a baseball covered with black signatures. "I think I got the whole Tigers starting lineup." Kaline and his wife laughed when Frank hesitated. "Take it. That's the strange one, the one I hit that was wrapped in the flag." Kaline put it in Frank's hand. "I'm going to use that same bat, too. I hope they bring us both luck."

"Geez! Thank you, sir!"

Ellie brought out her own prized Kaline souvenir. "Now we both . . . have your balls, Mr. Kaline," she croaked.

Kaline and his wife looked at Ellie, then at each other, and burst out laughing. Ellie realized what she'd said and hung her head. But Kaline reached out and lifted her chin.

"You certainly do, Ellie. And I couldn't have put them in better hands." He laughed again.

"Oh, you stop that, Al," his wife said. "You're only embarrassing her further. You'd better get going. Mayo's waiting. Win this one for all of us."

"I'll give it a heck of try." Number 6 tipped his game cap and was gone.

Frank held the magic ball from the flag, turning it over and over in wondering hands. It was a tight squeeze, but they were all right there, first initials and last names only: M. Lolich, N. Cash, B. Freehan, D. McLain, M. Stanley and the rest. Even Mayo Smith had signed. And, of course, number 6:

"To Frank – A. Kaline, World Series 1968"

"It's the least we can do, Frank," Mrs. Kaline confirmed.

Frank put his Kaline ball in his Kaline glove and just stared at them. It was like the ball had come home, to Frank's home.

Ellie tugged his arm again. "How's it feel, white knight?" Ellie still held her autographed ball and could only mouth the words, but Frank understood. And the power of the feeling amazed him.

"Lucky," Frank said.

thirty-four

Frank

"Wow! Look at that," Ellie rasped.

Frank watched in fascination as a brown-skinned man in a vaguely western suit, about to sing the American national anthem, was lead out onto the field—by a dog! He was carrying a guitar and wearing dark glasses. "Who's that?"

Beside Frank, Mrs. Kaline explained. "Frank and Ellie, that young man is José Feliciano. He's a blind singer and songwriter. From Puerto Rico originally, but now he's an American citizen. That's his guide dog, Trudy. Ernie chose him to sing the anthem for the game. Feliciano flew in from Las Vegas especially for this."

Frank knew "Ernie" was Ernie Harwell, the Tigers play-by-play announcer. Ellie grabbed Frank's arm, and then whispered three words at him. "*Light. My. Fire.*"

Frank got it. José Feliciano, sure! Jim Morrison and The Doors had taken their original recording of the song to number one on Billboard's Top 100 list for three weeks last year. Now,

Feliciano's version of *Light My Fire* was one of the biggest hits on the radio. It wasn't Motown, but even Smooth Daddy Groove was playing it.

"Cool," Frank said.

"O-oh, say, can you see . . . ?" Now Feliciano sang and played *The Star-Spangled Banner* in that same personal style, giving it a Latin rhythm and phrasing that was very similar to his rendition of the Doors' hit. All around the stadium, men doffed their hats, as did the Tigers and Cardinals players on the field. Frank did the same and held his Tigers ball cap over his heart. Ellie was into it, smiling and swaying to the Spanish beat. Amid the roar of cheers from the fans, Frank thought he heard some unexpected boos and hisses. Maybe a few people didn't appreciate Feliciano's Latin interpretation. Mrs. Kaline must have heard the hisses and boos too, because she was shaking her head in disgust. "He's an American," she insisted, beneath it all. Frank suddenly saw that, in the United States anyway, there were more racial issues than just black and white. He resisted thinking that this might be true of Canada, too. Yet, why not? He vowed to pay more attention to the whole complicated issue in future.

At the end of the anthem, Frank's head spun with momentary dizziness, yet the excitement of the start of the game made the tight pain in his back bearable. Before they sat down, Mrs. Kaline pointed out a man with smooth silver and black hair, just a few rows away, cheering his head off while holding a large hot dog slathered with bright yellow mustard. "Frank, Ellie, that's Michigan's governor, George Romney."

It was Romney, sure enough. What a contrast. Frank last saw the stunned politician on TV during the race riot the year before. A harried-looking Romney was doing anything but enjoying a hot dog and cheering, as his beloved Motor City burned around him. Frank wondered what the man had thought, enduring the ominous sound of rooftop snipers' bullets and the deeper, .50-calibre machine gun reply and jarring clatter of Huey helicopter gunships that overrode them all. Seeing Romney celebrating at the game now made last year's events seem an unreal nightmare.

Frank looked around at the mix of black and white fans cheering together, sharing seats and laughter and the desperate hope the Tigers could come back from near-impossible odds and, just maybe, begin the Motor City's healing. The governor's presence made this game five of the World Series look even more crucial to Frank. A lot more than just a World Series championship was riding on this game, he acknowledged, not for the first time.

"Faith, man. Don't forget the faith," Frank whispered, feeling a little harried himself. Didn't Al Kaline just put the personally autographed, World Series baseball into his hand a few minutes before, the miraculous ball charged with the streaming red, white and blue supernatural power of Tiger Stadium's flag?

Frank's eye continued its slow slide up the long white pole from time to time to take in the ripple and flow of the flag. Were the game, the series, the magic gone, almost before they had begun?

thirty-five

Frank

Frank glanced briefly to his right, at Ellie's worried face. He tried his utmost to believe, to beam all the pride and confidence he could muster at Al Kaline and the Detroit Tigers as they trotted out and took up their playing positions on the field for the first inning of game five of the 1968 World Series. It felt like every Tigers fan in the whole stadium was sitting there right beside Frank—on the edge of his seat. He had a fleeting wish that his father and grandfather were with him now, to share the burden of desperate hope shadowed by lurking doubt.

A minute later, every eye in the ballpark was held by a single player: the St. Louis Cardinals best series hitter, ace base-stealer and 1967 World Series champion, the incomparable Lou Brock. The all-star left fielder walked from the batter's on-deck circle and took up position at home plate like a star performer taking his accustomed place at centre stage. The St. Louis fans clapped and cheered and shouted his name, "Lou! Lou! Lou!" To Frank's ballplayer's eye, Brock's whole demeanour was one of calm and assurance, his movements fluid and natural, brimming with dangerous potential. Brock was a left-handed hitter facing the Tigers left-handed pitcher, Mickey Lolich.

On Frank's other side, Louise Kaline raised both hands in front of her face and crossed the first two fingers of each. Her lips were moving soundlessly in what Frank judged to be a silent prayer. Abruptly, Ellie hoisted and waved her poster, straining to speak out her own faith: "Go Cats! Bite Birds!"

The stadium speakers crackled with energy, and Curt Gowdy welcomed the now-bright sunlight and sixty-degree temperature in a resonant electronic voice, and informed the crowd that the fitful stadium breeze was now blowing from third base toward first and right field. Gowdy described the right field fence as "home run heaven" at only three hundred and twenty-five feet, and that conditions now favoured left-handed pull hitters.

Frank's unsettled nerves made it impossible for him to resist stating the obvious. "Brock hits left-handed. And he likes to pull the ball."

"But remember, Frank, Mickey beat the Cardinals hitters eight runs to one in the second game of the series," Louise Kaline said, "and gave up only six hits. Mickey can do it."

But can he do it in this game? With everything riding on it?

It needed only two pitches to give the answer.

Brock took Lolich's first pitch high and inside for ball one. The second pitch he crushed, not pulling it to right field but sending it high into left, to land between the pursuing Tigers outfielders, almost at the fence. The leadoff double, putting him quickly into scoring position, was his ninth hit in the series. St. Louis cheers echoed off the upper decks and rocketed around the ballpark.

"Damn!" Frank just caught Mrs. Kaline's muttered response and had to agree. Beside him, Ellie lowered her brave poster and leaned it against her knees.

Still, Julian Javier, the Cardinals bespectacled second baseman, hit a hard ground ball to shortstop Mickey Stanley, who made a perfect throw to first base, for the first Cardinals out of the inning and game. That brought a roar of approval and a stadium-wide flurry of orange, white and black pennants from the hometown crowd. "Cool," Ellie croaked, and Frank breathed a little easier. It did leave Brock on second base though, already taking his usual long lead, ready to steal third or even home on a Tigers misplay.

Brock didn't have to.

It was centre fielder, Curt Flood, who hit a bloop single to right and brought Brock all the way home like a sleek-running greyhound. The first inning had hardly started and already Al Kaline and Frank's beloved Tigers were down a run.

Then, like a forbidding message from the fickle gods of baseball, Flood stole second base and Orlando Cepeda, with a full count of three balls and two strikes, hit a towering drive over the left field fence for a home run.

As Flood, and then Cepeda, trotted around the bases and crossed home plate, to the raucous cheers of Cardinals fans and the welcoming backslaps of their waiting teammates, Frank could hardly bear to look at the left field scoreboard. The number 3 appeared like it was ordained and completely overshadowed the Tigers 0.

Ellie nudged Frank. "Look," she rasped. Frank followed her pointing finger to his right. Like a thick layer of red icing on a badly baked cake, the seven Cardinals supporters in their bright-feathered costumes were performing a manic conga up and down the aisle to the exploding delight of their nearby fans. The sight was bittersweet on Frank's tongue.

"Yeah . . . I know," Frank said, finally.

Beside them, Mrs. Kaline was silent, her fingers uncrossed.

Frank's attention slipped away and he gestured at the Tigers bullpen. "Uh, who's that?" Frank was sure he knew, but asked anyway.

It took Kaline's wife a few moments to reply, like she didn't want to acknowledge it. "That's relief pitcher, Fred Lasher, warming up."

To Frank and Ellie, and to every fan in the stands who had noticed, it meant only one thing: starting pitcher Mickey Lolich, the Tigers best hope on the mound, might be pulled from the game before the first inning was even half over.

Could it get any worse? Yeah, Frank admitted. The way this series was going, it could.

Ernie Harwell reminded the crowd that the Tigers were supposed to be the hard-hitting powerhouse in their home stadium. Instead, the Cardinals had completely dominated the series home games with their superior bat work.

Frank watched the Cardinals fifth batter, third baseman Mike Shannon, connect with a hard-hit ball to centre field. Frank's heart remained lodged in his throat even after Tiger Jim Northrup pulled it in for the second out; and Mickey Lolich struck out the formidable catcher, Tim McCarver.

The disastrous first half of the inning was finally over.

"Now it's our turn." Mrs. Kaline spoke with all the proud

confidence of the wife of one of major league baseball's greatest players.

Frank took a deep breath and felt Ellie's warm hand slip into his, and give a reassuring squeeze. "Gotta believe," she mouthed the words almost silently. Frank smiled, nodded and desperately tried.

Oddly, what Frank noticed most when the Tigers came in for their first at-bat and the Cardinals took the field, was that the Cardinals starting pitcher, Nelson Briles, had wide, mutton-chop sideburns almost to his jaw-line. They kept catching Frank's eye and distracting him. *Stupid.*

Sideburns or not, it didn't take Briles long to get Dick McAuliffe, and then Mickey Stanley, to fly out to center field for two quick Tigers outs.

Now Louise Kaline shook her head twice, as if to banish her fears, and watched intently as husband Al Kaline approached home plate with the big Louisville Slugger in his hands. Frank guessed it was the lucky one—the one that had sent a hard-hit ball into the wind-stiffened Stars and Stripes during batting practice. The hard ash wood bat looked so ordinary. When Frank glanced at the flag, it was still streaming in the breeze.

Was there really magic in it, or was it just foolish superstition?

Now it was Frank who sought out Ellie's hand.

Frank, Ellie, Mrs. Kaline and tens of thousands of desperate Tigers fans watched Al Kaline dig his spikes into the dirt of home plate; adjust his plastic batting helmet over his special game cap; measure the distance to the far side of the plate with his bat; lean forward and take up his hitting position in front of Briles.

Ernie Harwell picked up the commentary:

"Kaline has had a marvelous World Series, batting .353, and he's been outstanding in the field. Thirty-three years old, born in Baltimore, Maryland, and never played a day of minor league ball in his life. He's been a hometown Tigers favourite for fifteen years."

Frank watched Briles wet his lips before delivering the first pitch and Frank instinctively wet his own. It was a ball, and Kaline took it for 1-0. Ellie's hand was sweaty in his as Kaline fouled off the next offering, 1-1. He took the third pitch, but it was a beautiful strike on the corner, 1-2. Ellie groaned and squeezed Frank's fingers twice when Kaline fouled off the next two balls to keep the count at 1-2.

It happened almost before Frank could register it. Briles wound up, paused, and threw his signature outside curve ball. Kaline was caught reaching for it and looking awkward as the end of his bat missed the tantalizing pitch by a good two inches. The disappointed Tigers crowd massively echoed Ellie's next groan around the stands. Frank felt it from his head, to his aching back, and right down to his tightly laced Keds.

The Tigers were out in order.

thirty-six

Frank

Frank found it impossible to resist as the leaden weight of dread climbed up his stiff spine and settled onto his shoulders, more unbearable than Ellie's weight could ever be. From the end of the first inning, right up to the end of the third, Al Kaline and the Tigers were down three runs. Three!

Like the official herald of major league doom, George Kell's deep voice reminded Tigers fans that in the last eighteen innings, the equivalent of two whole games, the Tigers had produced only two runs.

Geez! Two pathetic runs. Frank hated it! Hated it!

He looked to his right along the first baseline to the Cardinals dugout. Lou Brock and Julian Javier stood casually at one end, arms crossed, ball caps tipped back, laughing and joking together. Frank didn't have to hear the punch line to imagine that the gods of baseball were standing there beside them in the St. Louis dugout, looking right at Frank, while they, too, shared the joke.

As the early innings slipped by, Frank's eye had continued its slow slide up the long pole from time to time to take in the ripple and flow of the flag. Were the game, the series, the magic lost, almost before they'd begun?

Now, in the bottom half of the fourth inning, deep in centre field, the big stars and stripes were still serenely streaming in the light breeze as Al Kaline and his teammates came in to bat.

Ellie motioned across the stadium to the center field fence below the flag. "There they go again, Frank. They . . . still believe."

Frank and Ellie both watched as, once again, two young fans in Tigers orange, black and white paraded behind the barrier, each holding one end of their long homemade banner: "SOCK IT TO 'EM, TIGERS!" The hometown fans around them stood up, made room, and cheered with all pennants flying.

Frank looked at Ellie, and as if on cue, they both jumped up and waved pennants in support. Mrs. Kaline was right there cheering and waving alongside them.

They watched as Tigers shortstop, Mickey Stanley, came to the plate. Briles took the sign from his catcher, wound up, delivered a hard-thrown ball inside, overbalanced—and promptly fell flat on his face in front of the pitcher's mound! For a few seconds, the whole crowd was speechless in disbelief.

Curt Gowdy recovered first.

"Well, I'll tell you, George, you rarely see a pitcher fall flat on his face like that."

The crowd around Frank gave out with raucous laughter and mock cheers for Briles' Barnum and Bailey circus stunt.

Was it a sign from the gods?

Four pitches later, Stanley pounded a ball down the right

field line. The hit bounced off the fence in fair play and away from Cardinal Ron Davis for a stand up Tigers triple with no outs.

Frank and Ellie jumped to their feet with the hometown crowd, waved pennants, held up her Go Cats! Bite Birds! O Yeah! poster and cheered with the fervid enthusiasm of true believers.

With Stanley in scoring position on third, Al Kaline stepped up to the plate to the rhythmic shouts of "Go! Go! Go!"

Frank could almost taste the triumph—when the unexpected happened—again! Briles' fourth pitch was way inside and hit the handle of his bat. Kaline turned away so quickly that he lost his footing and fell down at the plate! To make matters worse, the ball came fair off his bat handle like some bizarre bunt, and Kaline was thrown out at first base almost before he could scramble back to his feet.

"Damn!" This time Mrs. Kaline's comment was clearly audible.

Frank held tight to his autographed ball and slammed his fist into his glove in frustration.

He felt Louise Kaline's hand on his shoulder. The gesture reminded Frank of his mother. "It's not over yet, Frank." And his mother's words, too.

The good news was that Tiger Norm Cash's sacrifice fly to centre field scored Stanley from third. Soon after, Jim Northrup brought Willie Horton home from third base when Northrup's ground ball hit some invisible field debris, took an unexpected hop over the head of Julian Javier, and bounced into the outfield. As Horton crossed the plate to the jubilant cheers of the standing hometown fans and his Tigers teammates, Ellie was proudly waving her Willie Horton, autographed blue glove like a maniac.

Now Frank dared to look at the left field scoreboard as the Tigers 0 slipped from sight to be replaced by a desperately needed 2.

"Yeah, gotta keep the faith." Ellie's voice echoed Frank's own thinking like advice from a friendly bullfrog. Earlier, Mrs. Kaline had asked for a cup full of ice from one of the drink vendors, and Ellie had been sucking steadily on the frozen cubes. Her voice sounded a bit better.

thirty-seven

Frank

More innings slipped by and the score remained a stubborn 3-2 for St. Louis.

The only noteworthy event for the Tigers was the major league argument at home plate, in the top of the fifth inning, which had Ellie shouting hoarsely and waving her blue Horton glove even more avidly. The "incomparable" Lou Brock, the leagues' record-breaking base-stealer, actually jumped up and down in vigorous, undignified protest when umpire Doug Harvey was adamant that he'd missed the plate by three inches when he tried to steal home, standing up, all the way from second base. It was the strong, pinpoint accurate throw from Tigers left fielder Willie Horton that got Brock at the plate. Even St. Louis manager Red Shoendienst's rare display of shouting and temper couldn't overturn Harvey's ruling.

Tigers fans feasted on every morsel of Cardinals outrage!

Now, between the two halves of the seventh inning, Frank and Ellie, and Mrs. Kaline and the whole crowd, right around the ball-park, rose to their feet for the traditional "seventh inning stretch." The relief was emotional as much as physical. Frank tried to ease the pain and tightness along his spine by stretching forward and back, and side-to-side.

True to his promise, the doctor had come to check on them during the third inning. But Frank didn't expect the doctor back now! And he brought Mr. Fitzgerald, and Frank's father and grandfather with him! *Uh-oh!* Frank thought, and tried to smile through the stiffness. He saw Ellie smiling too. Frank nodded at her, and they both stood up, holding their smiles and beaming confidence for all they were worth.

Again, Frank decided to take the lead and looked at Louise Kaline. "Mrs. Kaline, this is my dad, Norm Phelan, and my grandfather, David Phelan, and, uh, Ellie's father, Mr. Fitzgerald."

Louise Kaline stood, smiled warmly, and extended her hand to each of the three in turn. "Very pleased to meet you all. You have a couple of terrific kids here. I still can't quite believe what they did, but my husband and I are truly grateful. I can't imagine Al being out there without his special World Series game cap."

Frank watched each man take Mrs. Kaline's hand and bow slightly, like he was meeting a queen or something.

It was Mr. Fitzgerald who spoke first. "I think I speak for all of us when I say we can hardly believe it either and heartily agree."

"How are you two feeling?" Frank's father asked. That was the doctor's cue to step forward and motion Frank and Ellie into the aisle, where he quickly examined them. Frank turned a little red as he sensed the fans around them staring in open curiosity and whispering among themselves when the severe bruising on his back was revealed.

Then it was Ellie who acted. "High-fives!" she said.

Frank smiled, raised his hand and slapped hers. "High-fives! Definitely!"

The adults around them couldn't help laughing, even the doctor. "I think these kids can play for a few more innings before we send them to the dressing room. But please, have your own physicians examine them tomorrow. You have my card." The doctor made his own slight bow and slipped through the special gate in the fence beside the Tigers dugout and disappeared.

"I'll continue to keep a close eye on them, sirs," Mrs. Kaline said.

Frank's dad looked at his grandfather and Mr. Fitzgerald. They both shrugged. "Thank you, again. And we'll keep our fingers crossed."

"And our faith in Lolich's fastball high." Once again, Ellie's dad put his hands together and gazed heavenward, drawing more laughs from the adults. Then Mr. Fitzgerald hugged Ellie once, made an "after you" gesture, and followed Frank's dad and grandfather back over to their seats near third base.

Whew! Frank looked at Ellie's tightly smiling face and knew she felt the same relief.

Then Al Kaline was there again, right in front of Frank and Ellie. "How are you guys doing now? Feeling any better?"

"Doing a little better than you are," his wife said with a smile. Yet Frank could hear the strain in her voice. It reflected his emotional state, as well.

"Yeah," Kaline said, "haven't exactly set the field on fire with my hitting."

"It's ok, sir," Ellie replied. "My dad's a Baptist minister and I know all about keeping the faith. You helped us when we were in trouble too, and gave us these great seats, right beside your wife, and she's been, uh, really nice to us." Near the end of her speech, Ellie began to sound like Jeremiah Bullfrog again, but still kept her smile. Frank thought she was pretty cool.

"It's true, sir," Frank spoke up. "No matter what happens, Ellie an' me will never forget this day. And I'll always be proud to wear your number 6." Kaline gave Frank and Ellie a major league grin and nodded.

"Like I said, pride's what it's all about. It's what makes real ballplayers like you and Ellie." Kaline reached behind him and pulled something black and dusty from his back pocket. He shook it out once. "Frank, you have that special ball. You should have the cap that goes with it."

"That's luck, dude!" Ellie croaked beside Frank.

"Ok, gotta go get those pesky Cardinals." Kaline trotted back to the dugout.

Frank looked at the sweat-stained ball cap. He could hardly believe what he was holding in his hand. It was the beat-up Tigers ball cap Kaline had worn under his batting helmet since the start of the 1968 season, more than one hundred and sixty games! Ellie punched Frank's shoulder as the reality sank in. This was the very cap his idol had worn on his head for months. The dust and stains and sweat were all Kaline's, and now, all Frank's.

"Turn it over." Ellie was making flipping motions with her hand. Frank deliberately flipped the cap over and took in the words written in black Sharpie on the underside of the well-worn bill:

"Best of luck to Frank from Al Kaline
World Series 1968
Pride"

Frank took off his own ball cap and slipped on the Kaline cap in its place. He felt a momentary dizziness. This time, it wasn't from his head injury.

thirty-eight

Frank

"Geez, geez, geez!" Frank whispered to himself. It was still the bottom of the seventh inning with one man gone for Detroit. The Tigers were down to their last eight outs in the game and maybe the whole World Series. Frank was super-worried. Tigers manager, Mayo Smith, had made the hugely controversial decision to let pitcher Mickey Lolich come to bat. It kept Lolich pitching for the Tigers in the remaining innings, after he had settled in and held the Cardinals to their three runs from the first inning. Maybe Louise Kaline had been right, and Lolich could do it. But—and it was a big BUT—it meant Mayo could not use a more experienced pinch-hitter. One with a higher batting average and a better chance of getting on base to even the score, if not put the Tigers in front, in this must-win game. And the most worrying? Lolich had struck out his first two times at bat!

Ernie Harwell seemed to side with Mayo Smith.

"Lolich is the best pitcher the Tigers have had in this World Series, so far."

"Wow!" Ellie rasped, not totally convinced.

"Double wow!" Frank echoed. Beside him, Mrs. Kaline bit her lip and held up both hands, fingers crossed.

Ellie sucked noisily on the last of her ice and water. "I don't know about this," she added.

"Mayo usually knows what he's doing, Ellie," said Mrs. Kaline. "Usually."

It was that second "usually" that had Frank's heart pumping. He pulled Kaline's autographed batting cap down harder on his head and squeezed Kaline's autographed ball tighter in his autographed Kaline glove.

Frank and Ellie, Louise Kaline, and every hometown fan watched with jaw-grinding trepidation as pitcher Mickey Lolich took his stance in the batter's box to face Nelson Briles, pitcher against pitcher. Once more, Frank was compelled to say it: "Mickey's career batting average is only .110, uh, so far." Barely one hit in ten at bats. One! Ellie nodded without looking at him. Mrs. Kaline put her hand on Frank's shoulder again. Her squeeze made the tension all but unbearable. . . .

Frank closed his eyes. He listened intently as Ernie Harwell announced the outcome of each succeeding pitch. At two balls and one strike, Frank heard the crack of the bat—a weak one—and his eyes flew open. Ellie grabbed his arm hard.

This time it was Frank's problem: "I can't see it! Where is it?"

Ellie yanked him to his feet to join the rest of the crowd and pointed.

The Cardinals right fielder, Ron Davis, was racing forward

with his eyes up and his glove out to the full extent of his reach. An instant later, Davis was flat out in the air and watching the ball hit the field, a scant inch in front of his glove, and bounce away. By the time he recovered the baseball, Lolich was stomping down on first base and Ellie about pulled Frank's arm out of its socket.

"Ow-w-w!" he screamed, at yet another strain on his spine. No one in the ballpark noticed, including Ellie. "Lolich has singled! He's singled!" Ellie strained. She jumped up and down beside Frank and waved her poster in delight. The whole Detroit crowd let out with an orange, black and white Tiger-sized roar as Lolich, a pitcher, not a seasoned hitter, made it safely to first base. Frank let out a breath he didn't know he was holding and tried to work out the agony in his shoulder and back.

Geez! Will I ever feel just, like, normal again?

In short order, Dick McCauliffe hit his own single, and Mickey Stanley drew a walk from Nelson Briles.

The Tigers had the bases loaded!

It certainly helped ease Frank's pain. The entire ballpark responded. With a tornado of sound pinballing around Tiger Stadium and raising the hair on Frank's neck and arms, the hometown crowd was more on edge than at any other time during the game. Frank couldn't remember getting to his feet once more, but in a living, rolling wave, most of the fifty-three thousand fans began to stand up and loudly voice their approval. The stadium was a Tigers Town blur of rippling orange, white and black colours. Then began the sharp, rhythmic reports of stadium seats slammed up and down in staccato bursts.

This time, in spite the pain or maybe because of it, the riot of noise jarred Frank into a state of hyper-alertness. His senses sharpened like a fine tuning fork responding to the waves of positive energy until his skin tingled with anticipation. The red and white pockets of Cardinals fans had no choice but to get to their feet to keep an eye on the action.

Five minutes later, the St. Louis pitching coach, Billy Muffet, had pulled Briles and his sideburns, and relief pitcher Joe Hoerner was on the mound, taking his warm-up pitches. Like Lolich, he was a left-hander.

Beside Frank, Ellie climbed onto her seat and pulled Frank up onto his. A sharp arrow of pain shot up his back, but Frank ignored it. Ellie kept a tight hold on his right hand and must have felt those tingling vibrations. She looked into his face and giggled like a maniac gargling sand. Frank squeezed Ellie's hand and giggled right back. He pointed down to the field at what both he and Ellie, and the standing crowd of fifty-three thousand, knew was coming.

The whole of Tiger Stadium was rocked to its venerable foundations by the shouting of a single name—

"AL! AL! AL!"

Frank didn't cast another look at the flag. This time, he didn't need to. Frank had the Kaline glove, the Kaline ball, the Kaline cap. He savoured the pride, embraced the faith.

Al Kaline, Mr. Tiger, stood beside the batter's box with what Frank was sure was the magic bat leaned against him. He reached up with both hands to adjust his perfect game cap and put the black batting helmet on over it. Taking up the rosin cloth, he wiped down the handle of the bat to remove any trace of dust or sweat and ensure a firm grip. On Frank's other side, Mrs. Kaline beamed her special faith at her husband with shining eyes, no crossed fingers needed.

For a long second, Kaline looked right back at her.

His face remained impassive, and what passed between them Frank would never know.

thirty-nine

Frank

"Bases loaded, one out, Cardinals lead by a run in the seventh inning. Kaline is seven for twenty in the series and batting a respectable .350. And the crowd comes alive here in Tiger Stadium!"

Commentator Curt Gowdy was right. Frank had never felt so alive.

The familiar stress, the anticipation, the fear mixed with faith that had caused Frank's whole body to vibrate was stilled. And here were Ellie Fitzgerald and Mrs. Kaline right beside him, and flush with a quiet pride no words need express. That wasn't all of the good feeling, but it was the most good feeling Frank could remember in his fourteen years.

Frank, and fifty-three thousand other fans, watched Kaline at the plate.

The big man took the time to knock the dirt from his spikes and square his batting helmet. It seemed to Frank that his idol's now familiar face remained neutral, as he exercised the special bat and went into his crouch, waiting for Cardinal Joe Hoerner's first pitch.

Frank knew Kaline had done this thousands of times, but this time was special.

On the seat beside him, Frank felt Ellie's hand slip into his with a familiar rightness and warmth. Mrs. Kaline watched her husband with eyes full of Tigers pride and a slight smile on her face. In that moment, Frank knew there was no difference between the three of them. Not country, not age, not gender, not skin colour. They were Tigers fans together.

Frank felt the air around him stir into life. He didn't need to look up and out to deep centre field to know. . . .

Joe Hoerner waited for the pitch sign from the Cardinals catcher, Tim McCarver. Frank's baseball savvy anticipated it would be a fastball. He wondered if Mayo Smith would take the chance of starting the Tigers base runners early. It might avoid a disastrous double play that would end the inning, and with it, the Tigers last best chance in the game and in the 1968 World Series.

Frank was glad it was the Tigers manager making the decision.

Hoerner bent forward with the ball in his left hand behind his back. He took the sign, nodded confirmation, and went into his wind-up. Hoerner paused, looked left, looked right, to check the runners on first and third. He delivered a fastball hard and low. The pitch headed for the middle of the plate but tailed away outside before it got there. Kaline swung hard—and missed.

"That's strike one to the veteran, Kaline. Hoerner's keeping the ball low, trying for the hit on the ground that will save extra bases and may manufacture the double play."

Frank felt Ellie's firm flesh, still warm in his hand, as Kaline stepped out of the batter's box to rub any sweat from the palms of his own hands. Kaline checked his bat, his helmet, stepped forward again and worked his spikes deep into the dirt of the batter's box for the next pitch.

For a short second, Frank risked a look away. Each team manager—the Cardinals Red Shoendienst and the Tigers Mayo Smith—stood at the end of his dugout. The managers' expressions were as unreadable as Kaline's. Frank knew that his father and grandfather, Ellie and her father, Louise Kaline, Curt Gowdy, everyone in the park who knew anything at all about the game, were certain Hoerner would throw another fastball.

Frank knew that Al Kaline knew everything about the game. His baseball hero had waited fifteen years for this pitch. He was ready at the plate when the fastball came.

Kra-ack!

The bat connected. It wasn't a ground ball. It was a fly.

The ball wasn't particularly hard hit, but cleared the infield and dropped into short right centre, in front of the Cardinals hard-charging fielder. Ellie's hand caught at Frank's in a shared moment of completeness. He laughed at the feeling but didn't look away. The universe paused and held its breath, and the crowd with it. . . .

It was enough.

Kaline's hit scored Lolich from third and McCauliffe from second. It left Stanley at third, Kaline on first, and Frank incandescent with joy. The Tigers were ahead for the first time in the game and still only one out.

Frank laughed again with Mrs. Kaline. He released Ellie's hand, leaned over and hugged Ellie once with both arms. Frank thrust his Kaline glove with his Kaline ball into the air, and waved his Kaline batting cap in mad, joyous, unending celebration with the rest of the crowd.

Frank's heart was too big for his chest.

Even with the crackling power of the Tiger Stadium speakers to amplify it, it seemed an age before Curt Gowdy could make his voice heard—

"Al Kaline has had a lot of hits in his career, George, but that may have been his biggest."

"It might have been the biggest hit of his life." George Kell, the Tigers other colour commentator, affirmed.

All around Frank, the elated crowd stayed on its feet.

Men waved their hats. The men without hats took off their suit jackets and waved them. The women waved handkerchiefs, brightly coloured scarves, and an orange, black and white sea of Tigers pennants. Shouts of "AL! AL! AL!" washed down and across the field in an exhilarating torrent of sound. The noise went on and on and on . . .

Frank didn't want it to stop.

If there was a still centre in this storm of celebration, it was Al Kaline.

Frank couldn't take his eyes off his idol. Al Kaline stood quietly at first base, his hands on his hips and one foot on the bag, staring into the middle distance above third base. It caught Frank. This coolness. This acceptance. The supreme grace of the moment. Could Frank ever understand it? Achieve it in his own game, in his own life, in his own way and time?

Beside Frank, Louise Kaline was clapping and watching her husband with the rest of the crowd. Frank again caught the briefest of smiles, knew the rightness of it all. This was Mrs. Kaline's moment too.

This was pride.

Kaline's single was the game-winning hit at 5-3.

At the end of the game, Frank and Ellie and the roaring crowd refused to sit down until they drew Al Kaline out from the Tigers dugout to receive their accolades. Kaline took off his special World Series game cap, held it high, and with it, turned in a slow circle to salute the crowd.

Thirty seconds later, Kaline was at the fence, leaning over and kissing his wife. Frank and Ellie and the crowd cheered even louder.

"Frank, you have the ball and my regular season batting cap," Kaline said, "but I think I'm going to keep that bat." Frank could only nod his head in agreement. "You and Ellie come back soon, now."

And Al Kaline was gone.

epilogue

Frank

"You got a letter, Frank!" Fancy was shouting at him from the bottom of the stairs.

"Geez! Not now," Frank muttered. He was arranging and rearranging his Tigers and World Series memorabilia on the headboard of his bed, trying to get it right. He'd just about decided to put the autographed Kaline baseball between Kaline's framed and autographed rookie cards, and the autographed Kaline ball cap.

Frank was almost at the door of his room when he stopped, remembered and went back for the cap. In the two weeks since Al Kaline and the Detroit Tigers had gone on to beat the odds and win the 1968 World Series, Frank had been nervous about leaving his souvenir alone in the room, even for a few seconds, even in his own house.

"You still wearin' that stupid old baseball cap?" Fancy scoffed. She was carrying Mr. Nibs in her arms.

"You still slobberin' over your stupid Barbie and Ken dolls?"

Frank replied. Fancy and Mr. Nibs both gave him "the look," but his sister held out the white envelope.

"It's from a girl," Fancy said, and waited. Frank kept his expression composed, said nothing more. He took the stairs back to his room, two at a time, with only a slight twinge from his healing back. He locked the door behind him.

"Ellie Fitzgerald, cool!" Frank read the return address before digging out his Swiss Army knife and slitting open the envelope. A small square of stiff paper fell out before he could remove the letter. It was a photograph with a printed note on the back: "For my white knight and favourite Canadian Tigers fan. Keep the faith! Ellie."

Frank turned the photograph over and saw Ellie wearing her Junior Tigers uniform and laughing into the camera. Her colourful Go Cats! Bite Birds! poster was leaning against her legs. Ellie's right hand was giving the camera a big thumbs-up. Her left hand held what Frank knew had to be her autographed Kaline baseball. "Lookin' proud! Just like I remember her."

Frank propped his pillows against the headboard, put his feet up and settled in to read the letter. There was some stiffness in his back, too, but the black and yellow bruises from Big Red's kicks had begun to fade, and the serious pain with them. His head also felt pretty good as the cut and bruise healed up. Still, if it hadn't been for Ellie and her fantastic pitch hitting home behind Big Red's fat left ear, Frank figured he might be some kind of drooling vegetable. And a crippled one, at that.

Doctor Seymour had examined him for the second time yesterday, after Thursday's junior high school classes. Frank couldn't have agreed more with the doctor's diagnosis. "I think the Tigers winning the World Series was better medicine than anything I could prescribe, Frank." Doctor Seymour was also careful to reassure Frank's parents, especially his mother.

Frank's father and grandfather were both well, and shared Frank's deep pride in the Tigers achievement. Not to mention the fact that pitcher Mickey Lolich had won the Most Valuable Player award for the 1968 World Series after beating the Cardinals formidable Bob Gibson, in the seventh and deciding game, by a score of 4-1. Still, his father and grandfather had been severely reprimanded by his mother and grandmother for letting all the rest happen, no matter how they tried to explain themselves, even with Frank's support. Frank was quick to emphasize that meeting Al Kaline, getting his autographed baseball and batting cap, and seeing his idol's key hit were also a big part of his healing process.

"You're going to have a pale patch of scar tissue from that head bashing, but I guess you can consider the mark an honourable war wound," Dr. Seymour concluded. "And do you ever take off that old ball cap?"

Frank had just stared at the doc like he was crazy, and didn't even try to explain.

Frank put Ellie's photo aside and unfolded the two sheets of paper.

Dear White Knight,

I hope you like the photo, Frank. I decided to write you because you weren't here in Detroit or around Tiger Stadium when the Tigers won game seven and took the World Series, against all odds. I know you probably watched the stuff on TV, but believe me, Frank, it wasn't like being there. Not even close.

After game five, I made my dad promise he'd take me downtown if the

Tigers won the series. Seeing what Kaline and the Tigers could do in game five, we both had the faith. And look what happened! The 1968 Detroit Tigers rule the World!

The celebration was wild, Frank. The crowds, the cheering, the Tigers pennants waving. My dad called it "a full-scale riot." And it was. But the good kind. People dancing in and out of the streams of cars on Woodward and Trumble. Drivers honking their horns like mad. Even the cops were smiling. My dad and me were both exhausted when we finally got home. But the good kind of tired. Except for the burned-out stores and stuff, you could almost forget that the race riot happened only last year. Gotta keep the faith, right?

And this is what I really wanted to tell you. My dad has made arrangements for us to attend the Baptist Union Fall Luncheon on Saturday, November the second, in good old Canada. Yep, Canada, man! It's being held in Windsor this year, inside the Jackson Park Pavilion. I'll be crossing the Detroit River and coming to Canuck-land for the second time in my life! Anyway, my dad and me would like you and your family to be our personal guests. We'll have four tickets waiting at the door in the name of Frank Phelan.

Lucky! Lucky! Lucky! DON'T YOU DARE MISS IT, White Knight! Cheers, from Black Knight, Ellie.

END

Acknowledgments

The author is indebted to the Clayoquot Writers Group for their valuable advice over the course of writing this novel. Author Ashley Little was the first to review a draft and suggest improvements. Author and editor, Joanna Streetly, provided the most recent edits that substantively improved the quality. Joanna then designed the black and white cover illustration that symbolizes the racism theme. Greg Blanchette did a masterly copy-edit. Eileen has been a loving wife, a help and a support in this, as in all aspects of our life together.

This is a work of historical fiction. The author has taken a number of liberties with the layout of Tiger Stadium, the depiction of major league baseball players and other elements necessary to the fulfillment of the story. Any errors and omissions are his alone.

David Floody's witness of the 1967 Detriot race riot, its extent and violence, are seared into his imagination forever. He attended Windsor's most racially integrated high school of the time, enjoyed its diverse culture and took pride in the friendships it encouraged. *The Colour of Pride* is his tribute to that time and place.

David now lives in Tofino, British Columbia and is a member of the BC Federation of Writers and the Clayoquot Writers Group. His first book, *Kittenstein and Frankenfur – the gambling cats*, reveals how mini-monsters from kitten hell can become their owner's last hope of salvation.

He invites you to visit him at www.davidfloody.com.